MY KIND OF CHRISTMAS

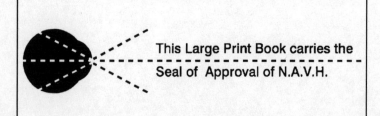

This Large Print Book carries the
Seal of Approval of N.A.V.H.

MY KIND OF CHRISTMAS

ROBYN CARR

WHEELER PUBLISHING
A part of Gale, Cengage Learning

GALE
CENGAGE Learning®

Detroit • New York • San Francisco • New Haven, Conn • Waterville, Maine • London

GALE
CENGAGE Learning

Copyright © 2012 by Robyn Carr.
A Virgin River Novel Series.
Wheeler Publishing, a part of Gale, Cengage Learning.

Wheeler Publishing Large Print Hardcover.
The text of this Large Print edition is unabridged.
Other aspects of the book may vary from the original edition.
Set in 16 pt. Plantin.

LIBRARY OF CONGRESS CATALOGING-IN-PUBLICATION DATA

Carr, Robyn.
   My kind of Christmas / by Robyn Carr. — Large print ed.
      p. cm. — (A Virgin River novel series) (Wheeler Publishing large print
   hardcover)
      ISBN 978-1-4104-5260-3 (hardcover) — ISBN 1-4104-5260-3 (hardcover)
   1. Christmas stories. 2. Large type books. I. Title.
PS3553.A76334M95 2012
813'.54—dc23   2012034388

Published in 2012 by arrangement with Harlequin Books S. A.

Printed in the United States of America
1 2 3 4 5 6 7 16 15 14 13 12

For Goesel Anson, MD,
who walks in kindness and beauty
and changes the lives of so many.
With appreciation and deep affection.

ONE

"I think a little vacation in Virgin River is exactly what Angie needs," Sam Sheridan announced as he looked around the table at his family, all gathered at his home for Thanksgiving dinner. Angie gave her grandfather a grateful smile, relieved to finally have someone on her side. "She's been through quite an ordeal," Sam continued, "and I think medical school can wait while she figures things out. A little rest and relaxation — a chance to visit with the rest of the family — it will do her worlds of good."

"Well, I think if anyone knows what's good for Angie, it's me," Donna replied sternly, glaring daggers at her father. "A visit with Jack, Mel and Brie sounds all well and good, but I'm her mother, and I've supported her from the day she was born. A vacation should be the furthest thing from her mind right now. The accident —" She hesitated, glancing over at Angie. "Well, let's be honest, Angie — the accident has really . . . affected you. There's nothing that needs 'figuring out.' You need to get back on track academically as soon as possible. That's where your focus should be. That's where it was before."

Before. It seemed for Angie as though things would forever be divided into life before the accident and life afterward. While there wasn't much that she remembered from the car accident itself, there were certainly a few moments that stuck out in her mind. She remembered how close she came to dying that cold, drizzly March evening, lying in an emergency room covered with blood, and that it was her long-dead grandmother who was attempting to help her cross to the other side. She hadn't told anyone in her family about that little detail. Why bother? Some of them already thought she was half-crazy.

On the day of the accident, Angie had been the passenger in a car with her friend. A car on the opposing interstate lane had lost control, crossed the median and hit two oncoming cars — including the one Angie had been traveling in. The crash could've been caused by a flat tire or from the driver's attempt to avoid another car, but there was no clear villain, no alcohol or drugs to blame. It was truly an accident.

The driver of the other car had been killed, everyone else injured, Angie the worst. She'd suffered a couple of serious fractures for which surgery had been required. She also lost her spleen, had a collapsed lung and a titanium rod had been placed in her left femur. But the big issue had been the head injury — there had been an impressive laceration on the back of her head and, while there was no open fracture, her brain began to swell and the neurosurgeon had needed to implant a shunt to drain the edema. After her surgery, Angie had been in a coma for three days and had to fight her way back to the world through a postanesthetic and pain-med haze. Friends, family and medical experts had wondered for weeks if this bright, driven young medical student would have any mental handicaps as a result.

She did not.

However, as often happens, the experience changed Angie forever. And those changes were what had led to the current impasse between Angie and her mother, a university professor who wanted to see Angie back in med school as quickly as possible. Today, Angie was fully recovered from her accident and could have gone back to school in September, but she'd chosen not to.

"Well, maybe a brief break from school is within reason," her father, Bob, said to Donna cautiously, once the rest of the family was happily starting dessert and the three of them had offered to start the dishes in the kitchen. Angie rolled her eyes. She knew he'd remain on the fence to avoid an argument with her mother.

But Donna wasn't nearly so reserved with her opinion. "This is completely unacceptable, Angie," she said stiffly. "You've worked far too hard to reach this point in your studies, and we've contributed far too much for you to waste it all on a whim."

Angie was shocked and suddenly angry. Concern was one thing, but this? She was done having her parents, mostly her mother, decide things like this for her. "I might not want to continue medical school! I might want to make macramé flower pot holders for the rest of my life! Or grow herbs! Or hitchhike across Europe! I don't know what I want to do right now, but whatever it is, it's going to be up to me!"

"Don't be absurd," Donna announced in her typically dismissive way. "You're not yourself at all right now. It's obvious the accident has affected your personality more than you realize, Angie. Once you get back to school, you'll be yourself again."

Personality change? Angie didn't agree, except that she'd grown surprisingly stubborn. "Actually, I think I've finally found my personality. And you know what, Mom? I think it's remarkably like yours."

If the accident had any affect at all, it had been through a close-up view of how unpredictable and tenuous life could be. One minute you're buzzing along the freeway, singing along to the radio, the next you're looking down on yourself, watching as medical staff frantically work to save your life and you see your dead grandmother across a chasm of light.

Once she realized she had barely survived, every day dawned brighter, the air drawn into her lungs more precious, the beat of her heart lighter despite the colossal importance of what had happened. She was filled with a sense of gratitude and became contemplative, viewing the smallest detail of living with huge significance. Things she had previously taken for granted now took on a greater significance. There was no detail she was willing to miss: she stopped to have long conversations with grocery-store bag boys, corner flower peddlers, librarians, booksell-

11

ers and school crossing guards. In short, life was different now for Angie, and she was enjoying every minute of it.

She'd also looked back at the life she'd lived so far and had some regrets — specifically about dedicating so much time to study that she had few friends. Many study partners, but only a few friends. She'd said no to far too many parties and dances for the sake of grades. For God's sake, she was already twenty-three and she'd had only two boyfriends! Both pretty inadequate, come to think of it. Was life all about books? Didn't well-rounded adults know how to play? While her few girlfriends were dating, traveling, exploring, getting engaged, what was Angie doing? Making Mama proud.

She was going to fix that if she could. "Mom, I love you, but I've made my decision. Medical school can wait. I'm going to Virgin River."

Angela LaCroix pulled up to Jack's Bar on the day after Thanksgiving and parked right next to her aunt Brie's car. She gave a double toot of her horn before she jumped out and dashed up the steps and into the bar. There they were, waiting for her — Jack, Mel and Brie. Angie's smile was so big she thought her face might crack.

"You made it," Jack said. He rushed around the bar and picked her up in his embrace. Then he put her on her feet and said, "I thought you might be bound, gagged and held prisoner in Sacramento."

"It didn't get physical," she said with a laugh. "However, Mom isn't speaking to any of you."

"That's a relief," Jack said. "Then she won't be calling five times a day."

"Come here, kitten," Brie said, edging Jack out of the way to hug Angie. Then Mel jumped off her stool and joined the hug. "It's so good to have you here," Brie said. "Your mom will come around."

"Fat chance," Jack said. "I don't know anyone who can hold a grudge longer than Donna."

"I hope I didn't cause a rift in the whole family," Angie said.

Jack walked back around behind the bar. "Sheridans," he grumbled. "We hang together pretty well in tough times, but we've been known to have a lot of differences of opinion. Bottom line is, you're welcome here anytime. You always have a place at my house."

"And mine," Brie said.

Angie chewed her lower lip for a moment. "Okay, here's the thing. I appreciate it, I do, and I plan to spend a lot of time with you, but I was wondering, hoping, that you wouldn't mind letting me use that little cabin in the woods." She took a breath. "I need some space. Honest to God."

Silence hung in the air. "Is that a fact?" Jack finally said.

Angie took a stool and her two aunts automatically framed her on their own stools. "That is a fact. Space . . . and I wouldn't mind a beer. And maybe some takeout. It was a long drive."

Jack served up a beer, very slowly. "There's no TV out there," he said.

"Good. But there's an internet connection, right?"

"It's slow, Ange," Mel pointed out. "Not as slow as dial-up was, but it's finicky. The internet connection in our guesthouse is much —"

"I think it's an outstanding idea," Brie said, smiling at Angie. "Try it out. If it gets a little too quiet, I have a guest room and Mel has the guesthouse."

"Thanks, Brie."

"Hey, when you're running away from home, you should at least have your choice of accommodations," Brie added.

"I'm not really running away. . . . Well, okay, I guess that is what I'm doing. Thanks, you guys. Seriously, thanks."

Mel laughed. "It's not exactly an original idea. Brie and I both landed here because we were running away from stuff. I'm going to go get Preacher and Paige. They've been so anxious to see you. And I'll call your folks to tell them you made it here safely."

"You had no trouble driving?" Jack asked.

"I like driving, but my dad insisted we swap cars. I have his SUV and he has my little Honda," she said. "But I wasn't nervous. Maybe because I don't remember the accident."

But Angie didn't want to dwell on what had happened. She was here to relax, to escape, to move forward with her life. Changing the subject, she asked, "And did everyone have a great Thanksgiving?"

"I might never eat again," Brie said. "How about you?"

"We were all at Grandpa's and it was good, except for a little melodrama about me leaving for a month. Between the aunts, uncles and cousins there seems to be quite a diversity of opinion on how I should live my life."

"I imagine. And what did Sam say?" Brie asked of her father.

"Grandpa thought it was an excellent idea to come up here for a little while and he

15

reminded us all that you did that yourself, Brie."

"And you know what? He was very supportive and encouraging at the time, even though he was at least as worried about me as your parents are about you. He had guessed I was in love. Your grandpa is a pretty modern, savvy guy."

"Yes," Angie said quietly. She was close to Sam Sheridan and had often wished, over the past nine months, that she could tell him she had seen Grandma and that she had looked wonderful. But she wasn't sure she hadn't been dreaming or hallucinating, and second, Grandma had been gone such a long time. She didn't want to stir up grief in her grandpa.

Preacher came out of the kitchen with a look of stun and awe on his face as he pulled off his apron and tossed it over the bar before grabbing Angie up in his big arms, spinning her right off her stool. "Aw, girl, girl, girl," he said, hugging her tight. Then he held her away and looked her over. "You are beautiful!" And then he had to let go of her to wipe his eyes.

"Preach," she said, laughing.

Paige slipped around her husband, giving Angie a warm hug. "I'm so glad you're here," she said softly.

"Your big scary husband is crying."

"I know," she said. "He's such a softie. He's the last person you want to meet in a dark alley, but he's so tenderhearted. He cries at Disney movies and Hallmark commercials."

"Yesterday I cried over football," he said. "It was pathetic all day. I'm just so damn glad to see you, Ange. Your uncle Jack was a mess while you were in the hospital, he was so worried."

"And as you can see, all is well," she said.

"Mel says you want a takeout. I'll make you anything you want — you just tell me what."

"I'll have whatever's on the menu and a bottle of wine. Do you have any sauvignon blanc?"

"Are you sure you're allowed alcohol?" Jack asked.

"Yes," she said with a laugh, holding up her glass. "Hence the beer I'm drinking. I promise not to get wasted. But, gee, some of Preacher's dinner, a glass of wine, a fire, a book, peace and quiet . . . Oh, Jack, there are logs out there, right?"

"You're all set," he said. "Do you know how to light the fire?"

She rolled her eyes. "Preacher, do you suppose I could do a little graze through your kitchen? Grab some staples — a few eggs, some milk, bread, that sort of thing? In case I wake up starving?"

"Absolutely," he said.

Although it was soft and low, Angie heard someone clear his throat. There, at the end of the bar in the corner was a lone man in an army-green, down-padded jacket. He had dark hair, an empty beer glass and some money in his hand.

Jack turned to him, took his money and said, "Thanks, bud. See you around."

"Have a nice reunion," the man said, moving to leave.

He was so tall — that was what Angie noticed first. As tall as her uncle Jack. And his dark hair had some red in it. Dark auburn. She'd never seen that combination before, unless it was on a woman and had come out of a bottle. Usually red shades were found in blond or light brown hair. The stubble on his cheeks had a tinge of red, too.

As he walked toward the door, their eyes met and Angie felt her cheeks grow warm — he'd caught her staring. He had the greenest eyes she'd ever seen. They had to be contacts. He gave her a half smile and then he turned and was gone.

18

"Wow," she said. "Whew. Who's the hottie?"

Brie laughed and said, "I think our girl is fully recovered."

Jack let go a little growl. "He's not the one for you," he said.

Angie looked around at all the smiling faces — Brie, Paige, Preacher. . . . "Gee, did I ask if he was right for me?"

Preacher chortled loudly, another thing the big cook seldom did. "Patrick Riordan," he told her. "He's here sitting out a little leave. He's Navy. I think he got hurt or something."

"Nah, he didn't get hurt," Jack clarified. "Luke said there was an accident during his last deployment and he decided to take a little leave or something. Riordans, good people, but that one's got troubles right now. You might want to give him a wide berth. I don't know all the details, but it sounds like combat issues. . . ."

"Yeah, we wouldn't want to get mixed up with anyone with *combat issues*," Preacher joked. And Jack glared at him. Preacher put a big hand on Angie's shoulder and said, "He's been kind of quiet and grumpy while he's been in town. If you got to know him a little, you know what? I bet he wouldn't cheer you up that much."

19

That made Angie laugh. "Well, how about that — we both had accidents. Now, what's for dinner, Preach?"

"Big surprise, turkey soup. It'll keep you very healthy. I boiled two carcasses all day. Homemade noodles — the best. Even though it's not raining, I baked bread."

Her mouth began to water. "I'm in."

Mel came from the kitchen. "I called Donna," she said. "Your mom would like you to email her when you're settled tonight and she promises to give you a little space to find yourself. She suggests you look at your med school transcripts."

Angie rolled her eyes. "Dropping out of school was far harder on Professor LaCroix than it was on me," Angie said. "I've never felt so free in my life."

After a little more small talk, and her beer finished, soup, bread and wine packed up along with some groceries from the kitchen, sun lowering in the sky, Angie was ready to head for the cabin. They stood around outside for a minute and Jack kissed her forehead. "Do whatever you want tomorrow, pumpkin, but remember if you decide to stay in your pajamas all day you'll miss the raising of the Christmas tree."

"You're putting it up tomorrow?"

He gave a nod. "It's a tradition. A bunch

of us went out and chopped it down this morning. It's loaded on one of Paul's biggest trucks. He'll meet us in town with the rest of his equipment tomorrow and we'll stand her up."

Mel gave her arm a pat. "It's not as much fun now that construction professionals are involved," she said. "It hardly ever falls and crushes whole buildings."

Brie hugged Angie hard. "I'm so glad you're here for a long visit."

Almost teary, all Angie could do was nod. Of all her aunts, she was closest to Brie. Brie had been only twelve when she was born. "Me, too," she said. "I'll be here for the tree-raising." Then she looked around at the little town, the lights shining from inside unfussy little houses, smoke curling from chimneys, folks pulling up to the bar and giving a wave to Jack, Mel and Brie as they went inside. The sky was darkening fast, gray clouds gathering and looking heavy with their burden. "Snow tonight?" she asked.

"Very likely," Brie said. "It's way overdue. Call if you need anything."

When Patrick got back to the cabin he was staying in — his brother Aiden's place on the ridge — one of his other brothers,

21

Colin, was sitting on a chair on the deck.

"What are you doing here?"

Colin lifted a bag. "I brought you some Thanksgiving leftovers."

Patrick sighed. "I was offered those yesterday at your house and I said no thank you."

"Jilly figured that by now you might have changed your mind."

"Why didn't you just leave them in the kitchen?" he asked. "The door isn't locked."

Colin just shook his head. "Look, kid, I don't pretend to understand everything that's going on with you, but I'm not going to invade your territory. I'll go inside when I'm invited inside."

Patrick walked around him and opened the door. He stood back and held it open. "Please," he said. When Colin stepped inside, Patrick said, "It's not complicated — I'm rethinking the Navy. But after four years in the Academy and quite a few in the cockpit, it's not an easy decision."

"Especially coming right after Leigh stepped out of your life and Jake dies . . ." Colin added.

"I think they're called life-altering events," Patrick said. "It's actually more complicated, though. I'm due orders. I'm going to get a squadron, and I'm not sure I want to take it. I've been given a little time to think about it, and not necessarily because of Jake." But that was a lie — it *was* because of Jake. The Navy shrink had ordered his leave.

"You're grieving."

"I'm *thinking*," Patrick returned emphatically. And then he looked away, remembering with some longing a time when he had been the least screwed up of the Riordan brothers. He had once been the least complicated, too.

"It might help to talk about it," Colin suggested.

That idea had been suggested before — many times. If his brothers knew how much time he'd already spent with the shrink, they'd either give up on him or get a lot more invasive.

"Colin, not that long ago, we all tried to get you to open up about your issues and it pissed you off because you were feeling very private. . . ."

"I was feeling very *secretive*," Colin corrected. "Because after I had augured in in the Black Hawk I was chewing Oxy like M&M's and couldn't risk letting anyone in my space."

"Even before that," Patrick said. "You were the brother who rarely put in an appearance at family things and, when you

23

did you didn't last long, so cut me some slack here. I need to be that brother for a while." In fact, the reason Patrick had chosen to come to Virgin River was because both Luke and Colin lived here, and Sean and Aiden were not so far away. He *did* want to see his brothers, just not too much of them. And because Patrick had been scheduled to be out to sea and not in Virgin River, the entire Riordan clan was planning a Christmas holiday reunion in warm and sunny San Diego. They had rented two large condos on the beach and his mother, Maureen, with her significant other, George, would go there in their RV. But Patrick would not be going to San Diego. By Christmas, he'd be heading back to Charleston to either accept the new assignment or pack up his gear and out-process. In the meantime, this little cabin of Aiden's — way up on top of the mountain — was sweet. And remote. And just what he wanted.

Colin put his hand on Patrick's shoulder. "Even before the Oxy, I had turned asshole into an art form. I realize that now. It took having my life gutted to turn me into the sweetheart I am today." Then he grinned. But he didn't remove his hand. "But you've always been the best one in the family. The most stable, sensitive, settled. It was always hard to picture you as a fighter jock. And now? It's hard to watch you in pain."

"I'm not in pain," Patrick said. "I'm in deep thought. Right now taking on a squadron commits me to the career path. I need some time to think about that. I'll talk about it after I've sorted a few things out. And I'm not completely antisocial — I made it to Thanksgiving dinner, right? I get to town for a beer almost every day." He didn't keep any alcohol at the cabin because the temptation to stay drunk for a few weeks was too strong. "I just need a little time, that's all. There's no reason for you to worry."

Colin removed the hand. "Okay, then. So, since you're not antisocial, hit town for a while tomorrow — they're raising the tree."

"The big tree?" he asked.

"Yep. Everyone gets into the act at some point. I'll stop by because I'm sure they'll need my advice. Luke will be in the thick of it. The general and Jack will compete for the boss position, but Paul Haggerty is the one in charge because he has all the heavy equipment needed to raise and anchor it. Getting it up and decorated is a two-day affair and the entire town shows up at one time or another. And then people start coming from all over this part of the state just to see it."

"I'll probably swing by in the next couple of days. . . ."

"Good," Colin said. He handed him the bag of leftovers. "Refrigerate. See you around."

"Yeah, sure."

After Colin left, Patrick made a phone call to Marie, Jake's widow. He called her every day. "Hey, it's me. How you doing today?"

"Holidays are kind of hard, but I knew they would be," she said. "I was with my whole family yesterday and they're a big crowd. My brother has a friend he says would like to take me to a movie, although I suspect my brother might have paid this guy."

"Nah," Patrick said. "Who wouldn't want to take you out? Are you ready for that — to go out, I mean?"

"Not yet," she said in a very quiet breath. "It hasn't been very long. . . ."

Just a couple of months, Patrick thought.

"And I was with Jake for a long time," Marie added.

Six years. Patrick knew exactly how long it had been. They'd dated for two years and then four years ago Patrick was their best man. Two years ago Jake's son, Daniel, was born and Patrick stood as godfather. He'd been on a mission with Jake when something went wrong over Afghanistan and Jake was shot down. They weren't the only two on that mission, but Patrick was their lead and the only one who felt responsible. Maybe it was more accurate to say Patrick had survivor guilt — why couldn't it have been him? Jake had a family who depended on him.

"I know, but can I just say that it's okay, Marie?" Patrick said. "Few weeks, few months, doesn't matter. If you feel like you can do it, go out and have a little fun with a guy, it's okay. Jake wouldn't mind. You know that."

"I know. When I'm ready, I will. But, Paddy, I have to get through all the special days without him first. All the holidays and birthdays and anniversaries . . ."

Is that what we have to do? Patrick wondered. "Did someone tell you that?"

"I've heard it here and there. I've been doing a little grief counseling with my church group and some people said that after you've been through all the important dates, things get a little easier. Or at least a little less terrible."

"Listen, Marie, I have all this free time. Want me to come back there for a while . . . ?"

"Seeing you is always good, Paddy, but

27

I've been surrounded by people since I came home to Oklahoma. I think it's better if you take care of yourself. I think you miss him as much as I do. You have things to work out, as well. Your own things."

Patrick was silent for a moment and then said, "I've been thinking about giving up the plane," he said quietly.

"Why?" she asked in a stunned whisper. "Because of Jake? Paddy, you love the plane!"

"Not because of Jake. Because in the long term . . ."

"And do what? Fly a desk? What?"

"Maybe not the Navy . . ."

"Okay, now I know you're all screwed up — you're more Navy than anyone I know. You're going to be a commander next and then Joint Chiefs one day."

Nah, he thought — never anything that elevated and political. He liked flying a fighter; he could exist commanding fighters. But after the accident, Patrick felt like everything in his life had suddenly changed and he wasn't sure which way to move next. "It's just something I've been kicking around," he said. "I might not get out of flying, but I have been getting sick of that big, gray boat."

"Now *that* I get," she said. "And that little

cot? And the night raids?" She laughed. "When you guys got home, Jake actually said he missed it all, if you can believe it."

"That's not what he told me," Patrick said, chuckling. "He said his sleeping arrangements had improved a hundred percent."

"Such a wild man," she reminisced sentimentally. And then with tears in her voice she said, "I don't think it's possible for me to ever feel that way about another human being again."

"It's too soon to say that," Patrick said. And his secret, which he didn't speak of, was that the only way he could get through ten more years in the Navy was with a woman like Marie as a partner. That's what had made Jake's life right; that's what he wanted — someone devoted to him. He was way too alone and he knew it. "We have to get through the year. . . ."

"Paddy, are you very lonely?" she asked him as if reading his mind.

"No, I'm getting by. My brothers are here." *The brothers I try not to spend too much time with,* he thought. Lonely wasn't his problem; as a Navy aviator he was constantly around a lot of Navy personnel — pilots, rios, mechanics, et cetera. On an aircraft carrier the only place to get a little privacy was in the head or up in the sky and *little* was the operative word — there was always someone in the next stall or in the rear seat of the aircraft.

But like an old married couple, he and Jake had never gotten bored with each other.

When they got back to Charleston, Jake was always with his wife and Patrick was usually with Leigh when she was in town and their schedules meshed. Jake and Leigh, his two closest friends. But then Leigh broke it off after four years and, not long after that, Jake had been killed. Next thing he knew he was spending his time in port with the Navy shrink, working it out. Or not working it out — he didn't have much to say to the doc and had never mentioned the breakup.

The shrink told his commander to give Patrick six weeks. Getting six weeks out of the Navy was pretty rare unless you'd had some horrible catastrophe like your wife dying of cancer.

Paddy was facing reassignment and he could just turn it down and walk away but his boss wanted him back; he wanted him to take a squadron. But doing that with nothing to look forward to, and without his two best friends — his girl and his buddy — was hard to imagine. He just didn't know if he was up to it.

He still had a hard time believing they'd left him.

TWO

The snow fell heavily on the Friday night after Thanksgiving and Angie was enthralled. Although she had done a little skiing in her time, she lived in a city that had to look up to the Sierras to see snow. The porch at the A-frame cottage was covered and for a little while she put on her heavy down jacket and sat out there just to watch it fall. So silent. So delicate. It was like being on the inside of a snow globe.

The fireplace in Mel and Jack's little cabin was large and warm and there was no need for any additional heat. She fed it logs and cozied up on the couch under the down comforter that had been on the bed. The sofa was soft and deep and she couldn't remember when she'd had a better night's sleep. They got a good six inches that night, and the morning dawned bright and clear with a thick, white blanket of snow on the ground and a delicious dusting on the pine boughs. It was like being on another planet — so far from that L.A. freeway where her life had been forever changed, so far from the house in Sacramento where she'd grown up, the place where she had revisited her childhood so many times during her recovery.

Yes, this was what she'd been looking for. A respite — some old-fashioned peace and quiet.

No one really understood how difficult it was to wake up from a bad dream, determined to change your life. She'd had partial memory loss for a few weeks after the accident, though she knew what she'd been doing, who her friends were, what her plans had been. This whole idea of being a doctor — she knew she could do it and do it well. She'd been groomed for this since her intellectual parents discovered her interest in science. But it was more like getting a plaque or trophy than about what it would bring to her life. After striving toward this goal for years, what was she to do with that feeling that it just wasn't enough? Perhaps after she watched falling snow, the orange sunsets, the explosion of autumn color and possibly a world-class geyser or waterfall she'd feel that enthusiasm return.

She still had the same friends, even if she

hadn't seen much of them. They were busy in med school and she had a rigorous rehab schedule, plus the relocation from L.A. to her parents' Sacramento home. One friend was still missing, though — her boyfriend. Alex. They'd been together for several months before the accident — he was a med student, as well. It happened all the time. Students tended to date one another more out of convenience than anything else, because it seemed to fit well with the intensity of med school. Alex left her at some point during her rehab — after the coma, before she remembered everything and could walk again. Strangely, his actions had remarkably little effect on her except to make her think, *Wow! Who does that? Leaves a girlfriend while she's recovering from catastrophic injuries?* That thought occurred every now and then.

The phone in the cabin rang, jarring her thoughts, bringing her back to the present. She tried to ignore it. It was still quite early, but she hadn't brewed coffee and didn't feel like cooking breakfast, so she pulled her scuffed-up cowboy boots over her torn jeans and grabbed her jacket. The phone was relentless, so with a heavy sigh she picked it up. "Hello."

"You're not staying with Jack," her mother said.

"Hi, Mom. No, I'm staying in his cabin."

"But I thought we understood each other — you would stay with Jack or Brie."

"Nope. That was your expectation. I'm very interested in seeing them but not living with them. I was hoping for the cabin or, at the least, Jack's guesthouse. I want a little time and space to myself."

"This is exactly what I've been talking about. You're not yourself at all. I've made an appointment with a neuropsychiatrist," she said. "We should get to the bottom of this."

Angie laughed. "Listen, Mom, do yourself a favor. Cancel it. You don't need much more than an everyday counselor to figure out that my brain is fine. The problem isn't me. I'm not doing things your way and it's making *you* crazy. I have to go. I don't want to be late for the raising of the tree."

"Angie . . . !"

"Bye," she said, disconnecting.

Neuropsychiatrist? Never gonna happen. Besides, she'd already seen at least one of those and no one, no matter how many degrees they had, could convince her that rejecting her mother's plan for her life automatically signaled a personality disorder.

The phone rang again, but Angie zipped her jacket and headed out the door. She stopped on the porch to indulge in a moment of remorse. Sadness. There was bound to be friction between a firstborn daughter and her strong-willed mother. Angie had always known how to please her parents and, in fact, usually had. Her mother proclaimed her a handful to raise, and yet, she'd managed to be Donna's pride and joy. Angie had never rebelled so thoroughly before.

Donna didn't seem to push back on Angie's younger sisters with the same kind of determination. When Jenna or Beth resisted their mother's plans, Donna seemed to let go faster. Easier.

"Dr. Temple, do you think my personality has changed?"

"It's possible. And there's always PTSD. Catastrophic accidents and long recoveries can have that effect."

"Do I have a disorder?"

"Disorder? I'm no expert, but I don't get the sense of a disorder. Do you think you have a disorder?"

"You know, I just feel like I finally woke up. I

feel as if I should change things. It's filling me with a sense of relief, of second chances, but it's upsetting my family. They're worried and angry, especially my mother. I'm battling with her over things like school. Battling like never before."

"Hmm. Well, have you asked yourself — do you like the new you?"

"I do. I want to be more independent. But I hate disappointing my mother. She's had it in her head I should be a doctor for a long time."

"I think, Angie, that you have to act on what's in your head, not your mother's. You're an adult, not her little girl anymore. Maybe you two need a little space to figure things out."

Not long after Angie had that conversation with Dr. Temple, Uncle Jack and Brie had stepped in. Jack called Donna and said, "The two of you are fighting like a couple of cats in a sack. You're not going to get better this way. Send Angie up here for a while. A few weeks. Let her get some perspective and take a breather. This is ridiculous."

It took a follow-up phone call from Brie, but Donna finally came around. She was persuaded to put off the head butting at least until after the first of the year.

Angie could almost hear her father breathe a sigh of relief.

When Angie arrived in town, she saw that even though the hour was early, the place was already a circus. The big flatbed with an enormous tree strapped to it blocked the street and mounted on another truck was a giant winch. The ground had been plowed free of snow right between the bar and the church, back off the road a bit in the area where, in milder weather, there were picnic tables. That's where the tree would stand. The sound of a hydraulic post digger assaulted the morning air as meanly as a jackhammer, and a lot of people stood around watching while the tree was being attached to the lift. Cables trailed off the tree — likely to be anchored to stakes in the ground to steady it.

It was so *big*.

Someone pressed a cup of coffee into her hands and she turned to see Mike V, Brie's husband, her uncle Mike. She had forgotten her desire for caffeine. "Thank you," she said, kissing his cheek.

"How's that little cabin working out?" he asked.

"It's perfect. I'm going to get some candles from the bar — I sat on the porch last night and just watched the snow. If I'd had some candles . . ."

"I'm sure that can be arranged, *chica*," he said, draping an arm around her shoulders.

As they stood together in the street, watching, chains were tightened, the motor on the lift was pumping away and more and more people who had been forced to park down the street were walking toward the tree-raising. Jack and General Booth stood near Paul Haggerty, talking and pointing and gesturing, but Paul seemed to completely ignore them as he directed his team.

It took long enough that Angie's coffee was gone by the time the tree was finally lifted off the bed of the truck. Four men holding four cables maneuvered the airborne tree so that the trunk slipped into the hole that had been dug right in the ground. Then the cables were pulled tight, straightening the tree. There was a loud, collective "Ahh" in the crowd of people gathered around to watch. There was a bit of muffled applause thanks to the gloves and mittens worn by most of the spectators.

Finally Jack and the general had major roles — they were standing across the street from the tree to judge the straightness of it before the cables were secured to the ground. They were gesturing right, then left, then right. . . .

And Angie saw him. He was standing on the porch of the bar, leaning a shoulder against a post. He was most definitely watching her. When their eyes met he did that smile thing again — half his mouth lifted. His eyes got just a little bit sleepy, but the glittering green was still overwhelming. She wanted a close-up of those eyes.

Real close.

Patrick lifted a coffee cup to his lips, but he never took his eyes off her, peering at her over the rim of the cup.

"You okay, *chica*?" Mike asked.

"That guy," she said, just taking him in. "Do you know him?"

Mike followed her eyes. "Patrick? I know his brothers. I've only met him once or twice."

"How long has he lived around here?"

"Just visiting, I hear. You okay?"

"He's staring at me," she said in a low voice, trying not to move her lips.

Mike cleared his throat. "Um, listen, if he's making you uncomfortable, I could have a word with him."

She grinned at Mike. "He's making me uncomfortable all right, but not exactly in a bad way. Don't say anything, all right? Don't make him stop. I don't think anyone has ever looked at me that way before."

Mike turned Angie toward him. His black eyes bore into her with intensity. "Ange, don't play with fire. I don't know much about Patrick except that he has some difficult situation going with the military. The Navy just gave him more leave to sit in Virgin River than they typically grant, which usually indicates a problem of some kind. You should at least talk to Jack before you do anything young and foolish."

She laughed at him, amused. "Wow, doesn't that sound fun, a chat with Uncle Jack about an interesting guy. Now I was kind of young at the time, but if I remember correctly Uncle Jack thought you were a bad idea for Aunt Brie. Do I have that right?"

Mike pursed his lips as he pondered this. "We were both older than you, for one thing. We had been through some real major crises, for another, which left Jack feeling a little on the protective side. And we were careful to take it slow — know what I'm saying? I don't know any details but I hear Patrick has had some issues — real problems. Hear me?"

"Absolutely," she said. "Fortunately, I haven't been through any crises or had any problems. . . ."

"Oh, man," Mike said. "Now you're scaring me."

She patted his arm. "I'll be just fine, Uncle Mike. I know it's hard for everyone to accept this, but I'm not a little girl anymore. I can handle this." She turned to look again at Patrick but he wasn't there. "Crap," she muttered. "I hope you didn't scare him away. I wanted to talk to him."

"I was on the verge of suggesting you don't talk to him."

"Yeah, I know," she said. "I think I need a refill on the coffee. Thanks. By the way, where is Brie?"

"I think she's in the bar with Ness, but, Ange —"

"I'll catch up with you in a while. Thanks for the coffee." She glanced at the tree and gave it a nod. "You might want to tell Jack it's leaning west."

Angie scored in the bar. Brie was there with little Ness, sitting at a table with Mel and Emma, chatting it up while the little girls made an attempt at coloring. There were only a few people in the bar since the tree-raising was occupying almost everyone in town. She noticed Patrick sitting at the far end of the bar on the other side of the room, all alone, far away from her aunts.

"Ah, my favorite aunts," she said. She

42

leaned down to give each of them a kiss on the cheek, telling them the cabin was awesome. She immediately excused herself to go to the bar for more coffee. They might've expected her back at their table after she'd gone behind the bar to serve herself. Instead, she paused, took a deep breath and hopped up on a stool right next to Patrick. She imagined that Brie and Mel wouldn't know how much courage she'd needed to do that. They knew she wasn't particularly shy, but they couldn't possibly know how little experience she had with men, especially a man like this — handsome, sexy and out of her age range by at least a few years.

"Hi," she said. "I'm Angie LaCroix." She put out a hand.

He stared at the hand for a moment, then lifted his gaze to her eyes. And, oh, sweet baby Jesus, he was *beautiful*. He took her hand in his much larger one. "To what do I owe the pleasure?"

Just go for it, she thought. *Why not?* "I thought we should meet, since you look at me like you're the big bad wolf. And you are . . . ?"

He couldn't seem to suppress a short laugh. "I bet you know exactly who I am."

"Ah, yes, Patrick Riordan, the youngest brother of a clan anchored here. Do I have that right?"

"More or less. I have a couple of brothers here and another couple not too far away."

"Right. So you're here visiting family?"

"Not exactly. I'm here because one of my brothers has a vacation cabin here and I had some time on my hands. Since the lot of them are planning a Christmas gathering in San Diego, there won't be a crowd of Riordans here for the holiday. That suits me fine. I wanted a quiet place to hang out for a while. I wasn't looking for a family reunion, but it's always good to see a brother or two. Just not too much of them."

She looked perplexed. "If you want to avoid them, why would you come to their little town?"

"It's complicated. The Riordans are extremely nosy and opinionated. They gather. They *swarm*. If I hadn't come here, they would have come looking for me. All of them. That's what happens in my family. We can leave one another alone for months at a time but then when something happens, like a brother at some kind of crossroads, accident or crisis, the troops are called in and the wagons are circled. When you're the one the wagons are circling, it sucks."

She was silent for a moment. "That's very grumpy of you."

"Well, you did ask."

"You know, we have a little something in common," she said. "I'm here for a little R and R myself and for a similar but not identical reason. I dropped out of school. I'm not sure I want to pursue my original plan and I need a break. My parents, who are both college professors, are going a little crazy on me. A little distance from them seemed like a good idea. In fact, it was Uncle Jack's idea." She grinned at him. "Though I suspect I didn't get far enough away. My uncle Jack can get a little . . . intrusive . . . protective. For example, he suggested I stay away from you."

"Me? Why? What's wrong with me?" he asked.

"Apparently you're scary and dangerous," she informed him with a sly smile.

"What? Dangerous? Me? Who said that?"

"It was implied," she admitted. "I've been advised by the older men in my life not to get involved with you, but no one has told me exactly why. So, why?"

He chuckled silently and shook his head. "Listen, I'm just here for a few weeks. Maybe you *should* stay away from me. And you look like you finished school a long time ago. You must be younger than you look."

"I finished college. It's a postgrad thing.

But . . . How old do I seem? Because you undress me with your eyes. Skillfully. And at a great distance, too."

He leaned toward her. "How old are you?"

"Almost twenty-six," she said, straightening, sitting tall.

"How almost?" he pressed.

She took a breath. "Twenty-three."

He groaned and looked down, shaking his head. "God. You're younger than you look."

"So how old are you?" she asked. "Forty?"

"Hey," he said. "I'm thirty-three."

She leaned her head on her hand, elbow braced on the bar. "Had a hard few years or something?"

"Whoa! You're brutal!"

But Angie was really starting to enjoy this adventurous, flirty side of herself. This was certainly new territory for her, but she suddenly had the urge to explore it. "The way you look at me should at least be considered a misdemeanor. Or a proposal, I'm not sure which. But it didn't feel that bad and I thought maybe if we talked . . ."

"What? You thought I'd ask you out on a date or something? Sweetheart, this is Virgin River. If we sit here and talk for even five more minutes, everyone in town will put us together."

"Let's take a chance," she said, amazing

herself. But then, she was on a mission. She wanted to know someone who she could relate to. Who could relate to her. And it sure didn't hurt that Patrick Riordan was smokin' *hot*. "Talking isn't against the law."

"What if I don't feel like talking? You don't want to mess around with the big bad wolf."

"Do you feel like listening? Because I can always talk. And we have things in common, you and I."

"I don't feel like fighting off the vigilantes who'll come down on me to protect your honor, so I think me going home right now is a better idea."

At that, Angie smiled so big that Patrick actually leaned back slightly. "So!" she said. "You do like me!"

"How the hell would I know?" he barked at her. "I don't even know you!"

"Then why do you watch me? Stare at me? Get mad when I suggest we spend a little time talking?"

"Because you're a cute little sexpot, and while you might be old enough for this flirtation, I can tell you're way too inexperienced for it, and you have a posse in town looking out for you and I don't need any trouble! Believe me, I have enough trouble!"

She glanced down at herself. Old jeans with a torn knee, a pair of battered cowboy boots that she'd been attached to for years, khaki canvas jacket and an oversize white sweater — and no makeup. . . . She looked up at him and laughed. "Sexpot? Jesus! Are you serious?"

He pursed his lips and put his hands in his jacket pockets. "Serious," he hissed.

"Well, holy shit, if this gets your motor running, I'm not going *anywhere*!"

"Angie . . ."

"You should see me when I get dressed up! I can look damn good."

"Angie . . ."

"Patrick," she mimicked.

Suddenly Brie was standing on the inside of the bar holding the coffeepot. She wordlessly refilled their cups without making eye contact and disappeared back to her table. Angie *knew* they were talking about her. She knew it and didn't care.

"I have an idea," Angie said. "Let's just have a cup of coffee. Then we'll reassess things. However, I have to warn you, I kind of like that you find me irresistible."

"Did I say that?" he asked, a slight tint creeping up his stubbled cheeks. "I didn't say that! I find you completely resistible."

"Touchy, huh? Maybe you should have something a little stronger than coffee."

He gave her a slow look, a full appraisal

that made her warm, a feeling she couldn't remember having before, and she liked it. She was growing more bold by the minute. Then with his eyes narrowed he said, "All right, we'll have a cup of coffee. You'll talk. Then I'll head home and you'll stop looking for trouble."

She stared at him levelly. "Do women actually find you scary?" she asked.

Patrick couldn't remember ever treating a woman like that, rudely looking her over, trying to make her uncomfortable to scare her off, running roguish eyes up and down the length of her. Especially a sweet young thing like Angie. In fact, he had always been the complete opposite, a gentleman to the core. Present circumstances had put a rough edge on him. Plus, his instincts told him it would be practical if not wise if she just didn't get too close. He was a wreck without much to offer. The only woman who had his attention right now was his best friend's widow, that's how sad his life had become.

But Angie wasn't easily discouraged. With a cup of coffee in front of him he said, "No young woman should come on to a man she doesn't know, especially after being warned away from him by her protectors. That sort of thing could get you hurt."

"Oh, stop," she said. She took a sip of her coffee. "Jack and Preacher and Mike said they know you a little bit and are friends with your brothers. They all said you were troubled by something but no one ever suggested you were dangerous — I made that up to flatter you. So guess what? I might be troubled, too. You might think I'm a little nuts, but the truth is I wouldn't mind having a friend who also has some things to sort out."

He just stared at her. "And what might be troubling you, miss? Dropping out of some cushy college program?"

"Exactly right," she answered. "But not because I was bored or disillusioned. I was in an accident and had to take leave. It was a medical leave."

He was startled and it showed in his eyes. He might've overheard something about a hospital at the bar, but the details were vague right now. "What kind of accident?"

"The kind that means having rods and pins put in you and lands you in physical therapy for a few months."

An image of Patrick's brother, Colin, lying unconscious in a hospital bed, barely alive after a Black Hawk crash, came to his mind. He shuddered involuntarily. "What happened?"

"Well, I had to learn to walk, of course, but —"

"No, what kind of accident?" he asked, genuinely interested.

"Oh — a car accident. Three cars, actually. And what happened is still being disputed — the driver at fault was killed. She lost control of her car, jumped the median on the freeway and hit two oncoming cars, the one I was in and another. There was a witness who said she was cut off by a speeding car that didn't stop. It was raining and the roads were slick. Another witness said there was no speeding car and that it looked like her car suddenly hydroplaned, like she lost control because of a flat or broken axel or something. Someone suggested she might've fallen asleep, but it wasn't like she'd just come off a twelve-hour shift or anything — she was on her way out to meet a date for dinner and hadn't driven far. I don't remember much. I remember lights, sirens, my girlfriend crying — she had a broken ankle, a couple of broken ribs and a really badly shattered wrist, plus lots of bad bruises and cuts. They had to pry both of us out of the car. She remembers that — the sawing and crunching of metal — but I don't."

He was quiet for a moment, in something

51

of a trance. "Man," he finally said in a whisper. "One killed?"

"Yes, and the third car was a family with little kids, but thankfully they didn't have any critical injuries. The kids were in their safety seats and they were in a big SUV. I feel terrible about the lady driver, though. There were no drugs or any alcohol involved. I think, in the end, what we have here is an accident."

"And you were badly hurt," he clarified.

"All banged up. I was in L.A. at the time, a student at USC, and my parents live in Sacramento so they jumped in their car right away. My dad drove like a bat out of hell so they could be there when I got out of surgery. My mom stayed with me for two months, until I could be moved home to complete my checkups and therapy. The whole time I was in L.A. there was a steady stream of aunts and uncles and cousins visiting to see how I was doing even though some of them had to travel a ways. I come from a big family and I'm the oldest grandchild. My grandpa was there several times. I don't know if you've ever had the experience of looking like absolute shit and feeling even worse and having thirty or so people stare at you. . . ."

"I'm pretty sure I haven't," he said.

"It sucks. And when I was back in Sacramento, there was even more checking in. I was never alone, never. So — there you have it. Well, no, you don't have it yet. The thing is, my mother is the toughest, strongest, least sentimental overachiever I know. She's Uncle Jack's oldest sister and she's been pushing him around for over forty years. She's a journalism professor at Berkeley. But having her oldest child hurt and in the hospital brought her to her knees. Kicked the stuffing out of her. She took a leave from the college and dedicated herself to my care, which was a wonderful thing to do, but I think she lost her mind a little bit. She's always been domineering in her way . . . bossy, you might say. The accident really amped that up. She was determined to get me healed and back on track. But suddenly, she wanted to bring my sister Beth home from her senior year at NAU in Flagstaff — she couldn't sleep at night thinking about her driving those mountain roads. And my littlest sister, Jenna, she wanted to keep in Sacramento at a state college even though she'd been attending UCLA."

"And what about you?" he asked.

Angie couldn't help but laugh. "She wants me to sleep in a helmet."

He laughed a little with her. "I bet you

want to sleep in a helmet sometimes, too."

"Well, that's where Mom and I have had a breakdown in communication. I want to *not* be afraid. I never want to be scared to live life because of one bad experience, as terrible as it was. It's not like I could've done anything differently — I was in the wrong place at the wrong time. So — should I live the rest of my life in a padded room?"

He shook his head. "No, but you shouldn't follow strange men into bars, either. Even bars owned by your uncle. You should have yourself a nice young man who has a normal life and calls you for a date, then picks you up and takes you someplace special."

"Oh, I had one of those," Angie said with a sigh. "I had him for months before the accident and he said he loved me. He wandered off sometime during physical therapy. . . . Haven't heard from him since."

Patrick felt the color drain from his face. And he found himself thinking, *I was one of those nice young men who did what his woman expected, and I was left. . . .* He couldn't believe people did that — abandoned their partner in a time of need. He'd never be so cruel as to run out on a person he'd once loved like that. Angie's experience with her former boyfriend was very close to the hurt he felt over the woman

54

who had left him behind. Leigh had said she loved him, too. Then suddenly she told him, unemotionally, that they weren't right for each other. She had a career of her own and wanted a full partner, not some Navy fly-boy. He hadn't been with another woman since then.

Yet what tore him up the most was the fact that when he'd called Leigh to tell her Jake was dead, she hadn't come to him. She hadn't comforted him beyond the telephone condolences of that one call. She hadn't come to the memorial. She'd sent Marie a card — she might have even had a card sent by one of her assistants — but she hadn't called her. That's when he realized they must never have been good together in the first place. If the tables had been turned and she'd lost someone close, he would have been there for her even if they were no longer a couple.

They'd spent so much time together, the four of them. Didn't she grieve Jake? Sympathize with Marie? Worry about Patrick's feelings? It had baffled and hurt him. He felt he had never known her at all.

He looked at Angie and said, "So he just kind of wandered off?"

"Yeah. At first he was too busy with school, then he said he just couldn't watch my struggle, it was too difficult for him. This guy wants to be a doctor! And he couldn't bear seeing me in pain? Pah! Then one of my friends said he was seeing someone else. I cried. For an hour. But something tells me I got off easy. I'm going to need a much tougher man in my life. I'll hold out for that."

He grinned suddenly. His immediate thought was, *And I'll need a much stronger woman.* Could it really be that simple? "You should."

"You don't look at all scary when you smile," she said in a rather soft voice.

"You said I didn't look scary before."

"Yeah, well, I didn't want you to get all bigheaded. So, Patrick Riordan, what's got you all messed up?"

He slid back in his chair. "I thought we agreed not to talk about me?" He took a sip of coffee.

"I certainly don't intend to insist, but when you're sharing, you know, there's usually a little give and take. . . ."

"I'm a Navy pilot," he said after a short pause. "I was on a mission and another pilot flying in the same sortie was killed. Shot down. Right beside me. We were flying cover for Marine rescue choppers near Kandahar, avoiding missiles, and then . . . The unexpected. A heat seeker came out of nowhere. He was my closest friend. I was his lead. He was my wingman."

"I'm so sorry. I can understand why you didn't want to talk about that."

"Someone would've told you eventually. Jake went down and it's time for me to get orders — a new assignment somewhere. I just feel like I need a little time to decide if I really want that life. I always thought I did. But lately I've been thinking that it might not fit with the other things I'd like to have — like a family, for instance. Jake left behind a wife and two-year-old son."

"But do you love flying?" she asked him.

"I always have, but that . . ." His voice trailed off.

"That's one of the things I'm struggling with, too, Patrick. But I've realized that there are fewer NASCAR drivers killed than girls like me who were singing along with the radio one minute and dead the next. None of those people on commercial jets on 9/11 were taking chances. Besides, if you're doing something you believe in and are expertly trained to do . . . But then, you might have to ask the woman in your life before you listen to me."

He just stared at her for a second. "There's no woman."

"Oh," she said.

"And my friends call me Paddy."

She smiled at him. "I like that."

"What's your next move, Angie?"

She took a deep breath. "Oh, I'll probably end up going back to medical school eventually, but not —"

"*Medical school?*" he asked, wide-eyed. "You mean you're not getting some degree in basket weaving or tennis?"

She laughed lightly. "Nah. I'm a brainiac with limited social skills, as you can probably see."

He shook his head, but his mouth was still open. He hadn't been ready for this. "You take chances, but now I think I get it. So, you'll go back to school?"

"Well, like you, I have to make a decision — I don't know if I *want* to go back to med school. The second I said 'doctor' when I was about sixteen my parents were on the case — going over my classes, my major and my transcripts, my med school applications. I missed a lot of life being the perfect student. While I was recovering, I had some great docs but there was one I was close to. Dr. Temple was never in a hurry. He talked to me. It's possible he was simply studying me, looking for signs of brain damage, but still . . ." She gave a shrug, then shook her head. "I've been fighting with my mother a lot. She wants me back in med school before too much time passes, and I'm not sure I'm ever going back. Next for me, Paddy, is a little more balance in my life. If I've learned anything from what happened, it's that you shouldn't miss opportunities to live life. It could always be your last chance. And not just if you're a Navy pilot. It could be your last chance even if you're just making a grocery store run."

"No one can make you go to medical school."

"I so hate to disappoint them. But I might be looking for something more."

"Going to become an adventurer?" he asked.

"That's not really what I mean. I think watching the snow fall in candlelight and cuddling a baby — those can be watershed moments, too."

She stood up from the bar. He stood, as well. "For today, I chased down an interesting guy — something I've never done before. I've had a nice cup of coffee, and now I'm going back outside to watch the decorating of the tree. I'm also going to try to talk my way into one of those cherry pickers, but I might have to get my uncle Jack drunk first." Then she laughed.

"I gave you a hard time, Angie," he said. "Sorry."

"It's okay, Paddy. You have stuff to work out, too. Big stuff, and again, I'm sorry for your loss. And," she added with a shrug, "I've been told I can be a lot to take. Especially lately . . ."

He grabbed her hand before she could leave. "No, you're not," he said. "Maybe you should have another cup of coffee."

She shook her head, but the look in her eyes said she was tempted.

"You started it," he accused.

"Aw, I think you did, with your green eyes and that look."

He put his right hand against the side of her head in an affectionate gesture and suddenly time stopped. He had a strange look on his face. His fingers rubbed against a raised, hairless spot behind her ear. She had long, thick, pretty brown hair streaked with blond but there was no mistaking a scar. He pulled away from her to look into her eyes.

"A shunt," she said. "I don't know why the hair doesn't grow there, but I guess it'll grow back someday. I think."

"Shunt?" The word was not completely alien to him, but he wasn't making all the connections.

"My brain swelled while I was in a coma.

They fixed it with the shunt to drain the edema but then they leave it in. It's not working anymore but they don't remove the shunt unless it creates a problem. We don't do brain surgery unless we have to."

He watched her eyes. "Coma," he said, still gently touching that lump. "Brain swelling. You had a head injury. A serious head injury."

"But really, I'm fine. Completely recovered. I mean, I think I am. Even given my chasing dangerous men into bars . . ."

"It was a bad accident," he confirmed. "Very bad."

She nodded. "Which explains why my mother thinks I have a personality disorder and wants me in a padded suit for the rest of my life. And maybe it also explains my resistance to that idea."

He smiled gently and said, "I like your personality."

"Thanks," she said, some confidence restored. "That actually means a lot to me." She gave him another smile, then turned and headed out to join the festivities.

THREE

Once Angie left the bar, Patrick felt a little short of breath. Meeting her was the last thing he expected. Or intended. He was still feeling emotionally wounded by Leigh. Leigh, who was a sophisticated, thirty-year-old society girl, the daughter of a rich, widowed senator out of Charleston. Leigh, so stunning and brilliant she made men gasp when she strolled by.

So perfect and, ultimately, so cold.

Patrick threw a couple of bills on the bar for their coffee and went outside. There was still a lot of activity around the tree, but he didn't see Angie. He left town to go home, but all the way there he found himself thinking about the differences between this young, warm, optimistic woman who'd cheated death and Leigh, who had everything and was grateful for nothing.

How had he not noticed that Leigh was so unfeeling when he'd been involved with her?

Patrick had only one picture of Leigh Brisbain with him, although there were still many in his Charleston home, a house Leigh had decorated to suit her tastes. In the picture he kept in his wallet, taken on a sailboat, she lounged against him, both of them hanging on to the rigging, windblown and smiling. She'd been out of his life for six months; all the pictures at home should at least be packed away somewhere. Maybe when he got back there, he'd do that.

Leigh had a place of her own in Maryland, a place he'd only visited when he was available to attend charity or political events with her. When Patrick deployed, Leigh spent all her time near the nation's capital, working full-time for her father. She never stayed in Patrick's Charleston house without him, though Patrick had always thought of it as theirs, together. Leigh loved D.C. and planned to make her life there. Her ultimate ambition was to follow in her father's footsteps. She'd run for office one day and split her time between D.C. and Charleston.

How had he managed to miss that they were so unconnected? It had ended so suddenly. He had come home from sea to find a picture of her in a newspaper where she was dancing with a smiling man. Not exactly a smoking gun — she attended so many political and charity affairs that this didn't alarm him in the least. He had casually asked, "Who's the guy?"

And she had replied, "I guess it's finally time for us to have this talk, Patrick. Our lives are so out of sync — you're committed to the Navy and I'm going for a career in civilian politics. You're going to transfer around and I'm going to have to establish roots to support my constituency and political career. You'll be flying — I'll be here or in Washington."

"Haven't we had this conversation many times?" he said. "You're not running for office right away, probably not for years. We have plenty of time."

She merely shook her head. "I don't think so," she had said. "I'm not going to be a Navy wife. I'm building a career. I need a partner."

"To do what? Go to dances?" he asked. "You seem to do just fine, attending with your father."

"That's not working for me," she said.

"Are you asking me to get out? After ten years plus four in the Academy? Is that what you want?" he asked.

And clear as a bell she had said, "I'm

afraid that won't work for me, either."

That had pretty much summed it up. Oh, they'd talked it to death for a while, but the actual conclusion had been reached in the first two minutes of conversation. She was done. It didn't matter how he viewed the future, she was done. That was six months ago and he wasn't sure if he missed her, was angry with her, wanted her back or wanted to send her hate mail.

He began to ask himself why they'd been together in the first place and was stunned to find the list of reasons was incredibly short. She loved dressing him up in his Navy mess dress for formal events in either D.C. or Charleston; she praised him often for being a quality escort. He loved looking at her, talking to her, touching her. She loved being connected to a decorated aviator who had been to war many times and he loved the convenience of having someone there for him when he returned to port. Had he loved her? He'd thought that *was* love.

Maybe what he felt more than anything was foolish and inexperienced.

He'd always been a one-woman man and playing the field held no interest for him. Even if she hadn't been there full-time, neither had he. The end of their relationship was probably as much his fault, as Leigh's. Not only had she taken the path of least resistance, but so had he.

Patrick had always known, even if he hadn't admitted it, that he didn't have the kind of relationship with Leigh that Jake had had with Marie. Jake was a frothing mess when he got home from a mission, grabbing Marie up in his arms like the wild man he was, going missing for a few days while he immersed himself in every possible ounce of her and even then being reluctant to let her get too far from his side. *That* was real love, and that was what Patrick had always wanted.

Now, two of the most important people in his life were gone.

When he got back to his cabin, he didn't even go inside. He sat on the deck and absorbed the view. He thought about what had brought him here to Virgin River. Damn, life could get empty real fast.

And then this little med student comes along with such warmth, sincerity and passion for life. What a breath of fresh air. It didn't hurt that she was adorable, gutsy and funny. He probably should stay far away from her, but he clearly was at her mercy — he admired her. Truthfully, he was enthralled. Life played some very strange tricks, sticking him with completely inappropriate feelings for a young woman he'd known for all of an hour. She was too young. On a totally different life path. Vulnerable but alluring. He had to admit, however, her mere presence had taken all the sting out of his loneliness for a little while. But she was not right for him.

Even though his brothers didn't know it, he'd given his word to Jake — he would take care of Marie and Daniel. Marie needed him.

A creature of habit, he decided to call Marie. "How are you today?" he asked once she picked up.

"Today is a pretty good day," she said. "Things are quieting down in the post-Thanksgiving haze. You?"

"Not bad, but things aren't so quiet. It's getting interesting in Virgin River. They're putting up the big tree, for one thing — it's about thirty feet tall and decorated in military insignia."

"Wow, that's huge for a little town."

"This town is only little on the outside," he said.

Ten minutes later he was on his way back into town to watch the tree trimming and to see if there was anything or anyone interesting in one of those cherry pickers.

67

■ ■ ■ ■

Jack was descending in the bucket of the cherry picker when Angie pulled into town and parked across the street by the clinic. She met him as he got out. "You went missing for a while," he observed.

"I was exploring a little bit," she said. "Is it my turn?"

"Awww, I don't know, Ange. . . ."

"Come on."

"I might need a note from your doctor."

She laughed at him, nudged him to one side and inserted herself in the bucket. "Explain the controls, please," she said. "I'll be very careful."

He sighed, defeated. Sometimes he got so tired of headstrong women. He explained the levers in the control box, though with the diagrams right beside the controls, it was pretty self-explanatory. "Now, listen, I don't want you over ten feet off the ground," he said.

"Seriously?"

"Do you doubt I'll climb up this boom and bring you down?" he asked.

"This is getting really old," Angie said, and with that, she rose to the task. She went up ten feet, then left, then right, then up a few feet more, left and right, then higher.

"Angela," he warned.

She went up a bit farther. "I'm fine," she said. "I love this. I think I might decorate the whole tree for you. At least the top part."

"Angela LaCroix," he called. "Lower, please."

She leaned out of the box and grinned at him. "Are you going to ground me?"

Mel was standing beside him, looking up. "Angie, see that red streamer to your left? Pull that one a little right please, it's all wonkie."

She reached out of the bucket and Jack flinched. "Got it," she said. "Tell me when it's straight."

"Better," Mel said. "Now move around and pull the white one over."

"Mel," Jack said. "She's just having a ride. I want her down!"

"Jack, take it easy, she's twenty-three, not three. Better, Ange. If I give you some balls, want to hang them up there?"

She leaned out of the bucket and stared down. "If I come down there to get them, your husband is going to grab me."

"No, he won't," she said. "I'll hold him down. Come on."

Jack growled and began to pace. He spoke softly to Mel. "What if she gets dizzy?"

69

"Then she'll come down. She's better off in the bucket than on a ladder. Angie, are you dizzy?"

"Of course not," she said, lowering herself. She leaned over and accepted a box of shiny gold balls from Mel. Then she quickly went up again to avoid Jack.

"Leave plenty of room for the unit badges we'll also use as ornaments."

"Will do," she said, raising the cherry picker while holding on to the ornaments.

Jack watched her some, paced some, grumbled some. The number of people in the street and around the bar grew, but Jack was focused on Angie. No one paid any attention to his worries; Mel continued to yell up at Angie to move a ball or fix some garland. Angie laughed happily as she ran the cherry picker down to the ground, then up again with more ornaments. Or possibly she was laughing at her uncle Jack.

Jack had been oblivious to what was going on around him until he noticed that Angie stopped in midair and looked across the street. Jack followed her line of vision to see Patrick Riordan leaning against his Jeep, watching her. As Jack glanced between the two of them, Angie gave a wave and Patrick waved back.

Crap, he thought.

Well, he should've known — it was written all over her face that she was smitten with Patrick's good looks. Jack stopped pacing because Angie was all done playing around in the cherry picker now that Patrick had appeared. She brought it down, stepped out and brushed off her jeans. Her *tight* jeans.

"Thanks, I'll take over," Mel said, as though there wasn't a thing in the world to be worried about.

"That was fun," Angie said to her uncle.

Jack glowered.

"What?" she asked.

Jack tilted his head and glanced to the right, across the street, where Patrick patiently waited for her to be finished.

"Oh, excuse me," Angie said. And she walked casually across the street as though this was perfectly fine.

It was *not* perfectly fine in Jack's opinion.

Mel was raising the bucket with her box of ornaments while Jack was following Angie with his eyes. But Angie didn't look back. She had Patrick in her crosshairs.

So Jack looked around until he spotted Luke Riordan with young Brett on his hip. He walked over to him and said, "Luke."

"Looking good, Jack."

"Look over there, Luke," he said, again

with the head tilt. "Your brother."

"Yeah, he made it to town for the tree. That's good. I think he spends too much time alone these days."

"What's up with Patrick, anyway?" Jack asked.

"Flying stuff," Luke said with a shrug. "You know. Threw him for a while, made him rethink the Navy. He just needs some decompression time. He'll be fine."

"What kind of flying stuff?"

Luke turned his head to meet eyes with Jack. "His wingman went down."

Jack just whistled.

"He got some leave," Luke went on. "He has a decision to make. He always planned on a Navy career, but I guess he's rethinking it. He has until Christmas to figure it out. Who's the girl?"

Right about then Patrick put a hand on Angie's shoulder. She looked up at him, he looked down at her. Jack shivered. "My niece, up for a visit."

"Nice," Luke said.

"She's been valedictorian twice in her life already — for her high school class and for her college class. She's a medical student, but she was in a car accident and had to take some time off. We're all hoping she plans to go back to med school after the

72

holidays. That's what everyone in the family wants. Listen, Luke — see this?" he said, looking across the street to where Patrick and Angie stood talking. "This is Patrick's second trip into town today. He's interested in Angie. I don't think this should happen."

"What?"

"My niece and your brother," Jack said irritably.

"Aw, lighten up. Patrick's a good kid."

"He's no kid," Jack said. "How old is Patrick?"

Luke shrugged. "I guess about thirty. Thirty-two. Or three."

"Angie is twenty-three. And she needs to go back to school."

"What do you expect me to do about it?"

"I don't know, exactly. Talk to him. Tell him the girl is barely out of high school and he needs to move on."

"Aw, Jack . . ." Luke shook his head. "She's out of *college*. And she's smart. I mean — valedictorian? I'm lucky I graduated high school."

"He's been in the bar, and I hate to say it about one of your brothers, but he's got attitude, Luke. Doesn't talk, isn't friendly, acts all fucked up and miserable. And you say his wingman went down? Angie can't take on stuff like that. She's just a girl. A

73

girl with her own issues."

Luke started to laugh.

"What's funny?" Jack asked.

"He looks pretty friendly to me," Luke said.

And sure enough, Patrick was smiling. Laughing. Touching her with familiarity.

Jack cringed. "Ah, dammit, he's playing around with her hair!"

Luke laughed a little harder. "I've played with hair . . . you've played with hair. . . ."

"She's too young! She's barely recovered from a bad car accident!" He grumbled something and then said, "I'm responsible for her."

"Well, she's over twenty-one so I bet she doesn't let you stand responsible for too much."

"You got that right," he muttered. "Her mother is my older sister. I really don't want to go a round with her. She's a pain in my ass."

"Then don't. You better ease up, Jack. I don't think you're going to have much influence here. And I could talk to him, but it wouldn't do any good."

"I don't want that to happen," he said glumly.

"Out of my hands. He's a Riordan. The fact that he's always been a real docile and

74

sweet Riordan makes no difference at all."

"Look, I like you Riordan boys just fine," Jack said. "But the lot of you — you're scrappy, you're ornery and you're like heat-seeking missiles. That's my niece!"

"Yeah, Riordans are a lot like Jack Sheridan," Luke pointed out.

"Irrelevant," Jack said.

"That Riordan . . . if he's got his eye on a target — hey, nothing any of us can do. That's just how it is. You of all people should understand that. Besides, at thirty-eight I married a twenty-five-year-old and no one had a headache about that."

"As I recall, her uncle was a little annoyed. . . ."

"We had some things to work out, me and Uncle Walt. But the rest of you old boys just laughed at me, said I'd be going to college graduations with a walker."

Jack ground his teeth. Then, while he watched Angie and Patrick, he asked, "You and Shelby planning more kids?"

"Why?"

"Because I wish a girl on you!" And then Jack stomped off into the bar.

Angie couldn't help how she felt when she saw Patrick standing across the street watching her. He'd come back. If he'd just gone into the bar, it wouldn't have meant as much, but he had no interest in the bar — he wanted to see her in the cherry picker. It was like he was rooting for her.

And she wanted him to see her.

She walked across the street to him. "You got your ride," he said.

"I did. Is Uncle Jack still watching me?"

"Oh, yes," he said, putting his hands in his pockets and laughing a little. "He's going to be a problem, isn't he?"

"Completely."

"How would you like to handle that?" Patrick asked.

"Do you think if we ignore him, he'll go away?"

"I have my doubts," Patrick said. "He's a little on the grouchy side."

"So are you," she pointed out.

"Aw, I'm coming around. He isn't going to beat me up, is he?"

"If he does, I'll never speak to him again and, trust me, that would sting. I'm his favorite. He doesn't admit that because he has a whole flock of nieces, but I am his favorite. But I'm getting a little bored with this — he's treating me like a twelve-year-old virgin."

Patrick risked his life by fingering a strand of her hair and slipping it behind her ear.

"You're not, are you?"

Here's where Angie might have a little trouble. She was smart, but she wasn't worldly. Especially with men. One of her regrets, actually. She was twenty-three and she'd had a couple of boyfriends and only one had been semiserious. Oh, Alex had been serious to her, but apparently he hadn't been serious *about* her. She just shook her head and said, "I told you, I'm twenty-three."

"I see," he said. "That was obviously half an answer."

"The whole answer is no."

He laughed at her and asked, "What are your plans for the weekend?"

"Tree decorating. And then since everyone is in town for the tree, Mel is going to give me an orientation at the clinic today so that Monday morning I can start helping her out. That's about it."

"I have an idea. Why don't you come to my place tonight. I'll cook."

"Dinner?" she asked. "Did you just invite me to dinner?"

"I did. I'm going to try to make up for being so unfriendly — I'm actually a nice guy. Too old for you, but nice. I'm going into Fortuna to get a few things — I make a mean chili and it'll taste good on a cold night. But if you say yes, I want you to tell Jack where you're going to be and that you'll be perfectly safe with that dangerous Riordan." He laughed and added, "I should've known this would happen — my brothers haven't all been easygoing. I got a reputation by association. So, any interest in a bowl of chili and a fire?"

"Do you have saltines? And shredded cheddar?"

"I will have. Will you tell your uncle?"

She shook her head. "Nope. But I'll tell Mel so if he's looking for me, she can keep him under control."

"I'm serious, Angie — you'll be in good hands. I'll treat you like the little sister I never had."

She smirked and said, "Sounds very exciting. I can hardly wait. What time?"

Later that afternoon Mel gave Angie a tour of the clinic, which was in an old house that had belonged to the town doctor before he died. He had willed it to Mel. The living room functioned as the waiting room and was decorated like someone's grandmother's living room. The dining room was the reception center and file storage. Downstairs also held the kitchen, two small exam/treatment rooms and a little office. Upstairs were a couple of bedrooms — one made up as a hospital room, one for a doctor or practitioner staying overnight, plus a roomy bathroom. Mel showed her where all the supplies were, where the drugs and treatment kits were kept and showed her how to operate the rather old-fashioned autoclaves for sterilizing.

"I love this," Angie said.

"We could use a lot of updating, but we're a poor town. Our ace in the hole is the ambulance, which allows us to transport patients to better facilities if necessary."

"I think it's wonderful. Do you know what a town in Ethiopia would give for something this grand?"

Mel was stopped in her tracks, focused on Angie's face. "Hey. What's going on with you? That was a pretty interesting comment."

"Nothing much," she said. "I just think this is —"

"Bullshit. I see those wheels turning. Talk to me."

"I don't know. It's just that . . . I'm having a hard time seeing myself as one of the doctors who treated me. I mean, they were all incredible and there's no question they saved my life. But it made me wonder — what happens to people who don't have

UCLA Medical? After the experience I just had, shouldn't I be ten times as inspired to get back to med school? And yet . . . Well, that's what I've been thinking about. I'll figure it out."

Mel smiled softly. "I've only known you for five years, yet in that short time I've grown accustomed to the way you think out of the box."

"But look at this place, Mel — you make a difference here, I know it. When people come here who don't have money or insurance, they get the help they need. Don't they?"

"We can't do everything, but they get our best."

"And I've heard you say — sometimes you're paid in eggs."

She laughed. "We're paid in very interesting ways. One very darling lady from back in the mountains fancies herself a well-known psychic — she offered to pay me by telling me my future."

Angie gasped. "What *is* in your future?"

"I can only guess! My past is shocking enough — why would I want to know my future?"

"But what if it's only wonderful?"

"Then it will still be wonderful when it gets here. Ange, I wouldn't go to a psychic.

I have enough to worry about."

"But I hear they never tell you the bad stuff!"

"Really?" Mel asked with raised brow. "Then what's the point? If they don't tell you what to look out for, what's the good of hearing about that stuff that will work out just fine, anyway?"

"Oh, there's so much more to it! I love the idea of a psychic! Maybe I'll go — do you still have your freebie?"

"I might, but I don't know . . ."

"Well, never mind. I have something to tell you." A slight blush crept up her cheeks as she said, "I'm going to be having dinner with Patrick Riordan tonight. He's going to cook for us. He insisted I tell Uncle Jack where I'd be and with whom, just in case there's some worry. But I'm not telling Uncle Jack — he's gone a little around the bend where I'm concerned. So I'm telling *you*."

"Oh, gee, thanks. I just love being the one to keep secrets from Jack," she said with a roll of her eyes.

Angie laughed. "If you sense Jack getting worked up about where I am, you can tell him."

"So things are getting interesting between you and Patrick?" Mel asked.

81

"Not quite. In fact, he assured me he would treat me like his little sister tonight."

Mel smiled. "Why does that make me feel better?"

"I honestly don't know," Angie said. "You should probably visit that psychic and ask her why it makes you happy to learn that your adult niece is going to be treated like an inexperienced child!"

"I don't need a psychic to explain that," Mel said.

FOUR

Patrick mixed up his chili and had it ready on the stove. He chopped onion and peppers, added them to the ground beef, then opened a bunch of cans — beans and diced tomatoes — and added packaged seasoning mix. It was a real poor man's chili, but delicious nonetheless. Then he headed for the phone to call Marie, even though he'd already talked to her for a few minutes in the morning.

When Jake had been killed, Marie left Charleston almost immediately. There was a memorial a week after the crash and then her family swept her away, headed for home — Oklahoma City. The Navy had ensured her move was swift and efficient.

"You don't have to go," Patrick had said. "I have a big enough house. Have the Navy put most of your stuff in storage and take your time. You have ties in Charleston — friends, a job, a city you know and like. . . ."

"The hardest thing to leave is you," she said. "You've been such a good friend to me. But you'll deploy again before long."

"Not too soon, and I'll be back. And we'll keep in touch."

But she just shook her head. "Navy wives are very supportive of one another, in good times and bad, but my friends shouldn't be responsible for holding me upright. I'm sure we'll always be in touch but, like it or not, the Navy part of my life is over. I'm going home."

A few weeks later, the Navy shrink told him that, rather than going back to the ship, he thought Patrick should take as much leave as the Navy would allow. At that point Patrick headed for Oklahoma City. He stayed in a neighborhood motel near Marie's parents' home, intending to be her support for as long as she needed. There was no mistaking she was thrilled to see him even though they'd barely said goodbye in Charleston. But after four days she had said, "Paddy, I don't know what I'm going to do without you, but you have to check in with your brothers, your family. You need healing as much as I do."

"We can heal together," he said. His guilt weighed on him. No matter what anyone else said, Patrick felt as though he had some responsibility in Jake's death. And now, the least he could do was offer himself up to Marie. He hadn't been able to save her husband. He should at least be able to save her.

"Right now I'm going to rely on my parents, sister and brother and figure out how to face the holidays without Jake. Go to your family and let them comfort you."

He tried to argue a bit; his family wasn't expecting him for the holidays — he was supposed to be at sea. Jake's death might've changed a few things for him but the Riordans had other plans.

"It's not like they won't be grateful for a visit," Marie had said. "And in some ways your wonderful vigilance makes this even harder. We'll be in touch and we'll see each other again soon when we're both a little stronger. Then we can spend more time laughing over the good times we had with Jake and less time crying and agonizing over our loss."

That's when Patrick had reached out to Aiden and asked about the cabin. No doubt he could have counted on either Luke or Colin for a bed, but he couldn't stay with anyone right now. He had to be alone because of the nightmares. They didn't come every night, but often enough. He'd managed to get all that leave without even mentioning the dreams, but he'd be damned if he'd wake up screaming in his brother's house. He said he needed privacy and quiet and everyone bought it.

There was a part of him that had been disappointed when Marie sent him on his way, but a part of him was enormously relieved. With Marie he could lick his wounds and have company while missing Jake, but it was all a reminder that there was no one special in his life. And that he'd put far too much stock in a woman who hadn't been there for him — Leigh. And it reminded him of how much responsibility he now carried. He had to look after Marie and Daniel, perhaps forever. He'd given his word.

But while his chili simmered, he called Marie *again*. "How are you doing?" he asked instead of saying hello.

"Pretty well, actually," she said. "I forgot to tell you — last week, before Thanksgiving, I made an appointment with an employment counselor. I'm going to see him next week. I know jobs are scarce in this economy, but I'm a certified radiology technician. Jobs might not spring up over the holidays, but I'm a qualified candidate and I'll be ready in the new year. And you know what? It feels kind of good to get started."

"You're committed to Oklahoma City?"

he asked.

She answered with a laugh. "What are my choices, Paddy?"

"Well . . . there's always Charleston."

"Aw, sweetheart, I don't have any family there and I have a son to raise."

"I'm still there."

"You're there a few months a year. Listen, that was a hard enough gig when I had a husband coming home to me. It's not going to work with my dead husband's best friend."

"It could," he said. "I will always be there for you."

"You are a saint and might live to regret it. I could be calling on you till I'm a lonely ninety-year-old widow. What you need, Patrick, is a woman."

"Oh, really?" he said.

"You and Leigh parted company a long time ago, and unless you're really good at covering your feelings, you weren't real surprised and not all that disappointed."

"I *was* very surprised and disappointed!"

"All right, all right," she said, surprising him with a laugh. "You bounced back well and good for you. What I'm saying is, you can find a good woman now. It no longer has the danger of rebound written all over it. Just look around, Patrick."

"In Virgin River? Right."

"They're forming a line in Charleston as we speak," she said, teasing him. "Paddy, you're there for me, I'm there for you, but, my darling friend, you're going to find the right woman before long. You just have to be open to it."

Having chili with a cute little package tonight, he thought. *Just not girlfriend material.* "Right. Sure. Meantime, I have a house in Charleston where you had a life — where you can still have one. Keep an open mind, all right? Because you and Daniel are family to me."

"You're very sweet," she said. "The best friend a widow girl could have."

He didn't say much to that, just asked after her folks, Daniel and the weather and then said goodbye. It was too soon for her to think of him as more than a friend. But he had begun to formulate a plan in his mind. He was almost thirty-four and wanted stability in his life — a woman he could depend on, a family, a future he could trust as much as was possible. And here he was — committed to his best friend's widow. Wasn't it smart to form a committed relationship with someone who was a best friend, someone he could depend on, someone he really knew? He wasn't in love with

88

her, at least not in the conventional sense, but how important was that in the grand scheme of things? She was an awesome woman, very pretty, extremely smart, an excellent mother and had unshakable values. He could step into Jake's shoes effortlessly. He could love her for a lifetime; he would never regret it. He was trying to remember what more there was to consider, to hold out for, when there was a knock at the door.

He opened it to find Angie huddling into her thick jacket, a fresh young beauty wearing a smile sent to earth by the angels. Her hair was thick and soft, her eyes large and dark, her cheeks flushed and lips full and pink. Had he warned her not to get mixed up with the likes of him? What a damn fool he was — the mere sight of her made him forget Marie and long to hold her. She tempted him beyond sanity. A young woman like this would be his downfall for certain. He needed maturity; he wanted the kind of woman he knew he could count on. What did a woman know at twenty-three?

"Your directions were fine, but because of the dark I missed the turnoff three times."

"Sorry," he said lamely, standing in the open door.

"Are you all right?" she asked.

He shook himself. "Sorry," he said again.

"I just hung up from talking to Marie, my friend's widow. I'll shake it off in a second. Come on in."

"Listen, if you need to cancel, if this turned out to be a bad night, after all . . ."

"Nah, come in."

She stepped into the cabin uncertainly. "It probably puts you in a kind of sad, grieving place."

"Not usually," he said. "I try to talk to her for a few minutes every day. Can I get you a beer? I saw you have a beer at Jack's so I bought a six-pack. Sam Adams okay?"

She laughed softly. "You bought it just for tonight? You might be the only guy I know who doesn't stock beer. Sam Adams is great, thanks."

"Chili's ready and keeping warm, but take off your jacket and relax by the fire for a while first."

"Wow — this place is awesome," she said, looking around the great room. "No wonder you wanted to take a little R and R here."

He fetched a couple of beers and joined her on the couch. "My brother's wife practically rebuilt the place out of a shack a couple of years ago." He handed her a beer.

"You're a good friend, you know. It's too bad your friend, Marie's husband, doesn't get a chance to see what an excellent friend you are, calling her every day."

Oh, he'd be very surprised, Patrick thought. What would Jake think of Patrick nurturing the idea of picking up where he'd left off? But he said, "He'd expect nothing less. And if I'd left a wife and child, he'd do the same. We've been tight since the Academy. Almost fifteen years. We haven't always been stationed together, but it never mattered." He couldn't help it, he looked down. "I wish we hadn't been assigned together a couple of months ago."

"I'm sure it wasn't your fault."

"What if it was?" he shot back. He wiped a hand over his face. "Okay, we shouldn't go there. The investigation showed it was hostile, but I was responsible for him. If I'm still a little scarred, it's probably reasonable. Quick, use your young, nubile, med student mind to change the subject to safer territory."

She grinned suddenly. "You find my *mind* nubile?"

Right, he thought, *like every other part of you.* Then he remembered that while she might look quite young, she was brilliant. She'd catch everything.

"All right," she said. "Tell me about what you were like growing up and how it was

91

with four older brothers, all very close in age."

"On one condition," he said. "You have to promise not to ask any of them the same question."

"And why is that?"

"Because they will tell stories."

"I'm not sure I can promise that," she said with a laugh. "Come on."

"Well, being the youngest, they protected me all my life, but the price was very high. They'd always be there for me, but they'd never let me forget a single slip or embarrassing moment. I'm thirty-three and I'm still hearing about the night I got caught making out at my girlfriend's house. By her mom and dad."

She looked a little nonplussed. "That's not exactly original. Everyone's been caught kissing."

"Her sweater was in my hand and her bra was draped over the lampshade. They came home early. . . ."

She laughed happily. "More," she demanded.

"I peed on the side of a highway patrolman's car."

"Awww, well, little boys sometimes have lapses in judgment like that."

"I was twenty-five. And had been out with

my brothers. I blame them."

"It sounds like they taught you everything you know. I was wondering about when you were much younger."

"It's not good stuff. I was the last one to give up a binky, the slowest to potty train, was lost several times — once requiring police intervention — and my mother thought I'd be taking my blanket with me to football camp. It suggests I *liked* being the baby. I didn't pay attention in school until my football and basketball careers were on the line, which started in junior high. But I was always very nice."

"What do you mean by that? Nice?"

"As my mother said, I knew where to butter my bread. Luke said I was a little con artist, Colin called me the family phony, Sean said I was an ass kisser, but Aiden always liked me and found me sincere. Aiden was the only one who was wrong. I was definitely a kiss ass."

This made her laugh and, since he liked the sound, he went on. "By the time I was ten, Luke had enlisted. When I was twelve, Colin went in, both of them Army warrant officers who flew helicopters. When I was fourteen Sean had an Air Force Academy slot with a pipeline to a flying job — you can only get jets if you go to an Academy these days, you can't enlist and sign up for flight school. Then Aiden headed for college on a Navy scholarship — he's a doctor. It was down to me. In my mind, the only choice left was deciding which branch of the military I'd join. I got an appointment to the Naval Academy. I went to the same senator Sean had gotten his recommendation from — you can't get into an Academy without serious political juice."

She sat back on his sofa, shock on her face. She took a drink of her Sam Adams and then continued to stare.

"What?" he asked.

"How'd you do in the Academy?" She wanted to know.

"I did fine."

"*How* fine?"

"Well. I did well. I graduated second in the class. Got a couple of awards."

"And flight school?"

He narrowed his eyes. First in his class. Every class. "Well," he said.

"You little pisser, teasing me about my *nubile brain.* You were an overachiever."

"Who spent about four years in diapers . . ."

"With a binky in your mouth. There isn't a single prescription for brainiacs, except it sounds like growing up with four older

94

brothers might have put you in want of a brotherhood and the Academy. Flight school and a military career would fit right into your pattern. And apparently you were a lot more social than I was."

"Do you know everything?"

"I read."

"I read, too. But not about stuff like that."

"I know. You're reading weapons systems, math, aerospace, combat strategy, et cetera. I'm a science major who loves psychology. My degrees are in biology and chemistry with a minor in psych. I'm kind of drawn to the study of genetics, statistics, environmental science, DNA studies, that sort of thing." She shrugged and said, "That's how I relax. Reading that stuff."

She was *scary*! "Your childhood," he said. "Come on."

"I'm the oldest, a completely different dynamic. I had slaves — two younger sisters who did whatever I told them to. And apparently I was a real load to raise, but I like to think I was only curious. I liked to take things apart. You know."

"Toys?"

"Well . . . when I was two. When I was ten I took apart a VCR, an old jukebox, a pool table and a computer."

"A *pool table*?"

"At my grandpa's house. I got the legs to fall off. It took my dad and grandpa all day to stand it back up because they wouldn't let me help. But I also liked to mix things for taste and to see the chemical reactions — like the time I figured out that baking soda in cola could make a volcano. This wasn't a problem all the time — I came up with some interesting concoctions out of the refrigerator. But when I got under the sink, we sometimes had trouble. My sister had to be rushed to the hospital because she got a whiff of the fumes from one of my experiments and it burned all the cilia in her nose, throat and lungs. She wheezed for hours. I was grounded forever."

"Jesus," he said. "You're not planning to reproduce, are you?"

"Actually, I hope to one day." Then she smiled and said, "You know what cilia is."

"It's a commonly known word."

"It isn't," she argued. "Do you have a Scrabble game around here?"

"I hope not. Why?"

"You could actually give me some trouble." Then she laughed.

Something told Patrick he'd be wise to spoon some chili into her and get her out of here, but that was far from what happened. Instead, they took their time with lots of talking and laughing before they even got to the chili. They went through the teenage and college years, jobs they'd had, trouble they'd been in, glorious moments, disappointments, dates — the good and the terrible. He'd had many more dates than she. Instead of sitting at the table, they finally ate in front of the fire and, afterward, Angie found them a Scrabble game online to play on his laptop.

And she beat him.

It was getting very late when he asked her, "Where are you spending Christmas? With your uncle Jack?"

"I don't know," she said. "I'll probably go home to Sacramento. I just needed a break from Mom and Dad. My mom and I have really been at each other and Jack suggested I come up here for a while. Dropping out of school really took its toll."

"Angie, are you a poor little rich girl?"

She roared with laughter. "My parents are teachers! Well, they're professors — an honorable profession, but not exactly the top of the economic heap. I grew up in the smallish four-bedroom house they will always live in. They don't have a boat or a lake house, but we always traveled a lot while I was growing up — I guess giving us an education in foreign countries was a priority to

97

them. Now I realize they just added us in to every conference opportunity they had. They're middle class. Very smart, intellectually ambitious middle class without much money. I get a break on tuition because they're professors in a state university and I have some scholarship money for other expenses. And there's help from Grandpa, that sort of thing. So what about you? Where are you spending Christmas?"

"I was supposed to be on a ship, but I have some leave. I'm planning to stop in Oklahoma City to check on Marie and Daniel on my way back to Charleston. I'll have Christmas with them. A few days, that's all."

"Ah. And then? Back on the ship?"

"I'm not sure. I'm still thinking. Back to med school for you?"

"Um, it's not looking that way. But, please, don't say anything. I don't need my uncle all worked up or my parents running up here to deprogram me. The more I've been thinking about it, the more I just don't know if med school's going to do it for me. I had almost a year under my belt before the accident, but I'm losing interest."

"What do you mean, do it for you?" he asked.

She scooted forward on the sofa. "Can I

98

trust you? I mean, *trust* you? Because I haven't talked about this with anyone. And I'd like to, but I've been kind of afraid."

He edged closer to her. He wanted to touch her, but didn't. He'd like to smooth her hair or grab her hand. All he said was, "I'm your friend. You can trust me."

"I'm thinking of taking a couple of years off before going back to med school. I'm considering the peace corps. Or something like that."

He stiffened in shock. "Are you kidding me?"

She shook her head solemnly. "I want to make a difference."

"Can't you make a difference as a doctor?"

"Eventually. But right now I want to give something back, to justify the fact that I'm here, that I'm alive."

"Ange, you don't have to do that! You have all the time in the world to give back. You're tough and smart — you'll live to be a hundred."

"Yeah, with a shunt in my head and a rod in my femur. But right now instead of studying microbiology I want to dig a well. Or give immunizations. Or mix up gruel with vitamins for children who need food."

He sat back and put a hand on the top of

his head. "Whoa." She laughed at him.

"Listen," he said, "they won't take you right now. It's too soon after a pretty serious injury — that's not their style. You have to go through a battery of exams and tests to get in the peace corps."

"How do you know?"

"Well, I don't, I'm making this up, but I bet I'm right. I'm right a lot — how do you think I test so well? I'm a good guesser. But aside from all that, how long do you think they'll hold your spot in med school?"

"No telling, but that's not my biggest concern. If I have to reapply, I can get in. I have a double major with an excellent GPA. I've been valedictorian twice and scored high on the MCAT. Even if I have to apply to a different medical school a couple of years from now, I like my chances. And I'll find a way to pay back my parents and Grandpa."

He stared at her for a long moment. "You're a little crazy."

"Do you think so? Because I make perfect sense to myself."

"What do you plan to do?" he asked, a little jealous that he didn't have a plan of his own. "I mean, right now, after your R and R, what will you do?"

"I think I'll get a job and study humanitarian organizations for a while. The downside is I might have to live with my parents while I work and look for the right organization to apply to — and trust me, my mother is going to turn the heat up. She's always had a plan that she expects me to follow and I've been a dissident. It could be very uncomfortable. I've given some thought to staying here in Virgin River just to avoid that. Maybe I can work in the bar."

"Angie," he said, serious as a heart attack. "Go back to school. There's lots of time — don't rush."

"Did anyone ever suggest that you put off flying jets for a while? Until you were sure?"

"Of course not."

"That settles it, in my next life I'm coming back as a guy. I get so bloody sick of people saying, 'Slow down, little girl, you're not ready.' I'm as ready as I'll ever be." She looked at her watch. "It's getting late. No one's waiting up for me, but I better get going before you get tired of me."

He was afraid he never would.

She stood up and he stood. She reached for her jacket and he said, "I think I should drive you. Or at least follow you home."

"Why?" she said, slipping into her jacket.

"I'm a little nervous about you going out to an isolated cabin in the woods by yourself."

She laughed a little. "Okay, think about this. I just told you I was planning to go dig wells in India or administer immunizations in Africa and you're worried about me driving fifteen or twenty minutes across the mountain to a lovely little cabin? Relax, Patrick."

"What if you miss a couple of turnoffs?" he asked.

"I know where they are now," she said. "Take it easy."

She walked to his door and he was right behind her. When she opened the door, they were greeted by a fresh snowfall — just a couple of inches.

She turned back and smiled at him. "I'll go slow. Try not to act like my uncle Jack."

"Wait," he said. "Wait right here." He went to the desk in the corner and jotted down the phone number at the cabin. He took her a slip of paper. "You're going to have to call me. If you don't, I'll call Jack and track you down."

"I'd scold you for that, but I don't mind that you're a little protective. I'd hate a steady diet of overprotective, but that little bit just now wasn't too bad.

"Now I'm going to drive slow, then I'm going to build my fire because I haven't turned the heat on, so it'll be a while."

"Just call."

"You bet." She started to walk toward her SUV, then turned back. "I liked the chili, Patrick. But that isn't why I came tonight."

He smiled at her, watched her leave and thought, *I am so screwed.*

While he waited for her phone call, Patrick thought about how awesome she was. He couldn't get involved, but she was a more than welcome distraction. He opened a beer and his mind began to wander. He thought about her beauty, her sexiness. Then he began to pace because she hadn't called yet, rehearsing what he would say to Jack, how he was going to explain that he needed directions to that little cabin because he had to go looking for her.

Angela and I had a perfectly nice, platonic evening of Scrabble and chili and I let her drive herself home even though . . . Yes, Scrabble and chili . . . No, of course we didn't have sex. . . . No, of course I wasn't tempted, she's much too young!

The phone rang before he could rehearse any more mental lies. He grabbed it as if it were a lifeline. "Hello?"

"That t-took a little longer than I thought it would," Angie said.

"Are your teeth chattering?" he asked.

103

"A l-l-little. The cabin was so dark — I should've left on a light. There was a moon when I left but the snow clouds came in. I had to l-leave the car running with the lights on t-till I could get inside and light the p-place up. I gave the horn a toot in case any nocturnal animals were visiting."

He laughed. "I think you know everything. Did you build your fire?"

"And put on my warmest pajamas, which was torture. It's no fun getting undressed in the cold. The quilt was still on the couch from last night. It's finally starting to warm up in here."

He couldn't help but laugh at her. He assumed she would be as adorable in footie pajamas as naked. Okay, not quite, but still . . . The combination of the warm fire and heavy quilt seemed to be working, since her teeth had stopped chattering. "Are you settled in now?"

"Oh, I don't think I'll move from this spot before morning. Except maybe to feed the fire a log or two."

"Angie, there's heat in the cabin, isn't there?"

"Sure. But this is fun. Reminds me . . . when I was in college a bunch of us rented a cabin for skiing and it was so expensive we just assumed we'd have heat, maybe even catering! We managed the puniest fire and had to sleep snuggled up against one another right in front of it."

He settled onto his own couch, chuckling into the phone. "I lived for nights like that. Did you fall in love?"

"Sadly, no, as I'm straight — it was a girls' trip."

"If only I could've helped. Who was your first love?"

"I think Dick, my junior year in high school, and he was a dick, as it turns out. We were kind of steady and he asked someone else to the prom. At the last minute. I think he forgot to break up with me first. I should've known he was shifty."

"Who took you to the prom?"

"I never went to one. I was a nerd who always envied the cheerleaders, pom-pom girls and stars in the school musicals. I was president of the debate team, a great chess player and went to the scholastic Olympics. I bet you went to proms."

"I did."

"With cheerleaders and pom-pom girls?" she asked.

He was embarrassed to say. "It's different for guys. They don't feel the same way about proms that girls do. Girls see it as a chance to feel like a princess. Guys see it as a chance to have sex."

"Did you? Have sex?"

"No. I clearly wasted my money. . . . But you should have gone to proms. You're pretty."

"Aw, that's nice of you to say. But a lot has changed in a few years. Lasik surgery for one thing — got rid of the big, thick, black-framed specs that kept sliding down my nose. Back in those days when things like clothes and hairstyles just eluded me, I'm pretty sure no one but my dad and uncle Jack found me pretty. I didn't have that instinct the other girls had about style, about flirting. But, hey, I had great instincts about things like chemistry and astronomy."

"Astronomy?"

"I have a kick-ass telescope. Unfortunately, I didn't bring it this trip. But the boys were never interested in looking at stars — they wanted to look at boobs. Another advantage I didn't have. Oh, and did I mention the pimples?" She laughed happily at that. "Oh, God, I'm so glad those days are over. Was there ever anything more painful?"

"This is coming from the girl who was in a disastrous car accident? Asking the guy who watched his buddy go down in a hornet . . ."

"I know, I know, but there was something about the pains we had as kids, the melodrama and agony over things that didn't really matter but mattered so much just the same. . . . This other stuff of ours, it's *real*. It's a grown-up challenge and it does mean something and . . ."

He listened with his eyes closed. He'd known her for a day. A single day. She was everything he avoided — youth, innocence, inexperience. And she had everything he wanted — guts, wisdom and compassion. He'd seen this personality in certain military women. But there was something about Angie that stood out as unique. They'd each been through the wringer, yet she approached her challenges with relentless optimism. The linchpin was probably that she had not lost her best friend.

He thought he was probably headed for trouble here. He wanted her.

"Angie," he said. "We have complicated lives. . . ."

"Oh, very. It's nice, Patrick, to have a friend who relates."

"Listen, Ange — we have things in common. We get along, have fun. You're young, but you're still a woman. Women pull this off without too much trouble, being friends with a guy. Men aren't as good at it. And now I'm holding one of your secrets — your peace corps secret."

"Oh, I can fix that," she mumbled into the phone. He clearly heard her yawn. He could picture her, snuggled under the quilt in her warmest pajamas in front of the fire. They'd spent five hours together and now what were they doing? Talking into the night on the phone, still somehow connected? He hadn't done this in too many years to remember.

"How?"

"Give me a secret," she said. "Then we'll be even."

"It's more complicated than just secret sharing," he informed her.

"Start there," she said. "I'm good with secrets."

He was quiet for a moment, breathing into the phone. He could hear her breath, as well, and it felt like high school when he'd call the flavor of the week and romance her into the late night over the phone, a lot of which was just heavy breathing.

"Okay," he finally said. "Here's one for you. My best friend's wife, um, widow, Marie — she's great. She has it all — she's pretty and nice and funny. She's very strong and brave, though losing Jake has really been hard on her, but what else would you expect? When we were on a mission, she hardly ever complained — she missed him but she had a life. Her first priority was always family — she's a great wife and mother." He paused. "*Was* a great wife. And she was a great military spouse because she understood — the work her husband was doing was vital and everyone involved made sacrifices so that work could be done. The men and women who served, the spouses, the kids . . .

"I don't know why I'm telling you this — you couldn't possibly understand. You're twenty-three — years away from thinking like this. But I'm older. I've had a couple of serious girlfriends that didn't work out. The last one I was with for four years and even though in my gut I knew we were on different paths, I thought we'd last. I should've known better. But now, at thirty-three . . . Well, I think a little differently.

"I was with Jake when he met Marie and, man, it hit him like a Mack truck. Two years later I was his best man. Two years after that I stood as godfather to his son. And two years after that I . . . I helped Marie bury him.

"They're my family, Angie. As much my family as Luke, Colin, Sean and Aiden. And here's what I'd like you to keep to yourself

— if my brothers found out I've been . . ." He took a deep breath. "Marie's the reason I've been reconsidering the Navy. Jake asked me to look out for Marie and Daniel, make sure they're taken care of, and Marie needs me. The truth is, I've always loved her. Not in an inappropriate way, not in a way that would have threatened her marriage, I swear to God. I loved her like a best friend. She has high standards, she's loyal."

He was answered with complete silence. Finally she said, "I'm, ah, speechless."

"You probably think I'm crazy, but I'm just trying to think practically. I gave him my word. I told him I'd look out for Marie if anything ever happened to him. I made a promise, and I plan to keep it."

"Do you suppose he meant for you to *marry* her?"

"I highly doubt it," Patrick said. "But making sure Marie is taken care of, that's important to me. Very important."

"Patrick, don't you think you should be *in love* before you marry someone?" Angie asked incredulously.

"It probably makes more sense not to be. It's about compatibility, Angie. Finding the kind of person who fits, you know what I mean? Even if you have to make some com-promises — like the fact that she absolutely wants to live in Oklahoma, and there's no Navy fighter squadron in Oklahoma. . . ."

She was quiet for a moment, just thinking. "You older men and your 'practical thinking' are a little strange."

"You're probably right," he said with a laugh. She remained quiet and he sensed he might have gone too far. He decided to say goodbye before he revealed any more damning information — though after this, he wasn't sure there were worse secrets left to tell. "Time for lights out, Tinker Bell. I'll talk to you tomorrow, I'm sure."

On the other side of the mountain, in Jack and Mel's cabin, Angie laid on the couch, the phone still on her ear long after Paddy signed off, eyes wide and mouth open slightly. *I'm going to marry Marie, but I'll see you tomorrow.* Really?

A regular girl would be angry. Jealous. Insulted. But Angie wasn't a regular girl — she was different and she knew it. She saw right through his plan. He was responsible; he put duty first. And he was so lonely, in so much pain, he had a plan to marry his best friend's widow because it was safe. She couldn't imagine the magnitude of such a mistake. She also knew that simply telling him that would never work.

Imagining how he might feel inside made her heart hurt for him.

FIVE

Angie spent Sunday morning feeding her fire, reading a dangerously romantic novel and staying under the quilt. Every now and then she'd let her eyes drift closed and pretend the characters were Patrick Riordan and Angela LaCroix. It wasn't until about three in the afternoon that she emerged, showered, put on clean clothes and ventured into town. Tonight would bring the lighting of the tree.

By the time she arrived, Jack was putting the final touches on the strings of lights and hooking up extension cords, Mike was hanging on to Ness and people had already begun to gather around, lending a hand here and there. Angie gave a wave to the people she knew and then made her way to the bar. There she found her aunt Brie behind the bar. "Hey," she said, smiling. "You've been pressed into duty?"

"I think the guys are worried about getting everything done in time to light it up at about seven. Cocoa? Soda? What's your pleasure?"

"Cocoa sounds great."

Brie poured and asked, "And how was your night with the youngest Riordan?"

"You knew?"

"Not till this morning," she said. "Mel didn't think you'd mind if I knew. Did you have a nice evening?"

"Mmm-hmm," she said, sipping her cocoa. "He made chili. Then I beat him at Scrabble." *And then he confessed he was probably going to marry another woman even though he flirted with me.* She thought about telling, though she had promised she was good at keeping secrets. Was Brie the kind of person who would know what a girl was supposed to do with information like that?

"Sounds pretty tame."

"Very tame," Angie said.

"You like him?" Brie asked.

"He's very nice," Angie said.

"That's not what I meant and you know it."

Angie put down her cup. "He says he's too old for me."

"Oh. Is that so? Well, do you agree?"

Angie took a breath. "Age seems pretty irrelevant. And I might have a crush. . . ."

"Really?"

She nodded, dropping her head into her palms. "As in, world-class. And it would appear to be completely futile. Hopeless. Possibly ridiculous. He'd never be interested in someone like me." No matter how he acted.

"And why is that?"

"I think there might be a million reasons, and age is just the first of them. And then there's the fact that I'm not the kind of girl men like Patrick end up with. You have to remember — I'm a student, a *nerdy* student. And he's a hero. A fighter pilot. A stud."

"Stud?"

"Figuratively," she added.

"I see," Brie answered, laughing. "And his type is . . . ?"

His best friend's widow? "I'm not sure," she answered. "Someone a lot more sophisticated, I would think."

"This brings back bittersweet memories," Brie said. "When I was a law student, about your age, actually, I was in love with a professor. We were about twelve years apart in age, but God I loved him. Or thought I did."

"I said crush," Angie reminded her.

"World-class crush, you said. So, I loved the beautiful young professor, loved his voice and his gorgeous face and sense of humor and amazing body. And his *brain —*

Oh, God, what a brain. I would have crawled across a sea of cut glass for a kiss, even though it was the worst idea in the world. I didn't care. I was young and romantic. Young, romantic, hormonal women do the most unbelievable things. . . ."

"You're suggesting this is *hormones*?" Angie asked, affronted.

"I'm suggesting *I've* had some. You're responsible for your own hormones. In the end, I got a little bit of the professor — we had a brief dalliance after I was no longer his student. For about a month I thought I'd died and gone to heaven. Then I realized heaven was full of women like me — he'd been very busy and young law students were his specialty."

"By 'dalliance' do you mean . . . ?"

Brie nodded gravely. "Boy howdy, as Mel would say."

"First, I don't know if Patrick is like that and second . . ." She blinked. Dammit to hell, her eyes had clouded as if she'd cry. "I don't have a second."

Brie grabbed one of Angie's hands. "My heart was so broken. I got over it, of course, but it really hurt for a while." She gave the hand a squeeze. "You're a little vulnerable, babe. Accident and all."

Brie was spot-on. But what Brie didn't

116

know was that Angie was thinking — what difference was there between having your heart broken after one night or after one month? What difference is there in intensity? But she knew the answer to that question — if he ignored her from this point on, she might wonder and even suffer some longing, but she'd soon move on. If she went further, got truly involved with him and then they parted ways, as of course they must, she was fairly certain she would be torn to pieces.

"Don't worry, Aunt Brie," she said. "I'm sure we'll never be more than just friends." But what she meant was *He'll never take the chance.*

"Probably for the best," Brie said. "Want to help put out cookies?"

"Sure. I bet this place gets really busy when the lights go on."

"Really busy."

After Angie finished her cocoa she went into the kitchen to scout around for cookies. She found Preacher at the stove and Paige busy putting cookies on decorative platters.

"Good, another pair of hands!" Paige said happily.

In no time at all, Angie was grateful for the kitchen chores. She thought more about

Patrick but it was too busy to look around for him. She arranged cookies on platters, carried them to the bar and saw the place begin to fill up with people. Paige put out punch and a big urn of coffee and, while it appeared the town of Virgin River would feast on cookies, brownies and sugary bars, Preacher had a pot of stew and fresh bread ready for anyone craving something a little more substantial. The platters emptied as fast as Angie could put them out and, as she refilled them, the time flew by. The sun was setting by five-thirty, the colorful lights inside the bar were lit; there were happy voices and laughter everywhere. Women began to add their own sweets to the collection. Tables had to be pushed together to accommodate all the offerings. Drinks were served — hot toddies, cocoa and the stuff that would warm bellies on cold winter nights.

"It's almost time, darling," Paige said to Angie. "Go outside. Don't miss it."

The crowd outside was growing; the cherry pickers, ladders and other equipment had been put out of sight. Jack stood at the far end of the porch, ready to join the extension cords. To get the best possible view, Angie crossed the street and stood near the clinic in the darkness, hands in her pockets, watching her breath cloud the air.

And then there were big hands on her shoulders.

There were any number of people who might do that, but she could feel it was *him*. Sense him. Then he bent his head and gently nuzzled her, making her smile. Oh, she was toast. She knew right then that she'd never be able to resist him.

As if he read her mind, he turned her around and stared down into her eyes for a moment before gently and briefly touching her forehead with his lips. And then he smiled.

"I thought you found me thoroughly resistible," she said.

"I find you thoroughly tempting."

"And would you call that practical?" she teased.

He made a face. "Part of being good with secrets is not taunting a person with them," he told her. "I can't help it if you're tempting."

"I'm sure that has mostly to do with being in a little town where there aren't too many temptations."

"Or it could have to do with you. How was your day?"

"Slow and easy. Lovely. I've eaten a lot of Christmas cookies. How is Marie?" She

119

cringed at the thought of sounding jealous, but she couldn't stop herself from feeling it.

"Having a good day today."

He turned her around toward the tree, but he kept his arms around her waist, pulling her back against him. She glanced over her shoulder at him and said, "I think my uncle Jack is watching."

"Try not to worry. I learned to fight from four big brothers. I can defend myself *and* keep you safe."

She was close to telling him that the number of women he vowed to protect was growing. . . .

And then the tree lit up and the lights were so grand in the town, the street was filled with the brightness of an afternoon sun. There was a chorus of "Ahhhhh," then applause. Patrick's arms tightened around her. She leaned back against him and enjoyed the closeness. She had barely begun her fantasy of what else might happen between them when a truck came into town, horn blowing. The street was filled with people and the old truck's horn was separating them, parting the crowd, until it finally came to a stop right in front of the clinic.

Angie, acting on sheer impulse, wiggled out of Patrick's arms and ran toward the vehicle just as a woman got out of the passenger's side of the truck. She was holding a very large child wrapped in a blanket — a blanket on which there was a considerable amount of blood. A bloodstained towel covered most of the child's face.

On instinct, Angie went toward them. At precisely that moment, Mel and Dr. Michaels burst through the crowd, running toward them.

"Frank?" Mel asked. "Lorraine?"

"It's Megan! She slipped — there was ice on the porch and a nail sticking out of the porch post got her right on the forehead. It's bleeding bad."

"Come inside. Frank, you come, too. Let's have the doctor look at it."

Angie turned to Patrick very briefly, holding up her hand toward him. That was her only gesture before following the man, woman, child and practitioners into the clinic.

It felt odd to her. First of all, no one questioned her presence there, as though she was already an assistant of some kind. Second, Mel began barking orders at her as if she had been trained in this clinic. "I'll need a sterile pack of four-by-four gauze, sterile water, not saline. Cameron? Want an antibiotic?"

"I don't think we need an IV, but I'll go with cephalexin, broad spectrum IM. She had a tetanus shot last summer but give me some Valium and lidocaine. I'll get a suture kit."

"Can you get that together, Angie?" Mel asked, handing her the keys to the drug cabinet. "I'll take care of the syringes."

"Yes. Please check my work, make sure I have the right things."

"Absolutely."

Angie got out the gauze and water and then went after the drugs, but what really had her attention was the fact that the little girl didn't make a sound.

"I'm going to put pressure on the wound, Megan," Mel said gently, softy. "Just for a little while."

Angie had only seen a little bit of this injury, the blood on her face, but the child was so silent. She shook like a leaf, however — either terrified or in shock. And Mel was dabbing at her face and forehead with gauze. "Easy, Meg, it's not bad," Mel was murmuring.

"Let's get this cold, bloody blanket out of here," Mel said, leaving a thick padded gauze over half of Megan's face. She reached into the cupboard behind her and produced a clean, warm blanket. To Angie, she said,

"Roll Megan toward you, then toward me — gently, now."

They wrapped her up in a fresh blanket while her parents waited as close to the treatment room door as possible. Then Cameron was back, pushing his way in close, pushing Angie away. His suture kit sat on the counter behind him and he looked at Megan's pupils with a flashlight, asked her to follow his finger with her eyes, asked her a couple of simple questions like her birthday, her brothers' names.

"Is it terrible, Doctor?" Megan asked, her voice quivering on the edge of tears.

"It's not, sweetheart," Cameron said. "It's going to be fine."

In the first year of medical school, a med student had very little, if any, clinical experience. In fact, the only experience Angie had came from following around an instructor in a clinic. Without that little bit of experience, she would have no idea what a four-by-four was or how to select drugs from the locked cabinet. And while the injury was a bloody mess, especially on the face of a little girl, it didn't overwhelm Angie. She knew even the smallest head wounds could bleed like the devil.

By the time Cameron had opened up his suture kit, the wound had been cleaned and much of the blood wiped away. That's when Angie had her first real look at the little girl's face and tried not to gasp. The laceration on her forehead didn't appear too serious, but the sweet thing already had a horrific scar on her face, already healed. It looked as though she'd been cut from the corner of her mouth almost to her eye; her mouth lifted on one side and her lower lid of her right eye drooped, exposing pink tissue. The scar was thicker in some places than others — it was vicious. Disfiguring.

The little treatment room was very crowded and growing quite warm. Cameron was working carefully but quickly on the laceration, cleaning and washing with lidocaine. "I think we can take care of this here, Megan," Cameron said. "It's going to need some stitches, but it's small. It won't hurt. I'll numb it. And because of the size and location at your hairline, I wouldn't fear a bad scar." Then he looked over at Lorraine. "Is that all right with you, Lorraine?"

Although the woman twisted her hands, she nodded.

"I don't think she has a concussion," he went on. "I'm going to ask you to keep an eye on her tonight — I'll give you some instructions before you take her home."

Mel drew a syringe of something while

Cameron donned sterile gloves. Then he leaned over her and said, "Tiny little mosquito bite, Meg, that's all. I bet you don't even have a headache tomorrow."

Angie leaned so close to watch Cameron suture that Mel smiled and Cameron looked over his shoulder at her as if to say, *Do you mind?* When the stitches were in and a bandage covered the wound, Mel pulled Angie out of the room.

"Cameron's going to ask Megan to just lie still for a while. He'll examine her again before sending her home with her parents. I'm going to write in her chart."

Angie followed her to the desk in the reception area. "Mel . . . ?"

Mel stopped, turned and quietly answered the question she knew was on Angie's lips. "Almost a year ago Megan fell and hit her head, her face, on a shovel that was lying on the ground partially buried by snow. It cut her cheek but, to tell the truth, it wasn't that bad. It was actually the treatment that worked against her. Cameron took her to the emergency room — he wouldn't dare try closing up such a large facial laceration on a child. But there was no plastic surgeon, the E.R. doctor wouldn't call anyone in because Meg's family is very poor and has limited insurance — certainly nothing that

125

would cover plastics, and he stitched her up himself. It didn't take too long to see scar contractures, which I can almost guarantee will only get worse. Megan is growing — the scar is tightening while the rest of her face and surrounding tissue is soft and elastic. It causes severe distortion. And then there's ectropion, scar tissue pulling down her lower eyelid. She needs plastic surgery."

"And why isn't she getting it? Is she afraid?"

Mel shook her head. "It's considered cosmetic. Elective. It would cost thousands of dollars, and that's speaking conservatively. This is a struggling family. They're doing well if they can keep the heat on all winter."

"She'll be disfigured for the rest of her life," Angie said.

"I keep looking for a break. A friend of mine, a doctor in Grace Valley, managed to get a morbidly disfigured woman help several years ago — there was a plastic surgeon with a surgical team who took on some of the most challenging cases for free, but it goes without saying — he can't operate on everyone with an ugly scar. Megan's is hard to look at and very sad — she's a beautiful girl — but it's not the worst we've seen. I'd be so happy if we could just get that eye fixed. That's going to give her problems. It could lead to vision trouble, if it hasn't already."

"But by the time she's a teenager . . ."

Mel put a hand on Angie's arm. "I'll keep trying. It's hard in places like this, Ange. This isn't a rich place. People work hard, but most of them don't work for employers that provide good benefits — we're a lot of family ranches and farms out here. Most can't afford hundreds of dollars a month for medical coverage. Lorraine is a waitress and puts in a long week, so they have some benefits — the bare minimum. But there's no coverage for plastic surgery that isn't considered a medical necessity. I've already argued with them about the eye."

"Have they seen pictures? The insurance company?"

"Oh, of course. I've done my best so far and I won't give up. But the hard reality is that the Thicksons will have trouble even with the deductible and twenty percent of the costs. Frank was a logger with a good job, but he lost his arm in a logging accident. He has a prosthesis now. Between his part-time work and a disability check, they get by, but there are four kids and it's tough for them."

"It's wrong," Angie said, shaking her head. "This shouldn't be so impossible."

"We do our best — we do as much as we possibly can. Let me update this chart now. You can go if you want to, Angie. I can manage."

"Nah," she said. "There's a treatment room to clean up."

Mel smiled. Then she pointed at the reddish brown stain on Angie's pretty yellow sweater. "Hydrogen peroxide on that — takes blood right out. Grab a bottle out of the supply cabinet and take it home with you."

It was nearly nine by the time they'd finished cleaning up and Angie was finally leaving the clinic with Mel. Megan had long since gone home with her parents and Cameron broke free to find his wife and twins. When Angie stepped outside the first thing she noticed was Patrick, sitting on the porch steps at the clinic. "Hey!" she said in surprise.

He stood up while Mel turned to lock the door. "I wanted to see how you were. I already know the little girl went home with some stitches."

"You must be freezing," she said, noting the collar on his jacket turned up and his hands in his pockets. "Did you want to go to the bar for a while? Warm up?"

He shook his head. "I'll just walk you to where you're going and be on my way. Hi, Mel."

She smiled warmly. "Nice to see you, Paddy. And how nice of you to check on Angie. She was a wonderful help, by the way."

"I have no doubt. Angie, are you headed for the bar?"

"Ordinarily I might, but —" she spread her jacket open to reveal the bloody stain on her sweater "— I think I'd better go home and get out of these clothes. I'm parked right down the street."

Once Mel had walked in the direction of the bar, Patrick looped his arm through Angie's and walked her in the direction of her car. "You okay?"

"Sure. Of course. A little distressed about the situation that poor little girl is in, but I'm fine."

"Tired? Hungry?"

"I think my cookies wore off, but I'm not fit to go anywhere with blood on me."

"Home," he said. "I could follow you and, while you change clothes, I can fix you something to eat. I'm not much in the kitchen, but I heat a mean can of soup, scramble some very fancy eggs, that sort of thing."

She laughed. "Between the two of us, we could starve to death. Come on, follow me. I think I could use the company."

"And I'd like to hear more about Meg's situation."

At the side of her SUV she stood on her toes and gave him a small kiss on the cheek. "Prepare to feel sad about that," she said. "I'll wait for you to find your Jeep."

As she was driving to the cabin with his headlights in her rearview mirror, she wondered if he had planned something like this all along — another evening together. She wasn't likely to be demure or shy away. She'd never known anyone like Patrick before. She'd known guys like Alex — the self-absorbed and spoiled science freak who was used to having his way with little effort. Alex was so strong academically that it never occurred to him he wasn't perfect. When they studied together, Alex treated her like an equal; when they made out or made love, he definitely acted as though it were all about him. He was greedy. Impatient. Since she wasn't experienced, the whole thing was usually a little clumsy. Completely dull for her.

But Patrick was bold. He was sure of himself; he acted like he knew what he wanted, what he was doing. She had no trouble picturing him on the deck of an aircraft carrier, coolly preflighting his F-18. Strong and confident, that's how he seemed. Yet there was nothing Neanderthal about him — no club in sight. He was considerate and thoughtful — his waiting for her tonight was touching. He seemed so powerful, yet at the same time was gentle and enticing. She wondered if she was giving him more credit than he was due and didn't expect the answer to that anytime soon. But she sure wouldn't mind learning a few things from the hands of a master.

And then, Angie knew, she would undoubtedly sob with longing all the way to her first peace corps assignment. Because even though she'd been in another relationship — even a sexual relationship — she'd never before met anyone who instantly set in motion all the fantasies of living with true love forever.

She pulled into the clearing and he was right behind her. This afternoon she had left a light on so she wouldn't be coming home to a pitch-black house again. It looked welcoming. Sweet.

Patrick got out of the Jeep. "So this is your hideaway."

"Isn't it cute?"

"Small."

"I know. But I'm only one person. Come on, it won't take me long to show you around."

They stood right inside the door while Patrick looked around — kitchen and living room right inside the entrance, with her quilt and pillows still on the couch. "I guess I didn't really tidy up," she said, only half-apologetically. "Three nights and I haven't made it to the bed yet."

"I'll build a fire. What am I going to find in the kitchen?"

"Well, that's the beauty of having an uncle who owns a bar and grill — I raided the bar's kitchen so I'm stocked with the essentials. Should we look through the fridge and cupboards together?"

"Nah, I can manage. Is there anything you don't like?"

"I'll eat anything. I'll only be a minute."

"Take your time. I think I'll be busy for a while."

"Then I might hop in the shower."

"Go for it. I'll get busy," he said, going first for the stack of logs beside the hearth.

Fifteen minutes later when Angie came out of the bedroom in a comfy sweatsuit, freshly showered, she found Patrick had made a few changes. He had pushed the trunk that served as a coffee table away from the sofa. The quilt and pillows were folded and sat in the room's only chair and the fire blazed in the hearth. His boots sat by the door and his jacket hung over a kitchen chair. He stood at the stove, sleeves rolled up and in stocking feet.

He looked over his shoulder at her and smiled. "Tomato soup and grilled cheese."

"My favorite. You're very handy."

"I found a couple of trays. We can eat in front of the fire." He had the dishes sitting out and began to serve the bowls and plates. "What would you like to drink? I helped myself to a beer."

"I think I have some wine left. I'll get it."

"Tell me about the emergency," he said. "Did it make you want medical school more or less? Did it change your ideas about the peace corps?"

"Oh, Patrick, I still have so much to learn. Megan's injury tonight, though probably traumatic for her and her parents, was relatively minor — a laceration on her forehead close to her hairline. It needed a few stitches. But almost a year ago she had an accident and her face was cut. Dr. Michaels took her to the emergency room for stitches and, because of insurance issues, they just stitched her up without a plastic surgeon. Now she's disfigured. If it isn't fixed somehow, by the time she's a young woman and her head and face have grown and matured, the scar won't have grown with her. It could be monstrous. I'm not exaggerating."

He handed her a tray and picked up his own. "I take it they can't afford to get her the proper surgery?"

"Exactly. My uncle Jack has been here quite a while now — I think about eight years. There are things I've known about this place for a long time, but until I saw Megan's face, I didn't put them into perspective. There is some bounty here — people with money, with successful ranches or vineyards or businesses. But there's also a lot of poverty, a lot of residents living from hand to mouth. Mel and Doc Michaels get a lot done and the town helps when it can — there's a powerful sense of community here. But some things are just out of reach — like plastic surgery for an eight-year-old girl whose family has very little money. As Mel puts it, just keeping the house warm all winter is a struggle for them."

Patrick followed her to the living room, carrying his tray.

She stood in front of the couch. "I take it you had the floor in mind, since you moved furniture around."

"If you're going to be comfortable."

"It's perfect," she said, falling into a sit, legs crossed, without spilling a drop of soup or wine.

When he was sitting beside her, balancing his own tray, she said, "They make a difference here — Mel, Jack, Doc Michaels and a lot of other people. They work where there's need. They're giving back or paying forward. I think the idea of the peace corps got points tonight."

"Most twenty-three-year-old women are saving for a party cruise or a car or the biggest, flashiest wedding money can buy."

She laughed. "Well, first of all, I don't really come from people like that. Oh, my mom and my aunts have a real penchant for nice things — but I think they fall into the purse and shoe category, not cruises or cars. My parents' idea of extravagance was a trip to Russia so we girls could learn about the tragic history of that country. I visited Dachau and Auschwitz at sixteen. It was bound to give me a different perspective from most people my age. And then you have to consider my accident. Things like that can change your life."

"I know," he said.

"Of course you do," she agreed softly. She stopped talking to take a spoonful of soup. It came out of a can, she knew that. But she said, "You're brilliant. A genius. This is the best tomato soup I've ever tasted."

He gave her that sexy half smile and said, "And you are an accomplished flirt."

Six

Patrick was sure it was inappropriate to compare Angie to Leigh, but it came unbidden. For all he knew, Leigh might have been just as idealistic at twenty-three, but it was very hard to imagine. She'd been raised by a politician; she was jaded and had very specific goals. At twenty-three she'd been working on a master's in economics, determined to understand budget and deficit issues and how those would translate into votes.

Angie wanted to make a difference in the world. Leigh wanted to win elections.

When Leigh left him it had hurt; he'd invested so much time and energy in her. But this was not the first moment he'd had the notion he might've dodged a bullet. Had there been good things about their relationship? Oh, many. He'd enjoyed their time together, most of which was spent in what he could only describe as high-end entertainment. If it wasn't the finest D.C. restaurants or A-list parties attended by the movers and shakers of Washington, then it was skiing, sailing, scuba diving, traveling . . . all first-class. Dachau and Auschwitz? Not in a million years. Leigh worked hard and played hard. And so did he — it had suited him fine.

In fact, laid-back weekends or evenings spent with Marie and Jake — a barbecue or movie and pizza — bored Leigh to death. She behaved herself very well; she understood that Jake and Marie were important to him. Likewise, he was cordial and debonair for those sophisticated Washington events that really lit her fire. It was only recently, since Jake's memorial where Leigh was a no-show, when it had occurred to him that perhaps Leigh liked having a decorated Navy fighter pilot as her occasional escort to the social events surrounding national government. He wasn't there because she loved his company — he was there to boost her public image.

Patrick had always felt that having a family was important to him, but it was after Leigh left and Jake died that he realized *how* important. He finally knew that if his life didn't take the shape he'd imagined — a stable relationship that included kids — something very important would be lost.

He knew his face had given away his troubling thoughts when Angie told him to put another log on the fire and relax. "I'll clean up," she said. "It'll only take a minute. Then I'm going to finish the wine and I think there's one more beer. Can I grab it for you?"

"You absolutely can," he said. And he leaned back against the couch while she headed for the kitchen.

Just a few minutes later, dishes done, fire stoked and libations replenished, she turned the conversation to him. "What compelled you to join the Navy?" she asked.

He draped an arm around her shoulders. "I think I always wanted to fly, but who knows how much of that was internal or influenced by my older brothers — three out of four of them took to the sky. But practically speaking, it was education — I come from a pretty simple family. My dad was an electrician and my mom was a coupon-clipping, soup-making stay-at-home mom most of the time. There were times she did secretarial or administrative work, but nothing that would cover the cost of school. The five of us were either going to get loans or scholarships or have to skip college. The oldest two, Luke and Colin, were into helicopters, but Sean introduced a new idea —

the Air Force Academy and fighters. With that idea, my brain caught fire! In my mind, that kind of flying looked like the way to go, high and fast. It involved a sophisticated education and an exciting life." He shook his head. "Gotta love that plane. It asks a lot, it's demanding as hell and it requires good instincts and reflexes. Then there's the mission — our ground troops and ocean vessels would be lost without the kind of air support the Navy provides."

She was quiet for a moment before she said, "Sounds like you've made up your mind about what comes next for you."

"Ah, I don't know. I want other things, too. When you deploy a lot, spend a lot of time on a ship, it's hard to keep a handle on the other things in life. Like a family. The woman who takes on a Navy fighter pilot spends a lot of time alone. It's not fair. It takes an amazing commitment and a special kind of woman. . . ."

"Like Marie."

"She would be a good example."

"No wonder you think of her as the ideal wife. I have a friend, Connie — I've known her since junior high. She's always loved firemen. She chased fire trucks and went to firefighter bars. No surprise she married one eventually. Now she still loves firemen but

140

she hates their hours. Her husband is gone a good third of every month and it's driving her crazy. She's stuck alone while he's out pulling women from burning buildings. She wants him to quit and go to work for her father. Now why would you marry a guy in a job you find powerful and sexy and then not want him to do that job? Or how about all the girls who want a doctor and then find out how hard it is to be married to a doctor? The way I see it, you pick the whole *person*. You have to look him over really carefully. If he has the qualities you need in a partner, you sign on. And he looks you over, making sure of the same things. If you do that, there's only one option — you support their career choice because there's no *other* choice. You can't remake people, for God's sake. You have to love them for who they are."

Patrick stared at her. His mouth might've been open a little bit. How had Leigh put it? *I don't think we're going in the same direction. I'm not going to compete with the Navy. I need a full partner.* In other words, she was looking for someone who could dedicate himself to *her* goals. And here was Angie, talking about choosing a partner based on the whole package, not on how well you can mold them to suit you.

141

"Are you sure you're twenty-three?" Patrick asked her.

"My sisters and I are not very much alike," she said. "We've always enjoyed different things. We sometimes throw in with one another when it's not our number-one choice. Baby girl is an athlete — I go to as many games and meets as I can because it shows support. I'm not going to dump her because her athletic events bore me or are inconvenient — she's my sister! But sometimes I read while she's running track or playing basketball and even that makes her think I don't love her."

"I'm almost afraid to ask — but the middle sister?"

"Piano and violin. Concert ready. I enjoy that a little more than basketball, track and other sports. But, hey, these are the same sisters I sent to the emergency room when I started experimenting with mixing household cleaners. I think I owe them."

He laughed at her. "I think you do. A piece of advice — before you have children, be sure you can afford full-time watchdogs."

"I know, right?"

He leaned toward her and kissed her briefly, looking into her eyes. "Your lips are soft," he whispered. "And perfect." He kissed her again, this time deeper. He slipped an arm around her waist and gently lowered her to the floor. He could feel her body responding to his, her hands reaching up to wrap around him, to encourage him. As much as he wanted to keep going, a small part of his conscience tugged at him. "Listen," he said, pulling back slightly, "we shouldn't. We're just passing through."

She simply looked up at him with those sweet, pretty eyes and, against his better judgment, he kissed her again. This time he tongued open her lips and played inside her mouth, moaning low in his throat. Her fingers tangled in his hair, as though trying to pull his mouth even closer to hers. Against her lips he whispered, "Why do you have to taste so damn good, feel so good. Angie, I want you and you're the last person I should be wanting." He leaned over her, his hands busy with her torso, running up and down her sides, grazing a breast, devouring her mouth with his. "My ears are ringing. Tell me to stop before this —" But Angie shook her head, her lips red and swollen from his deep kisses, her eyes filled with longing. "Stop me," he whispered. "Push me away. This is such a bad idea. Before I go completely deaf, tell me no. . . ."

"Patrick," she whispered. "Paddy . . ."

"Yes?" he asked, his eyes sleepy and sexy

and gazing into hers.

"Do you *always* talk this much?"

He smiled for just a second before he took her mouth by storm and rolled with her on the floor until his body covered hers. His lips on her neck, her ear, her temple, her mouth again, always looking for a better, even deeper taste of her. When he broke away for a moment she said, "I like that." She was a little breathless.

"We're going to go real slow, just take our time getting to know each other. Nothing happens that you're not ready for. All you have to do is put one hand on my chest, like this," he said, taking her hand and placing the palm against his chest. "You don't even have to say anything. This is all about you, Ange. I don't even have to kiss you again unless you feel like it."

She was still for a second. Then she grabbed the front of his shirt in her fists and pulled his mouth against hers.

Patrick took full advantage of her decision, moving along her with sweet passion. She moaned against his lips; her urgency thrilled him. Mouths open, tongues playing, lips sliding, tilting right, then left, he devoured her. He couldn't get deep enough into her mouth. This response from her had him hard in an instant, but he was determined to move slowly even though her body felt tight with needy determination.

Patrick knew that, by her age, a lot of young women had had more than one serious boyfriend; they at least knew what they wanted. Patrick had been with a number of women, beginning when he was seventeen, and many of them, though young, had things to teach him. He sensed this was not the case with Angie. She'd had other concerns — like being valedictorian to every class she attended, even coming out with two degrees. You didn't get honors like that by spending a lot of time making out.

He pulled her fully into his arms, her body flush against his, and kissed her wildly, madly. He gently and slowly toyed with one breast, waiting for that hand to stop him. Instead, she grabbed his wrist and slid his hand under the soft fabric of her sweatshirt where he found . . . *Ahhh, naked.* Her perfect, small breast filled his hand and he groaned, running a thumb over a hardened nipple.

His lips slid to her neck and he kissed his way from her ear downward. Then he whispered, "How do you feel about ditching the shirt?"

"Excellent. If you ditch yours."

"I can do that," he said.

He yanked off his own, almost ripping off buttons. *So much for slow,* he thought. He couldn't get down to skin fast enough and he hoped, no, he *prayed* she was ready to take a chance on going further. Once his chest was bare, he slowly lifted her sweatshirt over her head and just gazed at her as she sat in front of him.

There were a few scars — a small line a few inches below her left breast, a thin but longer scar along her abdomen and a lump on her collarbone where it looked as if it had once been broken. He traced each mark with his finger, then leaned forward and retraced the same path with his lips. Eager to see her spread before him, he leaned her back to the floor and entertained himself with her lovely breasts, stroking, kissing and licking them with equal attention. Angie sighed, her eyes drifting closed. Hovering over her, his thumbs teasing those perfect nipples erect again, he watched with a sense of pride as she moaned and arched her back, her breasts reaching up to him for more.

With a force he didn't have all that much control over, he was pushing his erection against the vee where her legs met . . . and she pushed back. She rolled her hips beneath him, wanting. Begging. He made use of a secret weapon — an erection in a pair of tough jeans right against her most sensitive part. He gently pushed apart her legs and held himself between them, rubbing those hard jeans against her. And then he dipped his mouth to her nipple and gently tugged it into his mouth, teasing with his tongue before sucking.

Her hands were in his hair, holding his head; her head tilted back and her back arched farther as she pushed against him. A soft primal sound came out of her. She stiffened; she shuddered. He held that nipple tight between his lips while nature took its course and had its way with her. *God, what a beauty; what a hot, amazing beauty.* It was a long few seconds before she collapsed beneath him and he traded the nipple for her lips.

"Sorry," she whispered. "It just happened."

He brushed her hair back at her temple. "You don't ever have to be sorry for good things that happen between us. It's a wonderful thing. You're a passionate girl."

"Woman," she corrected.

He smiled and then chuckled. "All woman," he admitted. "Baby, you have no idea how special you are."

He kissed her lips, ear, neck, chin, breasts,

leisurely getting to know her body. And then, giving her plenty of time to put that hand against his chest, he slowly slipped his own hand lower, skimming her stomach and moving down past the waist of those loose sweats. Once again, paradise came in the form of no underwear. As he slid his hand lower, she opened her legs and lifted her hips, welcoming him. He growled against her neck as his fingers pushed lower into the warm silk of her folds.

And she purred back at him, pushing against his hand.

"What do you think, Angie? Too much? Too fast?"

She just shook her head, biting her lower lip, eyes closed.

He stilled his hand. "Look at me, Angie," he whispered tenderly. "I have to see your eyes." She opened them dreamily, a small smile on her lips. He couldn't resist her. "I'll make love to you if you want me to."

"I want you to. You have to promise to tell me what feels good to you, though. I'm not sure I'll know."

He smiled down into her eyes. She had a look of satisfaction on her flushed face. "I promise," he whispered. "Somehow I think you're the only thing I need."

Because he was a gentleman, he disrobed

first so he wouldn't leave her naked and waiting. He sat back, pulled a condom out of his wallet and got rid of his jeans, tossing them after the shirt over the back of the couch. As he rolled on the condom, she raised onto her elbows to look at him.

"Hoo boy," she said softly.

He just grinned at her before gently sliding off her pants. She was so beautiful his mouth watered. He carefully lowered himself over her; all he wanted in the world right now was to be sure she never regretted this.

"You're trembling," she whispered.

"I know. I'm trying to be careful with you. But the truth is, I can't get into you fast enough. . . ."

She ran a hand over the stubble on his cheek. "I'm okay, Paddy. You can let go."

"Sweetheart, if I let go, I'm afraid I'll tear you apart, I want you that bad."

She reached down between their bodies and gave him a brief stroke before positioning him. He had barely touched her when, with a will of its own, he slid into her. Her eyes widened for just a second, then gently closed. He held her still, filling her, and the trembling stopped at once. "Better," she said.

Patrick moved cautiously, slowly at first,

but when she started to lunge toward his thrusting hips he pushed harder, loving the soft sounds of pleasure she shared with him. When she cried out, he took her mouth and kissed her ravenously while she gripped him with all her internal muscles. He held on. And on. And on . . .

When she had exhausted her pleasure and relaxed, he grabbed her behind and let himself go. The power of it shocked him. As he felt his orgasm release, it started another shuddering inside her and she wrapped a leg around him to pull him deeper. "God," he said. "God, Ange . . ."

It took a long time for him to catch his breath. He started to pull away from her and, that fast, the palm of her hand was against his chest. "Don't," she whispered.

"I won't leave you, sweetheart. Let me grab the quilt."

She allowed this, and in just one second, he had pulled it over them and was holding her. She was so soft in his arms. He turned her so that he could cradle her against his chest, her back against him, listening to her breathe evenly. *Don't talk*, he told himself. *Don't say a word, not a single word.* With her head on his arm, she curved into him. He held one hand against her chest and with his lips pressed against her neck, he began to drift off. He couldn't help himself. "Are you all right?" he asked.

"I'm better than ever," she whispered.

And they slept.

In the cool light of morning, Angie realized she was alone, but she could smell the pleasant aroma of freshly brewed coffee. Just as she was sitting up, Patrick handed her a cup. He wore only jeans — no shirt, no shoes. The fire blazed with new logs.

"Mmm," she said, taking the cup in both hands and bringing it to her lips. Nice. Patrick sat on the only chair in the room, elbows on his knees, leaning toward her. "Oh, Ange, what did we do?"

She laughed softly. "What did we do three times, you mean?"

"Are you going to be all right?" he asked.

"Why? Are you planning to bolt now?"

He shook his head. "No, of course not. But I have commitments. At the very least, there's likely a big gray boat with my name on it. And you have a world to save. We have to face the facts."

"Maybe I should be asking if you'll be all right," she said.

"Maybe so."

"Paddy, I can't stand that you're so sad on the morning that I'm so happy."

151

"Ange, I'm not going to want to leave you." He dropped his chin, looking down. "And I have to." He looked up. "Tell me you understand that."

"Wow, another revelation in the emotional growth of Angela LaCroix. I thought men handled flings effortlessly."

He was quiet for a long moment. "Not necessarily," he finally said. "So, a fling? That's how you look at this?"

"Well, you've made it clear that you aren't available for the long haul. You have your 'commitments.' But I'm a grown woman who happens to have really enjoyed our night together. I don't see why it can't continue on just like this." She looked right into his eyes, hoping she could convince him — convince herself — that she could be nonchalant about all this.

"Listen," Patrick said, his face a little red, "we should try to be discreet."

"Are you embarrassed?"

"Not even slightly," he replied quickly. "But there's no point in upsetting or worrying people. I mean, I doubt anyone would be worried about me. But you . . ."

"Please, I'll be fine," she said. "I'm a big girl." She took a sip from her cup. "Hmm. You know, I think having fresh coffee delivered to me in the morning is almost better than sex."

He smiled at her then. Relaxed again. "I'll have to work on my technique."

"I appreciate the gentlemanly overtures, but I believe it was consensual. I wasn't ambushed."

"I didn't think that was likely to happen when we'd known each other for about two days. I thought maybe eventually, but . . ."

"I knew in the first five minutes. Besides, it was three days." She ran a hand through her hair and it practically stood up, full of static electricity. "God, I must look like the wrath."

"You look like dessert."

"You're not dumping me, then?"

He shook his head. "I think it would be easier to give up an arm. But, Angie, I have no choice about leaving. I already have my plane ticket. I booked round trip."

"When will you go?"

"The twenty-third. My leave is up on the twenty-seventh. And I promised . . . Well, you know. I'm checking on Marie at Christmas. I promised."

"You're a good man, Patrick," she said. And even though she thought she might be losing him to that woman, to Marie, she meant it from her heart.

"And do you realize your uncle Jack is going to kill me?"

"Patrick, let it go! Do you think I tricked you into sex to get some kind of promise out of you? Seriously?"

"I don't know everything about you, Ange, but I'd bet my life there's not an ounce of cunning in you. I'm having a little trouble getting over the fact that you're . . . Well, you're twenty-three."

"And life is damn short, even for old guys like you," she said, getting to her feet without dropping the quilt or spilling her coffee. "I promised to help in the clinic and I'm going to keep my promise. I'm headed for the shower." Since she was naked, she dragged the quilt with her. At the door to her bedroom, she turned. "By the way, I'm free this evening."

She loved that he grinned hugely. "Are you now?"

Alone in the shower, with the hot water washing away the scent of him around her, she let down her guard a little bit. Despite her bravado, she knew she had loved him almost instantly. She had been extremely curious and fiercely attracted. He was brave, she could see that. He was loyal — even planning to marry his best friend's widow, believing he could make her happy, keep her and her son safe. Angie didn't exactly like those plans, but she certainly admired them. There was something about a selfless, giving man . . .

But she was going to have to fake it from now on, since there was no way of knowing how a situation like this would play out. Her heart felt raw and open, but she wasn't about to let him see that. When she stepped out of the shower, she listened. There wasn't a sound coming from the little living room. She wasn't surprised that he'd left. That's how casual flings were meant to go. Now that they'd had their morning-after talk, cleared up a few things, he would go.

While she dried her hair and dressed, she couldn't help but think about their night together. It drove her right up the mountain again — she'd never in her life had a night like that. In point of fact, she'd never even had a whole night. There had only been Alex, and he'd never actually *slept* with her. While Alex looked like a harmless nerd, he had been pretty impervious — he never once asked her if she was all right, for instance. He had gotten very excited, asked her if she was willing, boinked her and went home to his own campus apartment. She had accused him of needing her for chemistry — it was one of her degrees and he wasn't that good at it. He had responded

155

that it was far better than needing her for sex and she supposed that was probably as sensitive as he could be.

Well. Long ago and far away. It wouldn't take much of a lover to surpass Alex. However, she suspected that Patrick was more lover than she would ever meet again, and that thought was chilling. But despite how perfectly they seemed to fit, it had been clear from the first time they talked that their lives weren't meant to intersect beyond this vacation.

And yet, to her surprise, he was still there in the cabin when she emerged from her room, showered and dressed. He stood up from the chair, now wearing his shirt and boots, his jacket hanging on the kitchen chair. The small room was in order.

"I could make you breakfast," he offered.

Angie thought, *He's not going to stay with me, I knew that. But Alex would have been gone by midnight, so this really is an improvement.* "No, thank you, Patrick. I'm not much of a breakfast person."

"Most important meal of the day," he said.

"I know. Since the accident, my mother's been shoveling it into me as if it might prevent future accidents. I'm more a midmorning snack kind of person. Is there anything I can get you?" She flashed the best flings-

156

are-easy smile she could muster, though it felt fake, even to her.

"I'll shower at home, since you're headed for the clinic. I waited for a reason," he said. Then he came to her, put his arms around her and kissed her. He had perfected that kissing thing. In fact, she thought he perfected everything.

"Hmm. If I didn't have commitments . . ."

"But you do," he reminded her, breaking away from the kiss.

"So I guess I'll see you later?" she asked.

"Definitely. How about my place tonight. Is noon too early?"

She loved that. "I'll be there at six. Lay in some food."

SEVEN

When Angie arrived at the clinic, Cameron was just leaving, medical bag in hand, off to make a house call. He was standing in the reception area with Mel. "Good morning," Angie said. "I'm ready to help out. What would you like me to do first?"

"Cameron's leaving so let's plan the day over a cup of coffee."

"Excellent," she said, heading for the kitchen to start a pot brewing.

A few minutes later, Angie sat at the kitchen table with a pen poised over a yellow pad, ready to take down her instructions.

Meg poured them each a steaming mug and handed one to Angie. "Okay, kiddo — how do you feel about what happened last night?"

Angie's cheeks flamed as her eyes widened in shock. Had news already spread about Patrick spending the night? "Huh?" she asked, dumbfounded.

Mel frowned as she pulled out a chair and sat across from her. "The injury, Angie. Megan's injury and the emergency. Did it upset you?"

Oh, way to be discreet, Angie, she thought, looking down and taking a deep breath to pull herself together. "I'm only upset for Megan — that scar. I've been thinking about it a lot. I have a question."

"Shoot."

"If she were to get plastic surgery, what would the procedure entail? Just how complicated would it be?"

"Probably removal of the scar by incision, rejoining by an expert, possibly a very minor graft. Maybe something to lift that lower lid. I don't really know — but I did a little internet reading on it. She would very likely end up with a thin, barely visible scar that wouldn't contract or distort her facial features. Something she could conceal with a touch of makeup."

"Not extensive?"

"I wouldn't think so, but before you ask — it would still be very expensive for the Thickson family. It would require pre-op blood work and exam, an O.R., anesthesia, a nurse and O.R. tech. I don't think it would be a long surgery, but nonetheless . . ."

"I know, I get it. Has anyone asked around for donations?"

"I'm pretty sure the pastor, Noah Kincaid, has a fund started, but he has a fund for many things in this town, as does Jack. There are plenty of people around here who live comfortably but far more who barely squeak by. Everyone pulls together admirably and there's no question that a surgery for Megan is a good cause, but so is medication for Adie Clemens, who lives on social security, or Burt Jackson, who's losing the farm that's been in his family for generations. There's a whole flock of women who can't afford mammograms and we've managed to get a nonprofit organization in here now and then to do free ones. Cam and I do wellness exams for the cost of lab work in an effort to keep people healthy. We do what we can. We can't do it all."

"But you don't mind if I look into it? Research a little bit?"

"In fact, I'd appreciate it," Mel said. "You have a good heart, Angie."

"I just wish I could leave here knowing Megan's scar is going to be fixed."

"Well, my advice is that everything seems to boil down to knowing who to call. I've tried a lot of agencies and foundations on this one with very little positive feedback.

Having someone else take over the computer and phone will be helpful."

"I'll bring my laptop with me tomorrow. I might have a few people I can ask that you haven't thought of yet."

"I would love that. Now . . . is there anything else you'd like to talk about? Asking about last night seemed to get a pretty strong reaction."

"I think I'll take a rain check," Angie said, but she couldn't seem to help coloring up again.

Mel smiled. "I just want to be here for you if you ever have anything on your mind that you want to talk about. I'm not going to make judgments and I promise not to give advice unless asked."

"That's not very Sheridan of you," Angie said with a laugh.

"I'm a transplant. I don't carry all the Sheridan traits. Plus, it helps that you're not my daughter. We all tend to lose objectivity when it comes down to someone we desperately feel we have to protect."

"That would explain my mother's behavior," she said.

"And your uncle's, to some degree."

"But . . . how did you know there was something . . . ?" She couldn't say it. In case any part of her night was still a secret, she wouldn't go out of her way to reveal it.

"Well, either you've been snowmobiling or you have yourself a little whisker burn there." Mel raised her eyebrows, giving Angie a pointed look.

Angie's hands went to her cheeks before she could stop herself. She laughed. Okay — no secrets. Except the details. Delicious, wonderful, mind-blowing details.

Patrick knew that comparing the women he'd had intimate experiences with, even when done secretly, was not gentlemanly. And Patrick was, if nothing else, a gentleman. However . . .

His relationship with Leigh had been satisfying in its own way. It must have been — he had never strayed. But even in the beginning he wondered what more he could do to satisfy her, to arouse her, to really make things exciting between them. It always seemed as though she had little interest in sex — in any sort of intimacy, now that he thought about it. There were times, of course, when this was understandable — sometimes they fell into bed tired after working long hours. After a couple of years, he reasoned that they'd drifted into a certain complacency because they were so comfortable; they'd just grown so accustomed to each other. Perhaps they took each other for granted. But there were other times when it chafed — like when he returned from deployments. He had missed her while he was away; he hungered for an obvious sign she had longed for him, too. He would have welcomed some wild lust. Some hot, crazy, sweaty, button-popping, fabric-ripping sex. Hell, he'd have been happy with a really good kiss. Anything to show him that his absence had affected her.

But Leigh wasn't made that way. She was emotionally reserved and even more so when it came to sex. The woman was so damned beautiful and socially vivacious, it felt as though she should be an erotic dream come true, yet she was always so busy perfecting her social image that there was hardly any time left to spend with Patrick. She assured him he was a wonderful lover and that she desired him more than anyone else. And she said she loved him. He bought it, too. Until she left him and never looked back.

Angie, on the other hand, couldn't seem to get enough of him during their night together. She was Leigh's polar opposite in bed — and Patrick loved it.

Patrick drove all the way to Fortuna for breakfast. Under the circumstances, he

163

didn't think he could hold a conversation with Jack. And Jack liked to talk. Chances were good if Jack looked deeply into Patrick's green eyes he would see images of his niece burned into the irises. Patrick's palms still tingled from where he'd touched her.

He made a run to the grocery store. He was a passably good cook, but he didn't want to spend a lot of time cooking or cleaning up that evening, and he wasn't sure what Angie liked to eat, so he played it safe — chicken stir-fry, brown rice, wine. A little cheesecake in case she had a sweet tooth.

Once that was finished, groceries safe in the car in cold weather, he drove out to Jilly Farms to visit with Colin. As luck would have it, Luke was there. Colin, who had a titanium rod in one femur, was holding the ladder steady while Luke used a staple gun to affix multicolored lights to the eaves. This was a brilliant stroke of luck and Patrick had a strategy here — if he spent a little time with them, declined any offers of dinner, his evening would be his own. And he had plans for the evening.

"Great timing, Paddy," Luke yelled from the top of the ladder. "We're done."

"I pride myself in good timing," he said with a laugh.

Luke made his way down the ladder and once his feet were on the ground, Colin lowered the extension and picked it up to put away. Teamwork. The interesting part was that until this past year, these two brothers, eldest and second-born, were fiercely competitive and often battled. Now they were Mutt and Jeff. Frick and Frack. Ozzie and Harriet.

Luke looked at his watch. "Lunch," he said.

"It's ten-thirty!" Patrick said.

"I had breakfast five hours ago."

"I had breakfast one hour ago," Patrick said. "But I can watch you eat."

"What have you been up to, kid?" Luke asked as he crossed the porch and went into the house.

Thirty-three years old, flown a hundred missions in war zones on at least ten deployments to sea and he was still *the kid*. The youngest. The one who should be taken care of. "Reading," he said with a little attitude.

"Reading what?" Luke asked.

"You taking a survey?" Paddy returned.

Colin had leaned the ladder against the porch and was right behind them, following them into the house. "Sometimes if you just let him take your temperature, it satisfies him and he stops asking questions."

"*War and Peace,*" Paddy said.

"My ass," Luke shot back.

"Actually, I have been reading, but not *War and Peace.* I'm catching up on the DeMille books. That's what we do at sea — read. Watch DVDs. We play video games and work out a lot. And fly. I haven't had any significant downtime when the ground isn't rolling under me in about ten years now."

"How's it working out for you?" Colin asked.

"All right, as a matter of fact. This was a good idea. For a few weeks, anyway."

"Come to San Diego with us," Colin invited for at least the tenth time.

Paddy shook his head. "I have commitments."

"Yeah?" Luke asked. He opened the refrigerator. Though Colin lived in this big old Victorian with Jill, Luke apparently put himself in charge. He pulled out bread, lunch meat, cheese, lettuce, mayo, mustard, pickles and tomatoes. "What commitments?"

"I told you, but you never listen. I have to be back in Charleston right after Christmas and I promised to check on Marie on my way. I'm going to spend Christmas with her and little Daniel."

"Is that carved in granite?" Colin asked, putting a couple of plates on the work island. "Because maybe you can wrangle a few more days out of the Navy, come with the family to San Diego . . ."

He shook his head. "I told her I'd be sure she was all right at Christmastime. It's Jake's wife," he said.

"Widow. Did she ask you to come?" Colin wanted to know.

Patrick shook his head. "In fact, she said I didn't have to. But I have to. You guys didn't really know him — Jake. And you never knew him with Marie." His shoulders lifted slightly in sentimental memory. "They were so crazy for each other, sometimes it got ridiculous." He laughed. "They could finish each other's sentences. When we got back to base after a deployment, they couldn't be disturbed for days. While we were home, they had date night, alone, every week. I know a hundred couples that wouldn't be as wounded by separation as Marie and Jake — they were like a blended person. She's doing well right now, but it's been brutal. So I'm going to see Marie. Besides, if it wasn't for the crash, I'd be at sea over Christmas, anyway, and you'd never think twice about me missing it."

"You seem a little better," Colin observed.

"I said this was a good idea. I had to get the hell away from that boatyard. A little distance, you know? I remember when the smell of jet fuel got my heart pumping and all of a sudden . . ." He shook his head. "Probably just some PTSD."

"Even after my Black Hawk went down, I was ready to climb right back into one," Colin said.

"Yeah, because it was yours, not one of your boys. That changes everything. But I'm working through it."

While Patrick talked, Luke spread out bread and dealt cold cuts and cheese onto the slices. He slathered them with mayo and mustard, then sliced a tomato. The tomato slices went on two of the four sandwiches, lettuce on all four.

"Missed a couple," Patrick told Luke.

"I don't want tomato. That's Colin's — since his woman grows 'em, he has to eat 'em."

Patrick couldn't help it, he laughed. "You two," he said. "For about forty years we couldn't keep you two from fighting, day and night, and now look at you. Like two little old ladies taking care of each other. You're totally mellowed. It's the girls, that's what it is."

168

"Probably," Colin said. "For me there were a lot of factors, but I'll be the first to admit Jilly is the best of all those things. She just has this calming effect on me."

"How much older are you than Jillian?" Patrick asked.

Colin shrugged. "Eight years or so, I guess. Luke's the one who robbed the cradle."

Luke took a huge bite of his sandwich, chewed, swallowed and said, "I've got almost fourteen years on Shelby, the crazy little witch. Young is good, trust me."

Patrick leaned toward him. "Don't you feel just a little bit like a dirty old man?"

Sound and movement stopped so suddenly, it was almost surreal. Only eyeballs shifted between Colin and Luke. Luke slowly put down his sandwich. "Shit," he said. "You did it. You and the little one, Jack's niece. You did the nasty."

"What are you *talking* about?" Patrick said indignantly.

Colin put down his sandwich. "Yep. Not DeMille's books relaxing you, Paddy. Something else altogether. *Someone* else. Aw, man. You had to go for the mayor's niece?"

"Mayor?" he asked. Patrick stood up from his stool, yet Luke and Colin finally sat down on theirs. The older brothers looked a little weary. "There's no mayor here!"

"Okay, the king, then. Jack's pretty much running this town. Don't tell him that, though. He seems oblivious," Colin said. "What he's *not* oblivious to is his niece. He's been clear — he doesn't want her mixed up with any Riordan hooligan."

"It was consensual," Paddy said before he realized how awkward that sounded. Obviously all the wonderful sex had killed off some of his brain cells. He certainly hadn't engaged his mind before opening his mouth.

"There we go," Luke said. "He did the teenager. Crap."

"She's twenty-three! She has two degrees! Two impossible science degrees — biology and chemistry! She's been valedictorian of every school she's been in! She's extremely smart."

"I know this," Luke said. "Jack told me. In fact, he told me at the same time he pointed to you and Angie and said, 'That can't happen.' So now what, genius?"

"Nothing happens, that's what." Paddy said. "We're friends. We're both stuck in a weird holding pattern in our lives right now. She knows all about my situation, about Jake, about the Navy. And I know about hers, about her accident, her indecision about continuing med school."

Luke looked at Colin. Colin looked at Luke. "Think Jack is going to buy 'weird holding pattern'?" Colin asked.

"I wouldn't count on it."

"Screw it!" Patrick said, storming toward the door. He whirled back toward his brothers suddenly. "This isn't about Jack. It's about us, me and Angie, sitting out rough waters in Virgin River. We're adults. I might be a little more of an adult if you're counting years but I bet I have a lower IQ, so that puts us pretty much even. So mind your own goddamn business, all right?" Then he stormed out the door and walked toward his Jeep.

"Hey!"

He turned around to see Colin standing on the porch. Colin, the king of badasses until his Black Hawk crash and Jilly.

"Lighten up, kid," he said. "No one accused you of anything."

"Really? Really? Because it sounded like you were pretty goddamn judgmental in there. . . ."

"Nah, we were pretty Riordan," Colin said. "Take it easy, Paddy."

"I'm telling you, she's a good person! She's smart enough and mature enough to make a decision and I wouldn't —"

"Hey, slow down, Paddy. Riordans have a

lot of rough edges, missed a lot of training growing up, but there was never a Riordan man who didn't take special care where women were concerned." Then he grinned. "Even, you know, the kind of naughty ones . . ."

"She's not naughty!" he nearly shouted.

Colin put up his hands. "Hey, I wasn't talking about the little Sheridan niece, pal. My thoughts drifted more toward Luke's taste for pole dancers."

"He always said it was you who favored —"

"We treat women right," Colin said, cutting off his younger brother. "We Riordans don't have a lot of sterling qualities, but we're good to women. And our friends. And, in tough times, to our brothers. Ready to settle down now?"

"She's good people, Colin," Patrick said. "I don't want either of you saying one negative thing about Angie."

"Patrick, man, no one would. But you have to tell her she's been outted. You wouldn't want word to get around to Jack and have her broadsided."

"I'll take care of her."

"Of course you will. You probably don't have to be told this, but she's a little . . . tender."

And with that, Patrick dropped his chin, looking down. He couldn't help feeling the weight of that. God knew he didn't want that to be the case — he wanted her to be as tough as she talked. That way he could leave her when he had to without feeling like a piece of shit.

"It's okay, buddy," Colin said. "You can't always help who gets your attention. At least she's over twenty-one."

"Then why the reaction?" Patrick demanded.

"Because, kid — you have complications right now. 'Commitments,' as you call them. Just let me know if you need someone at your back."

Patrick was quiet for a minute. "Thanks."

"Want dinner here tonight? I'm cooking for my little farmer."

"Sorry, I can't."

Colin studied him for a long moment. "Of course you can't," he finally said.

The Riordan men weren't known for sensitivity, though they did stick together. In fact, they could be rolling in the dust fighting one minute and the next backing one another up. Patrick, being the youngest, had never had great conflict with any of them. It was Luke and Colin who fought the most.

Then it was Luke and Sean. Then it was Sean and Colin. There were times it was Luke or Colin and Aiden. But no one could stay mad at Paddy.

He'd had about enough of being called *kid*, however.

So, the old boys — Luke and Colin — had mellowed out beyond anything Paddy had expected. He was convinced it was their women. Two of the scrappiest Riordans got two of the best women — Shelby and Jilly. Nothing wrong with Sean's Franci or Aiden's Erin, either, but the latter two women hadn't had nearly as much challenge in taming their men.

Colin was right in what he said to Patrick — Angie was tender, even though she tried to appear worldly and brave. He should probably break things off before he added to her struggle with her family, with her uncle. They were going to part ways eventually, anyway. Probably better if it happened sooner than later. But he couldn't even think about it. Patrick hadn't had the kind of experience he'd shared with Angie with another woman in so long he couldn't . . . Oh, hell, he was pretty sure he'd never had that kind of experience with a woman, and he was not without experience.

Once home, he got his stir-fry ready —

chopped and marinated so that all that was left was to throw it in the pan. Then he settled in to call Marie.

"Hullo?" she said thickly.

Oh, please, he prayed. *Let it be a cold.*

"How are you today, Marie?"

She sniffed and snuffled. "Oh, Paddy," she said, crying. "I don't know what's wrong with me. I let myself have a bad day — I think I lost my mind a little bit."

"What happened, honey?"

"It was so crazy. My mom was watching Daniel so I could do a little Christmas shopping at the mall. It was crowded, it was festive, lots of lights and music and . . . I was feeling so good. I kept finding things I couldn't resist — perfect presents. I went through a ton of stores and bought armloads of things and then . . . Oh, God, Paddy! I realized I'd bought presents for Jake!" And she melted into tears.

"It's okay, Marie," he said. "It's okay. . . ."

"Shirts and sweaters and pants and shoes. Electronic stuff he would love. All for Jake. Like I was going to go home, wrap it all up, put it under the tree and he'd —" He could hear the sobs across the phone line.

"You can take it all back," he said, trying to reassure her, to comfort her.

"I don't want to take it back! I want him

to come home!"

"Aw, Marie . . ."

"Do you ever ask yourself if it's true? If he's really gone?"

He shook his head, although she couldn't see him. This might be a good time to tell her Jake sometimes visited his dreams, joked around with him, poked fun at him. But then again, no . . .

"Unfortunately, I know he's gone," he said quietly. "But I think I'd rather forget that sometimes and buy him Christmas presents by accident."

"No, you wouldn't."

"If I could have an hour of him being alive, I'd take it."

"I don't know what to do," she whimpered.

"Ask your mom or sister to return those things, Marie. Or give them to charity and send me the bill. If it makes you feel better to look at them, touch them, fondle them for a while, then do that for a week or so. It's Christmas — it's hard. But it'll pass." He wiped at his eye.

"For a while it really felt like he was alive," she said weakly. "What's the matter with me?"

"Nothing," he insisted. "Normal confusion — he was your soul mate. The loss

176

is . . . It's just hard, especially right now. You talk to anyone in your grief group?"

"I don't want to right now. I just want to . . . you know . . ."

He chuckled through a fat tear. "Wallow?"

She chuckled back but it caught on a hiccup. "Exactly."

Patrick found himself thinking about their shared grief, how quickly sobs could turn into laughter and vice versa. They'd done this together since Jake's death. Even though Marie had a loving family, it was Patrick and Marie together who mourned Jake the most, the hardest. Even little Daniel, at barely two, didn't really feel the loss. His father had been deployed so much of his young life, anyway.

"Maybe you should sleep with the presents you bought," he said, teasing.

"Or wear them?" she teased back. "Oh, God, it's so embarrassing. I'm afraid if I tell my mom how I lost my mind, she'll put me in a treatment center."

"Nah, she won't do that. But you better not tell her until you're ready to part with all those presents. Hey, I think I'm Jake's size. . . ."

"Nice try — I didn't buy those things for you."

"But I'm coming for Christmas. You don't

have to get anything, but if you're already loaded up . . . What electronics?"

"Stop," she said, laughing. "Oh, Paddy, no one can bring me back to life like you can. What would I do without you? I love you so much. But I've already told you, you don't have to come for Christmas."

"Why the hell not? Aren't you looking forward to seeing me again?"

"Patrick, of course, but you have family. Spend time with them while you can."

"You're my family. I promised Jake a long time ago that if anything ever happened to him, I'd take good care of you."

"Oh, Paddy, if only you could give me what I need. I love you, and you're my dearest friend, but we have to find a way to move on." She sniffed loudly. "It's hard right now, but we'll do it. We'll find a way to do it."

"I'm coming," he said. "My family has other plans."

"Patrick," she said. "You are pure gold."

"No, I'm not — I already have my ticket. I'm reserved at the motel."

"I'm just not sure this would be good for either one of us. I don't want to depend on you too much."

"It'll be good," he said. "I guarantee it."

After a little more chat, they said goodbye and Patrick sat in his small living room and thought about her pain and loneliness. He had to be there for her and he would be. Maybe with a little more time he could convince her that together they could keep Jake alive and have a good life.

For the second time in twenty-four hours he made up his mind — the best thing would be to set Angie free to pursue her dreams while he went to Charleston by way of Oklahoma City and on to the next part of his life. He'd propose the idea to Marie — that they could do it together. Best friends forever. An excellent concept.

And then there was a light tapping at the cabin door. He opened it and there stood Angie, Christmas lights wrapped around her, twinkling. Her eyes were alive, her smile infectious.

"Oh, God," he said. "What's this?"

"I'm your Christmas present!" she said on a laugh. "Do you have any idea how big the battery pack has to be to do this?"

How do you turn down a Christmas present? He snatched her against him and went after her mouth with every ounce of passion he felt inside. He didn't stop until they were both almost freezing from standing in the open doorway.

EIGHT

Patrick pulled Angie inside and held her on his lap in front of the fire, lights and all. "Tell me about your day, sweetheart. It's bound to lead up to the lights."

"I had a good, productive day. It started off with a conversation with Mel about Megan's scar. Mel isn't sure, but she thinks it could be a fairly simple correction. Still costly, still out of their reach, but . . . Well, let me start with this — I mentioned Dr. Temple, my neurosurgeon, didn't I?"

"I think so."

"I had a lot of doctors, techs, nurses and therapists after my accident. It was pretty easy to get close to some of them, but he was the one I loved. I think my shunt has his initials on it." She smiled and absently touched that place on her head. "He spent much more time with me than seemed necessary. He was the one practitioner who was never in a hurry. I've even stayed in touch with him a little — emailed him a few times, called him twice or so. The most wonderful man."

"You crushed on him," Patrick said.

With an impish grin, she kissed him quick on the lips. Then she said, "I would have married him in a second. He was around sixty, however. But I loved him and today I learned something about him I didn't know. I called him for advice about how I might help Megan and I found out he gives an average of a day of every week providing neurosurgery for people who couldn't otherwise have it — that would include the underinsured, the poor who can't get help from Medicaid, the people who make too much money to qualify for Medicaid but can't afford both medical benefits and food. Megan and her family fall into the underinsured category. Dr. Temple said he'd be happy to work with me on that if I would be the point man. He's not the guy to do it, but he offered to reach out to some plastic surgeons. He gave me a list of things he thought I should look into to get this process started.

"And guess what else? I told him about the peace corps or a similar organization and he thought it was a great idea. He said I'd learn more in humanitarian relief than

181

anywhere else. He also said he didn't think they'd resist my application because of a titanium rod or a shunt, as long as I'm in good health. And I'm in excellent health."

"I can see that," he said with a bright smile. "You're all lit up."

"Will you help me out of these lights? And my jacket? This fire is getting hot. . . ."

"I'd be glad to help you out of all your clothes. Stand up," he said. He pulled on the end of the string of lights, she twirled around in front of him and, in just a minute, the lights were off. She shrugged out of her jacket and he pulled her back down on his lap.

"We did a little decorating around the clinic and I borrowed this string of lights with the battery pack. I'm sure Mel thinks I'm going to use them in the cabin. If I had an ounce of courage, I'd have come naked, strung with lights."

"Thank God you didn't. You might've found yourself making love on the front step. What else did you do today?"

"Talked to my mom, for once a nice talk, had lunch with Mel and Jack, asked my aunt Brie what I should do to set up a foundation with a bank to start to fund Megan's surgery — Brie's a lawyer. And I went on a house call with Mel — an elderly woman

182

back in the mountains seems to have bron-chitis. It was a wonderful day. I felt so . . . useful."

"Angie, I hate to put a damper on such a great day but . . . there's something you have to know." He hesitated. "We've been outted. My brothers guessed we're having a — What is it we're having?"

"I'm not sure," she said. "I guess we settled on 'fling'?"

"It's more than that. All day long I've been thinking that it would be smart, maybe even kind, to stop this thing before it goes any further."

She ran her fingers through the hair at his temples for just a moment before she grabbed his head in her hands and went af-ter his mouth like it might be the last kiss of her life. When she finally broke free she said, "You talk too much and you think too much."

"I don't want you to be hurt," he said.

"Then try not to take off too early! I know you have a plane ticket. I wrote the date in my calendar. Until we get to that date, I'd like to enjoy myself. You know, Paddy, I'm not some naive little girl. I know this isn't a happily-ever-after sort of thing — and I'm okay with that." She shook her head. "Leave it to me to pick a guy as controlling as my mother. Here's a good rule of thumb, Paddy. Don't do anything 'for my own good'!"

He couldn't help but laugh at her. "Are you sure you want me to employ that rule, my little hussy?"

"Not entirely," she said softly.

"My brothers are afraid I'm going to hurt you by leaving. After our little 'interlude.' "

"Interlude. I like that. Is that what usually happens? You love the girls and break their hearts?"

He gave a short laugh. "No, not so much."

"Oh?" she probed. "Care to share?"

He laughed a bit uncomfortably. "Seems like it was either a mutual decision that things weren't going anywhere or . . ." He rubbed a hand across the back of his neck. "Or I was dumped."

"Oh, Patrick. If we'd met under different circumstances, I'd hold on to you until you begged me to let go."

"Would you now?" he asked, smiling.

"If I'd met you last year, if you lived and worked nearby, if there weren't so many weird complications and — Listen, Paddy, things change when you almost die. In fact, I suspect I did die, if briefly. This little time we're here together in Virgin River — it feels like it could be a watershed experience.

Hmm? I'll go with it if you will."

"You suspect you died?" he asked. "What's that about?"

She cringed. "Listen, I haven't told anyone except Dr. Temple . . ."

"We're telling each other a lot of things never told before," he said.

"I saw myself," she said. "From above. I was looking down at myself while a whole bunch of people were working on me, around me. I saw my grandmother, who died years ago. She looked wonderful. I don't know if it was a dream, something I was programmed to imagine under the circumstances or if it was the real deal. She was in a halo of light and she lifted her hand and said, 'It's okay, Angie. Everything is going to be all right.' When I woke up, three days had passed and I was on the vent."

His lips were parted in either disbelief or awe. He finally closed his mouth and swallowed. "You were close to her?" he asked.

"Very close. My mother was her eldest — I'm the oldest grandchild. We were together a lot when I was little."

"Do you ever . . . see her in your dreams? Get messages from her in dreams?"

"I think she's been in a dream or two, but not like that night. That night there was all that light." She shook her head. "I don't want you to think I'm crazy, but —"

"I don't," he whispered. Then he seemed to shake himself. "So, I'm not opting out. Tell me how you'd like to spend this interlude. When you're not working or researching this gift of surgery, of course. When you can fit me in."

She smiled devilishly. "Well, I've got plenty of time right now . . . and I have a pretty good idea of how I'd like to spend it. . . ."

And his smile widened. "Yeah, my kind of girl." He lifted her in his arms. "Do you need food first?"

"I can eat anytime," she said. "Right now I'm just craving you."

Patrick nuzzled Angie's neck in the early morning. "You had sex on the first date. And the second."

"When you're me, you're a little more afraid of not living than of living too much."

He brushed the hair away from her brow and placed a kiss there. "I'm starting to understand what has your family a little freaked out. Might be your 'commitment to living,' as it were."

"I have no intention of being reckless," she said. "I just don't want to waste away in a lab or library while life goes on around me. You know why I haven't had boyfriends? Real boyfriends? Because I've been so focused on school. Because the only place I could compete in life was with grades, with scores. I always had to be the best in my class. It felt like the only way I could measure my success, my self-worth. If you knew the time I put into preparing for the MCAT you wouldn't believe it — it verged on OCD. It's that insane."

"And did that get you the highest possible score?"

Her gaze shifted away as if it was something to be ashamed of when, in truth, her fellow students had envied her. "Forty."

"Is that good?"

"Ninety-ninth percentile." She looked into his beautiful eyes. "But I'm tired of living my life behind a textbook, of being awkward as soon as I venture out into the real world. And . . . I'm sick of being lonely. Sometimes I have no one to talk to."

He laughed at her. "You? Shy? *You* came on to *me*. You let me undress you. You wrapped yourself in lights for me!"

"For some reason, I'm comfortable with you. You make it easy. Well, it was easy to let you undress me. Special circumstances . . ."

"Oh?" he asked.

She rolled over so she was on top of him. "Do you know the scariest part about this interlude? It's not the fact that we'll part ways soon, going off to do what we have to do. It's the thought that I might never find another man like you. I don't know much about getting myself a good boyfriend, but you might have raised the bar." She shook her head. "What if I'm alone forever *because* of you?"

Angie did research and made phone calls from the clinic so she could be on hand if Mel needed her help — even if it was just for sweeping up or sterilizing instruments. For someone who wanted to do more living, she had trouble managing idle time.

Her first order of business was finding a surgeon but getting through to one proved impossible. She was reduced to leaving her number and the subject of her business. She was thrilled when Dr. Temple called to check on her progress — he'd left messages with a dozen plastic surgeons he knew who he thought might help if their time permitted. He offered to email her the information.

"Have you made a decision about your next move, Angie? Peace corps? VISTA? Anything?"

"I've read a few websites, but my goal is to get this little girl set up before I pursue my own next move. What about you? Doing anything exciting?"

"I'm taking two weeks in March to go with a team to Honduras. There are a lot of patients who've been waiting a long time for medical and surgical aid. It's a private foundation operated by a senator's wife who happens to be a surgical nurse. She does all the front work, selection, scheduling, purchasing, acquisition and facilities. We'll load up a C-130 transport aircraft, see patients and operate ten hours a day."

Angie actually gasped. "I would love to do that!"

He laughed at her excitement. "You will one day, Angie. I have no doubt."

Brie was working out of her home office that day so Angie drove out there for lunch, and in a fever of excitement told her about Dr. Temple's philanthropic project. Then she described her own progress, or the lack thereof. Getting a doctor to even call her back would be a dream come true and having one sign on to donate his services — well, that was something she realized she was going to have to work very hard for.

"I'm so proud of you. But what I want to know is what you're going to do next. Any chance you're going back to school? You must realize your mom calls Jack and me every day."

"Even though she doesn't admit that to me, I assumed as much. What does she want to know?"

Brie leaned across her small kitchen table and took Angie's hands in hers. "Ange, she says you hang up on her."

Angie pulled back her hands. "When she puts on the pressure, I do. When she says she's made an appointment with a psychiatrist because I haven't made arrangements to go back to med school. When she asks me — daily — if I've had a chance to think things over and come to my senses. It's insane! She's so convinced that there's something wrong with my brain — simply because I'm not interested in doing exactly what she wants me to do. The truth is that *she's* the one who seems to have a problem, not me. Oh, Brie, how am I going to go home? Ever?"

Brie's brows furrowed in empathy. She shook her head. "Has anything changed? Have you made any possible plans? I mean, besides helping Megan get her operation?"

Now Angie grabbed Brie's hands. Her voice was soft. "I haven't said anything to my mom yet, but . . . yes. I think I'd like to do a couple of years in the peace corps or a similar organization, and maybe while I'm there I'll think about med school."

Brie's eyes got large, and she leaned back, startled. Then she groaned and let her head drop to the kitchen table. "Oh, man."

"You don't approve? Brie, I thought you might find it exciting!"

Brie lifted her head. "It's definitely dramatic."

"It's honorable! It's positive! People do it all the time! Why wouldn't you — ?"

"I'm going to go ahead and suggest you not hit Donna with that one right now and I'll tell you why. It's not a bad thing in any way, Ange. You're right — it's honorable and positive. And it's a dramatic change in course — *change* being the operative word. You went from being a student with very specific goals to a dropout with a whole new plan. And all this follows you being in a catastrophic accident — it smells like a paradigm shift. That worries people who love you."

"You?"

Brie shrugged. "Not so much. You don't seem too out of character. You've always been a generous person with a big heart. But if you start freeing zoo animals or chaining yourself to trees . . ."

"Oh, please — I'm not even getting slightly radical."

"Plowing fields in Africa versus attending classes at USC is something of a radical shift. Listen. Your mother is wonderful and I love her and she's helped me through more than one crisis in my life, but she is rigid. She doesn't like change. She doesn't adjust well — it takes her a long time. She's very comfortable being in control — not so much when the people she's controlling step out of line."

"Thus, the hang-ups," Angie said dryly. "But this whole thing just doesn't seem like such a big deal to me. Sure, it's a big change. But isn't it expected — normal, even — for a person to change their perspective on life after a near-death experience? The accident helped me to see what is really important in this world, and it showed me that I'm strong enough to be a part of it. I thought my mom might understand that."

"You and your mom have had a very close, very mutually supportive relationship. We need to get that back for both of you before you spring something like this on her."

"I'm not going to pretend to follow her trajectory for me just so we can be on good terms. I want my own life, not the one she outlined for me. And I love her, too. But, Brie —"

"I completely understand. But can we at least slow down a bit and ease her into the idea that you want something of your own design? That you're ready and capable of deciding some things for yourself? Can we be more reasonable about this?"

"When she pushes on me, I just can't deal with it. I have to hang up."

"Or maybe try something like, 'That's an interesting suggestion, Mom, let me think about that for a while.' "

Angie ran a hand through her hair. "That doesn't slow her down. She can be relentless."

"Follow with 'Let's talk about this later, Mom. Brie needs me to babysit.' I'll cover for you. Let's just give her time, that's all I'm saying."

"It's not like I'm shipping out tomorrow. It's not that easy to get into the peace corps, you know."

"I know. And given all you've been through, I don't find it a strange idea," Brie said. "How about your stay here so far? Almost a week in that little cabin, hanging out around town, helping in the clinic? How's it going?"

Angie grinned. "I love it so much. You

people really have it made, in a rough sort of way. I know you have lots of challenges here but you have exceptional beauty every day. And the challenges have made all of you closer. Look at me. I just got to town and I've already found a project that needs me. I love Mel's clinic — it's perfect. The town relies on her — do you know how great that is?"

"I do," Brie said.

"And you were running away to this town to fall in love — and look at what you bring to the whole county. I'm sure it's not as high dollar as Sacramento County D.A.'s office, but doesn't it feel good?"

"Most days," she agreed with a smile.

"I do love it here. I always have," Angie said.

"And how about that little crush we talked about last weekend?" Brie asked. "What's up with that?"

"Brie, it was never little. . . ."

"Oh, that's right — you described it as world-class."

"Yes. And full-blown." Then Angie's cheeks pinkened, though she tried to smile through it.

"Full-blown?" Brie asked weakly.

"I'm seeing him. We're trying to be discreet so Jack doesn't get . . . you know, how

194

he gets."

"Seeing?" Brie asked. But she shook her head. Did she not want the answer?

Angie took a deep breath. She closed her eyes as she answered. "He's wonderful. I adore him. And until I have to give him up, I'm going to love every inch of him."

"Oh, God . . ." Brie's eyes grew round and her mouth hung open, then she let her head fall to the kitchen table with a *thunk*, again.

Brie and Angie had always been close. When Brie was a tot, her big brother Jack carted her around, spoiled her, fussed over her. And then he went off to the Marine Corps when she was only five. When Angie was born, twelve-year-old Brie couldn't be around her enough. She was more a big sister than aunt — her babysitter and confidante.

While both of them were devoted to Donna, there were also times it felt as though they shared a common enemy. Donna was strong willed; she could be a force of nature. Also, Donna would often be the one to step in during a crisis large or small and take charge, manage the situation, resolve the problem. She seemed to be able to do that effortlessly.

When Donna and Brie's mother died, Brie leaned on her big sister heavily, and there was no question she'd have been lost without her. Angie leaned on both her mother and her aunt. Together, they all propped up Angie's grandfather, Sam.

Everyone knew Donna was a good, strong woman.

She could be difficult and hard to satisfy, tough to please.

She could also be so warm and compassionate.

Brie remembered too well a time when she was Angie's age, a law student messing with a professor. Donna had had a hissy. Brie would've died before listening to Donna, though. In fact, she wondered if it was Donna's warnings that might've driven her into the professor's arms. And, still, when her heart was breaking, Brie ran to Donna, who consoled her.

And here they were, full circle. Brie had learned a few things since she was Angie's age, things she hoped she could remember when her own daughter was twenty-three. For now, Brie pulled Angie into a hug and said, "Please be careful."

"Of course I will."

"Would you like to have dinner with us tonight? At the bar?"

Angie laughed. "Not a chance."

After saying their goodbyes, Brie made her way to the bar for dinner. Mike was meeting her there, as was Mel with her kids. This time of year the place had an even bigger draw than during deer-hunting season, given the tree and that amazing star on top. It was a crazier place — people came from miles to see the tree and it was only natural to stop into Jack's for dinner or dessert. And fortunately, Brie's daughter, Ness, and her cousins Emma and David were big enough now to sit at the table, feed themselves, maybe do a little coloring, sometimes sneaking off to Preacher's quarters to play with Dana and the toys.

Even with that advantage, the bar was not conducive to quiet conversation. And yet, Brie really needed to talk.

"Can you spit it out?" Mel asked, once they'd all settled at a table.

"Are you psychic or what? Because I don't recall saying I wanted to talk."

"You and Paige have been my best friends for going on five years. Both of you chew on the inside of your cheek when you've got a problem. Don't ask me why both of you do that. . . ."

"I'm going to stop immediately," Brie said. "I honestly don't know if I should be

197

talking about this."

"Patrick and Angie?"

"She *told* you?"

Mel shook her head. "I guessed."

"And she admitted it?"

Mel shook her head again. "She got red as a beet when I mentioned him. Dead giveaway. Even if I hadn't already noticed her bright eyes, distracted behavior and whisker burn."

"Shew. You should really be a cop."

Mel laughed.

"What are we going to do?" Brie asked.

"I think nothing."

"Do we tell Jack?"

"I think definitely not. Angie might see that as a betrayal. Besides, it's not going to take Jack long to figure it out himself."

Brie leaned back and took in the scene of the loud, packed room. Mike was behind the bar, as was Denny Cutler, Jack's part-time help. Preacher and Paige were serving; every few minutes Denny made a swing through the room with a large tub and bussed and wiped tables. "Maybe not at this time of year," Brie observed. "He's awful busy."

"He'll get around to it," Mel said.

"Did you talk to Angie about this . . . this . . ."

198

"Love affair?" Mel asked. She shook her head. "She seems very private about it. Shy. I don't want to shake her confidence or worry her."

"But, Mel!"

"Are you really surprised?" Mel asked. "Why would you be? I guess because Angie has always been most impressive in the academic arena, not the social. But, Brie, there are a few things I've learned about the women in your family — you're all so smart and so passionate and so loving. Angie was bound to do something like this eventually. Didn't she have a serious boyfriend last year?"

"Alex. But he was a wiener. I don't know why they were together, anyway, and when he disappeared while she was in the hospital, it didn't seem to bother her too much. I suspect she was glad to be rid of him."

"This one is not a wiener," Mel said. "He's a Riordan. If anyone can match the passion of the Sheridans, it's a Riordan." She fanned her face.

"But isn't this one, Patrick, in a bad place right now?"

"Isn't Angie?" Mel asked, lifting a brow. "I'm probably too sentimental, but I think people find each other when they're supposed to. When they need to. And, no, I

199

don't fantasize that this will all work out sweet and happy — in fact, I think there might be tears and heartache. But does she need this right now? I don't know. Maybe. Can we stop it? No way. Brie, that ship has sailed. Listen," she added, leaning close, "if I could be in charge, I'd work it out so that we always gained our greatest wisdom from the easy, fun stuff. That makes more sense to me. But it doesn't seem to be the case. It's usually the roughest waters that teach us the most."

Brie thought for a moment about her own heartaches, long ago and far away. The professor, the slime-ball; her ex-husband who had an affair with her best friend, the unfaithful turd. And then came Mike, who she would never have found but for the series of catastrophes she'd had to survive first.

"I don't want her to hurt," Brie said.

"Me, either," Mel agreed.

"Donna's going to flip," Brie added.

"She better not. That would be the kiss of death. At some point she's going to have to give up."

"Ninety percent of the time Donna and Angie have a great relationship, but hoo boy, that ten percent! Do all mothers and daughters go through this?" Brie asked.

"Did you?"

"My mother passed away quite a while ago, but I went through it with Donna in her place!"

"Listen, I know you sympathize with Angie," Mel said. "So do I. I just want to ask that you remember Donna's burden isn't light. She wants to protect her daughter just like she probably wanted to protect you. And I bet she takes a lot of heat for trying. Strong women can be so underappreciated unless you're screaming for their help."

Angie's plan was to go home to the cabin, light the fire, grab a shower and call Patrick. They hadn't made plans but she was willing to bet he was flexible. She had no idea what he did during the day while she was busy at the clinic, but she took great comfort in the fact that his plane ticket home wasn't until the twenty-third.

When she pulled into the cabin's clearing, her heart leaped. His Jeep was parked there. He'd decorated the cabin! The eaves were adorned with colored Christmas lights. There was a wreath on the door. A curl of smoke rose from the chimney and there were lights on inside. When she opened the door her senses were tempted by a wonderful aroma. He sat on the sofa, feet up on the coffee table trunk, and smiled at her.

"Well, my favorite B and E man," she said.

"I didn't have to break in. The door was unlocked. Come here, you delicious little thing."

She dove to the couch, right into his arms. "Cooking?"

"Sort of. A frozen lasagna, bread, a salad from the deli in Fortuna. Hungry?"

"I am. It was my plan to get a quick shower and then call you. . . ."

"I can help with that," he said.

"It's a very small shower."

"We aren't going to need a lot of room for what I have in mind."

I'm getting too old for this, Jack thought. The stress of this whole tree thing was driving him into the ground. People started arriving at five, about the time the sun was going down. He'd had to light the heaters on the porch because the size of the crowd meant there'd be a long wait for a table. But standing around outside and enjoying the tree didn't seem to bother anyone. And they stayed late — the bar was busy until after ten.

This year he and Preacher had to suspend the early breakfast four days a week to compensate for staying open later. Friday through Monday they didn't open until nine in the morning, even though typically, especially during the fall hunting season, they had the fires lit by six.

On this particular night, Jack left the bar at nine-thirty even though there were still quite a few people there. Denny offered to take over for him, and the kid was amazing — he could handle anything. Denny was a partner out at Jilly Farms and the month of December was nothing but greenhouse work, snow removal and relatively easy days. But the bar was hopping, so Denny took the opportunity to put in more hours. His young wife, Becca, was busy with the Christmas pageant at the church and the Christmas program at the elementary school (where she was director, teacher, treasurer and custodian), so if he was late getting home, it was no big deal. Besides, all that work at the bar brought in extra cash, and Denny and Becca were saving for a house of their own.

Jack was anxious to get home to his own wife. By now the kids would be asleep and Mel would probably still be up, reading or something. It was his favorite time of day.

Even so, he drove out to Angie's cabin instead. He hadn't seen her all day — she'd gone to Brie's for lunch and turned down an invitation to the bar for dinner. Who could blame her, it was a zoo. But to be sure she was eating well, he had Preacher pack up some brisket, some mashed potatoes and gravy, green beans and a cherry pie made from preserves from Jilly. To prove he wasn't such an old stick in the mud, he'd grabbed a bottle of sauvignon blanc, too, her brew of choice as far as he could remember.

When he pulled up to the cabin he found the lights out, smoke coming from the fireplace and Patrick Riordan's Jeep parked next to Angie's SUV.

I am so an old stick in the mud, he thought.

He backed out and went home. He left his take-out dinner and the wine in the kitchen, took his boots off by the back door, dropped his shirt and socks on the washer — he smelled like grease and beer — and followed the light to the bedroom.

Mel was sitting cross-legged on the bed, her laptop balanced on her lap. She looked up at him, smiling as she closed the laptop. "Hi, darling . . ."

But he was frowning. "Tell me the truth," he said. "Did you know?"

"Know what?"

"I took a sack of takeout and bottle of wine out to my niece and guess what? Paddy's Jeep is parked out there and the lights are out."

She studied his face for a moment. A long, stretched-out moment. Finally she asked, "What kind of wine?"

NINE

When Angie entered the bar in the morning, it was empty. She went behind the bar, helped herself to a cup of coffee, then went back around to sit up on one of the stools. It was only a couple of minutes before Jack came from the kitchen.

"Hi," she said. "Mel said you wanted to have a cup of coffee with me."

"Yeah, thanks."

He got out his own mug and filled it. She couldn't miss the fact that he wore a troubled frown, that he was contemplative.

"Ange, I went out to the cabin last night. I got off a little early and since I hadn't seen you all day I wanted to surprise you with some takeout and a nice bottle of wine."

"Aww. How sweet."

"Well, obviously I didn't make it inside. I thought it might be awkward, what with the lights out and Patrick's Jeep there." He looked at her pointedly.

"He surprised me. When I got home from the clinic he was there. Did you see the lights? He put up Christmas lights and a wreath. I'm thinking about a small Christmas tree, but I don't have ornaments. I could string popcorn or something. We used to do that —"

"Ange, Patrick was there. It was nine-thirty."

She looked at her watch. "He was there at eight-thirty this morning, too."

Jack groaned, leaned on the bar and put his head in his hand. "Angie, Angie, Angie."

But she held firm, looking him straight in the eyes. "I like him. He's a great guy."

Jack lifted his head. "He's a Navy pilot from Charleston."

"I know this. On leave until the twenty-third. Then back to the base . . . and probably the ship."

"So you know it has no potential? That it won't last? That you're having a little . . . ?"

She leaned toward him. "Jack, he spent the night. I have very high standards, especially since that last boyfriend dumped me before I even remembered who he was. Paddy is a perfect gentleman. Uncle Jack, I'm twenty-three. I'm not a child, and I'm certainly not a nun."

"You seem so young to your poor old

uncle Jack. . . ."

She shook her head sadly. "Emma's going to have a hard time with you. My mother was engaged at twenty-three."

"Your mother was engaged *twice*," he corrected.

Angie sat back. "Really? I didn't know that!"

"The first one was a mistake. Angie, I worry about Patrick. There are things bothering him."

"His best friend was killed right in front of him! Recently. You're right — of course it bothers him."

"I think he has PTSD stuff going on."

She laughed. "Jack, I have PTSD!" To his shocked expression she said, "Oh, I get it, you thought PTSD was reserved for the military. Most of my issues are very different from Paddy's, but it's amazing how much we have in common. PTSD is something you have to work through — it doesn't mean you're permanently damaged goods. And you know what? I thought I dreaded everyone knowing, but I'm glad it's out — now maybe we can get dinner here or order takeout or be seen together. I'm kind of tired of all this sneaking around."

"This was supposed to be a break from your mother until you two could learn to get along better, not a chance to get involved in something even more complicated."

She took a sip of her coffee. "And thank you — it's been much more fulfilling than I dared hope." He groaned and dropped his head in his hands again. "Stop reading into everything," she said, laughing. "I'm working on getting Megan Thickson some help — surgery on that scar. And I'm actually making progress. Just a little, but I have some good people trying to help me. My old neurosurgeon for one. I really love that guy."

"Angie, I don't want you to get hurt."

"Jack, where were you when I was sixteen, sitting in the living room in my prom dress with Grandpa and his camera waiting, with my sisters giggling, with Mom and Dad and Aunt Mary and Aunt Brie all set to snap pictures for a date who didn't show, who not only stood me up but took someone else instead?" She shook her head. "You know what my first choice would be? That I lived in the same general area where Paddy lives, or is stationed, and that we could date for months or years, like my mom and dad did. And my second choice? For you to let me make my own decisions for three more weeks."

"Have you told your mother?"

"I haven't *told* anyone, but around here there aren't any secrets, I guess."

"What will your mother say?" he asked.

"I don't care what she says, if she even finds out. I'm not a baby or an invalid and the bunch of you better get that straight or I might do something dramatic, like run away. Again." She stood up. "Really, I'm glad it's out. Wrap your brain around this, Uncle Jack. I like him. I'm not giving him up. Now I have phone calls to make, so I'll see you later."

"Angie, those Riordans . . ."

She turned back to him.

"They're good guys, don't get me wrong. But they're not pups. They're warriors, every last one of them. Rugged. Not exactly . . . *docile.*"

"Yeah," she said with a big grin. "I know." And with that, she turned and left.

"You could've warned me," Angie said to Mel.

"Angie, I didn't discuss you with Jack. Not much, anyway. I said it was true I suspected you and Patrick but that we hadn't talked about it and it was none of my business. I also told him that my experience with young women is that the louder the protest against their decisions, the firmer they become." She took a breath. "How'd he do?"

"He's batshit crazy. His little kitten is getting boinked by a fighter jock."

Mel couldn't help it, a laugh burst from her. She covered her mouth with a hand. "God," she whispered.

"Well, there's no one left to be discreet around. We can officially go steady. For three weeks."

"Like summer camp," Mel said. "Only this time in the dead of winter. Listen, while you were with Jack, there was a phone call. Dr. Hernandez?"

"Really?"

"Is he one of yours? Or a plastic surgeon?"

"Plastics. He left a number, I hope."

"On the desk. He'd like you to speak to his PA."

Angie bolted for the phone. In fifteen minutes she was back. "Okay, here's what we've got. The doctor wants to see her for an evaluation. If he can help, he will. His assistant will help me tally the other costs so I know exactly how much money I have to raise. Monday at 2:00 p.m."

Mel grinned largely. "Where?"

"Davis. I'm crossing my fingers that this is a relatively simple procedure. He must be a good man. He's waiving the office fee."

"Do you want me to take her?"

"No, please let me. But I'll have to go talk to her and her parents."

"I have a suggestion," Mel said. "She's very close to the elementary school teacher, Becca Cutler. And you're close in age. You might want to talk to her, enlist her help, maybe take her with you to the Thicksons'. It could give Megan peace of mind."

Angie waited until the end of the school day to drive over to the elementary school and introduce herself to Becca. When she arrived, she found the day care staff of three still busy with small children in one room and in another she found a pretty young blonde woman on her knees in front of a miniature table, scraping glue and clay off the top. There was a bucket of soapy water beside her.

"Hi," Angie said. "Are you Becca Cutler?"

She sat back on her heels and smiled. "I am."

"I'm Angela LaCroix. Jack Sheridan is my uncle."

"I heard you were coming up for a visit." She stood up, wiping her hand on her jeans. "Nice to meet you."

"So, this is the new school," Angie said, looking around. There were colorful tubs and baskets full of supplies, mats on the floor, little tables and chairs, desks lined up in one corner, a sink, blackboard and a bookshelf.

"K through fifth," Becca said. "The sixth graders go to middle school, then there's the high school in the valley. This was your uncle Jack's idea. Isn't it awesome?"

"He can really surprise me sometimes," Angie said. "I came to talk to you about one of your kids. It was at Mel's suggestion. It's about Megan Thickson — I've been helping Mel with a special project." When she explained what she'd been trying to do and the upcoming doctor's appointment, Becca teared up.

"Oh, God, could it really happen?"

"I have a long way to go," Angie said. "If the plastic surgeon decides it can be done, the next step is to calculate the cost. Even if he donates his services, there's still the cost of the outpatient surgi-center, lab work, post-op, et cetera. His assistant will break down the expenses. Then I go hunting for money," she finished with a shrug.

"How expensive could it be?"

"I have no clue," Angie said. "One of my uncles had a rotator cuff repair. He was knocked out for an hour and the surgery cost twenty-seven thousand dollars. Of course he had good insurance — it was covered. But who knows how costly Meg's surgery might be? Mel has called all kinds of organizations and agencies and had no success in getting affordable help for Megan.

"But let's not get all worried about that part yet — I haven't even begun to go looking for money. Right now I have to convince the Thicksons to let me take Megan to Davis for an appointment with the doctor. That's the first step. Would you come with me? We have to find a way to do this without letting her think it's all set — we have to explain this is only a possibility. I just can't break a little girl's heart, so I was hoping you might be able to help her understand."

"Of course I'll go with you. I'd do almost anything for Megan. She's one of the reasons I'm here, teaching, married to Denny."

"Really?" Angie asked, lifting her brows.

"I'll tell you all about it on the way to the Thicksons'. I love that little girl. I think she changed my life. I'll do anything I can to help."

Once Becca had finished organizing her classroom, Angie drove them to the Thicksons'. Becca lived right down the street and walked to school in the mornings and her car, a small sedan, wasn't snow and mountain ready. If she had anywhere to go that required all-wheel drive, she took Denny's truck.

"How did you end up here?" Angie asked.

"I came to find Denny. We dated years ago but he broke up with me before leaving for Afghanistan — it was a dark time in his life and that was one of many things he did that made no sense. I hadn't seen him in three years but I really had to know if it was time to move on or if we deserved another chance."

"That's so sweet!" Angie said.

"There were quite a few bumps along the way," Becca admitted with a laugh. "But that's when I met Megan, the sweetest little girl. She's had such a hard road, starting with her father losing his arm in a logging accident, her mother taking a job that made it hard for her to keep up with the family, and Megan's self-esteem was really suffering because her teacher last year didn't give her any encouragement. When Jack came up with the idea of this school, I was helpless. I had to say yes."

"I guess it didn't hurt that Denny was here."

"He'd made a life for himself here, but he was willing to come home with me to San

Diego. I never expected to end up here, but in the end it's the best decision I've ever made. Turn left up here, Angie — it's a fairly long road through the trees before we get to the house."

Angie was surprised to see a number of houses tucked into this woody, hilly, snow-covered area.

"Another left — it's that small one up there. They're sitting on several acres."

"It's very small," she said. "How many children?"

"Four — Megan's the oldest. They manage with two bedrooms. Things are much better for them now than when I first met them. Now Frank — Mr. Thickson — has a prosthesis and Denny was able to get him part-time work out at Jilly Farms. Lorraine has a hard job but she gets some overtime, which really can come in handy. This is a hard-working family that's had some real challenges. I think saving for Megan to have surgery is a priority right now, but I don't think they have much to spare." When Angie parked, Becca brightened and said, "Come on. I can't wait to hear their reaction to your news."

Once Angie and Becca had said their hellos, they sat with Lorraine and Frank at the kitchen table and Angie explained the whole story. "This appointment would be just the first step and there are many steps. The doctor's assistant will put together an estimate of costs — even with the surgeon's contribution, there are still lab, staff and surgical center costs. But first things first — we'll find out if it can be done, then how much we need, and then I can go on the hunt for contributions."

Frank looked down at the scarred table top. "Charity grates on me."

"This is important," Angie said. "The sooner that scar is repaired properly, the better the chances there will be no disfigurement in her teen and adult years. Try to remember, Mr. Thickson — this isn't about you. It's about —"

"I know," he said. He lifted his arm and rested his prosthetic limb on the table. "I'd do anything for Megan."

Lorraine reached across the table and squeezed his natural hand. Just then, Megan joined them in the kitchen.

"I'd like to take Megan to Davis to see the doctor on Monday. We'd have to leave early, but we can do it in a day. Will you trust me with her safety?"

"You would do that?" Lorraine asked.

"I'd be so happy to. Becca would come along if she could but the school can't spare her. But you're welcome to come if you have the time."

"I'll check at the diner. I'd like to come with."

"Just let me know. You can call me at the clinic."

"And if this doctor . . . ?"

"The first of many steps," Angie said. "Here's what I hope — I hope I can at least line up the providers and most of the funds before I go home at Christmastime. If I can get that much done, Mel would have no trouble taking it the rest of the way." She smiled at Megan. "I believe this is going to work, Megan. I have a good friend who is a surgeon — not the kind you need, but a wonderful man. He's been walking me through the process, telling me what I need to do. It might not be quick, but I really believe it's going to happen."

The little girl looked at her for a long moment before she let her lips rise in a small smile. And a tear ran out of her good eye. "Thank you," she said in a whisper.

And Angie's heart grew so large she thought it might burst.

By the time Angie got Becca back to town, it was after six. She dropped Becca off and then headed for the cabin, not knowing what she would find but hoping to see Patrick so much. It had been such an eventful day and they hadn't made plans; they never had.

When she pulled into the clearing and saw his Jeep, she was so relieved. The fire was obviously lit, the lights on the eaves were sparkling and there were lights on inside. She burst into the cabin and found him relaxing in front of the fire. As she was peeling off her jacket she said, "I'm so glad you're here. I had things I had to do and if you hadn't been here, I wasn't sure how to find you. Or if you'd even want to be found!"

"If?" he said, putting his beer on the coffee table. "Come here."

And it was in that moment that Angie created a very dangerous fantasy that she knew could lead to her downfall. She longed to come home to him or to be there for him when he came home. But she couldn't even count on that kind of commitment from him right now, so it was definitely out of the question for the future.

She went to him and let him pull her into his embrace. "My uncle Jack knows."

Patrick pulled back. "Well, that explains it. I stopped in for a beer this afternoon and he wasn't exactly cordial. I didn't ask him what was bugging him because I didn't want the answer. Did you tell him?"

She shook her head. "He was going to surprise me with some takeout and a bottle of wine last night and found a Jeep parked next to my SUV. And the lights off."

He ran the fingers of one hand through her hair. "Did he give you a hard time?"

She shook her head. "I think it's hard for him to relate to this strange place we're in, you and I. I have to admit, I've never been in a situation like this before."

"Me, either," he said with a smile.

"Not a girl at every port?"

He shook his head. "I've never been one to play the field. I've always been on the lookout for something solid, and if it looked temporary at best, I wasn't usually game."

"I thought men considered that a bonus — temporary."

He pulled her closer. "Not this man. This is a definite first."

"Well, the upside is, there's no reason for hiding out anymore. We're a Christmas fling and if we want to have dinner in town, why not?"

"And if I want to take you to my brother's house, will you go?"

"I'd love that," she said. "I want to meet these brothers! And wait till I tell you about the latest on Megan."

When she'd gone through all the details and her plans he said, "Let me take you to Davis."

"Why?"

"Because I'm interested in this project. And because I'll be able to spend the day with you."

She couldn't have thought of a better reason herself.

Brie looked at her caller ID before answering the phone. "Hey, Donna," she said.

"Baby sister. How's my girl getting along?"

"I'd venture to say this is one of the best vacations of her life. She seems to be having a wonderful time — busy every minute, looking healthy and happy."

"She told me about her project — the little girl."

"She's after it like a bulldog. She had to make dozens of calls to find a surgeon with the time and inclination to help. According to Angie, many plastic surgeons have full schedules months in advance. And without a doctor's exam, she can't put together a plan and cost analysis. She's remarkable, Donna. You must be so proud of her."

"I am, of course I am, but I'm worried. Do you know her latest? She wants to plunge into the peace corps or some similar organization rather than going back to school. After barely recovering from her accident? After all we've invested in getting her this far in school?"

Brie took a breath. "God. No wonder she hangs up on you!"

"What? Isn't this a reasonable reaction on my part? My daughter, who was always dedicated to medical school and to her goal of becoming a doctor, had a terrible life-threatening accident. And now, ever since she woke up from the coma, it's as though she's a different person! No more medical school, always fighting against me . . . I just want her to take her time — is that too much to ask?"

"Asking is too much to ask, Donna. Don't you feel her moving farther and farther away from you? You can stop this, Donna, and you'd better. Or you're going to lose her."

"I'm trying! I'm giving her space. I'm trying so hard to keep the judgmental tone out of my voice even though I think some of her decisions and ideas are so out of character and way too risky! I'm trying to —"

"Stop talking?" Brie asked, cutting her off. "Because, Professor, one of the things you do best is push your agenda on people. I know it comes naturally, and you've had many students to corral in the right direction, not to mention four younger siblings and three daughters to raise. Have you ever tried just saying nothing?"

She apparently was giving it a try because there was dead silence on the phone line. Eventually, Brie heard a deep sigh on the other end of the line. "Well. That hurt."

"I know," Brie said softly. "I'm not trying to hurt your feelings, but sometimes you're too pushy. And this isn't the first time you've heard that."

"Angie didn't think I was too pushy when I took a two-month leave to take care of her, to help her to the bathroom, read to her and cheer her on during all her painful physical therapy sessions."

"I think the important difference right now is that she doesn't need help to do all those basic things and doesn't like being treated as though she does. If you don't back way off, my darling big sister, she's going to run. Run fast and far. You have to let go. You have to let her make her own decision and, yes, even her own mistakes."

Donna's voice was uncharacteristically small when she said, "I only want her to be okay. . . ."

"Of course that's what you want. You're a good mother. And now I'm going be a good sister. I'm going to get you through this, Donna. Just give me a chance."

"Because you're all wise and experienced?" Donna asked, a bit resentfully.

"In a way. I might not have raised a young woman in her twenties, but it hasn't been all that long since I was one. And I remember how people getting in my space and my business made me crazy. I know that when I was determined in a certain direction — like dating some idiot who didn't deserve me — criticism of him would only make me more determined. I remember when I was planning a wedding and all my sisters had advice about what I should do — always exactly what I didn't want to do — and it made me furious . . . and mean. It made me mean. If you stretch your memory, I know you'll remember being in that place — young, idealistic and determined. And damn angry when anyone tried to change your mind."

She was quiet for a moment. Finally she said, "Creepy Calvin."

"Ah," Brie said with a laugh. "Your practice fiancé!"

"Engaged for four months. Mom and Dad hated him and asked me what I saw in him. Jack didn't like him. My girlfriends kept asking me if I'd lost my mind. What was I thinking?"

"Maybe you were thinking you could make up your own mind. So let me ask you something — if everyone had backed off, would you still have done it? Accepted his lame-ass proposal?"

"Oh, undoubtedly. But I would have broken it off sooner. I hung in there for a couple of months after I realized he was a controlling, small-minded doofus just because I couldn't bear the thought of anyone saying they tried to warn me."

"And what would you have liked your friends and family to have said to you instead?"

She thought for a moment. "Oh, something along the lines of, 'You're a smart woman, Donna. You'll do what's best for you.'"

"There you go," Brie said. "Practice that."

TEN

Nothing could have prepared Patrick for the experience of taking Angie, Megan and Lorraine to Davis for an appointment with the plastic surgeon. He had offered simply because he wanted to spend the time with Angie and because he was curious to see for himself the evolution of this special project she'd taken on. And the revelations were stunning.

When they arrived at the Thicksons', he was struck by their poverty. This was a hard-working family, yet they lived in a small, poor farmhouse that looked as if it would collapse if he kicked the right stud. Then there was his first full-face view of Megan's scar, and he'd had to concentrate to keep from wincing. The angry line that ran from her mouth to just under her eye made her look almost clownish. And she wore an expression of despair that he wasn't sure was an expression of her sadness or just the result of her tugging facial muscles. Even when she smiled, she looked forlorn. Angie was right — she could not go into her teenage years like this.

The drive to Davis was quietly light-hearted. There was a lot of talking among the women. There was a little song-singing and laughing. Megan nodded off for a while — she'd been up very early for the trip. And as they neared Davis, he could feel the nervousness settling in. Certainly Megan and Lorraine pinned desperate hopes on this visit, but Angie was his main concern. He knew she must be so afraid of failing at this — more than at any other challenge she'd taken on. Looking over at her as they drove, he could see that fear weighing on her.

But when they got to Dr. Hernandez's office, Angie's confidence was back. Despite the nervous pink splotches climbing up her neck, her voice was strong and confident. That's the thing with overachievers, something he knew only too well — people always thought it was easy for them, that it was effortless, or lucky. She flushed slightly as she explained why they were there but she forced her voice, which trembled a bit, to be strong.

Angie had told him she felt academically and intellectually strong but struggled with feeling socially awkward. He wondered if anyone else noticed her slight hesitancy when she spoke, her pinkened cheeks. She was determined, but he could tell it wasn't easy, selling her case to the doctor's office staff. She'd blushed a little the first time she had talked to Paddy, but it had passed so quickly he had forgotten about it. Around her friends and family, she seemed so self-assured. But in this setting, with Megan and Lorraine depending on her so thoroughly, it was clearly a struggle to keep up that appearance. He could sense in her an over-powering urge to duck and run. But she fought it valiantly.

After a brief wait, the nurse escorted them all to an exam room and even Patrick went along — he didn't want to miss anything. He was determined to be her extra set of eyes and ears, to pay close attention to the details. And no one questioned his presence within the group.

She smiled in relief, comfortable when she met Dr. Hernandez. "This is Megan, the girl we spoke about," Angie said. "And this is Mrs. Thickson, her mother, and Patrick Riordan, who brought us here, a very good friend."

"A pleasure," the doctor said, nodding at them all. "Let's get right to it. Let me have a look, Megan, and then I'll talk to your mother about the details. Is that all right with you?"

Megan nodded and the doctor helped her up on an exam chair that sat high off the ground.

Angie leaned close as the doctor placed gentle fingers on the girl's face, moving her skin around. He lifted her lower eyelid slightly with the end of a swab, asked her to smile for him, to open and close her eyes. And after just a few minutes he smiled at Megan and said, "I have some ideas, Megan. I want you to go with Sandra while your mother and I talk. Sandra will find you a magazine or you can watch TV. And, Sandra, will you please send Catherine?"

When it was all adults in the room, he began writing and talking at the same time, explaining that it was a simple but delicate procedure to repair the eyelid, and that would prevent vision issues due to severe drying in the future. He said there would still be a scar, but nothing as severe as she had now. Because of the way he would close the wound, it wouldn't tug or pull at her features, and it would be thin, not unsightly. Because of her youth, he thought it would be unnecessary to adjust the other side of her face at the same time so her features would be symmetrical. There would be some swelling and bruising for a while, but recovery should be uneventful. "The most important thing is this — her skin and tissue, young and elastic, will recover and heal nicely."

Then a woman came into the room. "Catherine will take you to her office. She can give you a detailed and itemized estimate. We've already discussed this and, rest assured, we'll shave costs wherever possible. We'll get it down as low as we can. That's a priority. And you say you've already exhausted possible grants and foundations?"

"My aunt has, yes," Angie told him. "She's the midwife and nurse practitioner who runs the Virgin River Clinic. She couldn't find help for Megan anywhere, but we're not done trying to get it done. And soon, before it gets worse. She's a beautiful girl."

"My only girl," Lorraine said. "She's kind and smart — I want her to have every chance to succeed in life. I can't stand the thought that something like a scar from a stupid accident would hold her back. It's just not fair."

"We'll do our best," the doctor said, holding out his hand to Lorraine. Then he looked at Angie and said, "You have a champion in Dr. Temple."

She flushed a little at that. "He was my neurosurgeon," she said, and whenever she said that, she unconsciously touched the shunt scar behind her ear.

"He told me about the accident. And you're a medical student, he said."

She nodded. "Only a year, but —"

Hernandez gave a chuckle. "Well, brace yourself." He put out his hand to Angie. "Why don't you sit down with Catherine and see what we have. And I'll be seeing you soon, I hope." Then to Lorraine he said, "Try not to worry, Mrs. Thickson. I've done this before." Then to Patrick he said, "Nice meeting you. I have a feeling you have a bigger stake in this than driver."

Far bigger, Patrick thought.

Soon they were all seated in a small office. Patrick, Angie and Lorraine faced the desk while Catherine sat behind it with her computer screen off to the left. As she clicked away, she explained certain things. No fee for the doctor, a very generous gesture. A discount at the surgical center. Operating room staff discounted. Presurgical lab work — sorry, no help there.

"We'll get the lab work in Virgin River — my aunt Mel might have connections there."

"We just need the results. I'll write up the order. There's one night of post-op observation. We usually have a nurse stay the night and, rather than hospital costs and germs, Dr. Hernandez keeps a room at a local hotel. This is nonnegotiable, given her age, anesthesia and the delicate work — a medical professional has to be on hand to watch for that rare complication. The first twenty-four hours post-op are the most important."

"Maybe the hotel will donate the room? Maybe I could find a nurse?" Angie suggested hopefully.

"I'll leave it on the estimate for now, but you're welcome to ask. Dr. Hernandez might prefer a nurse who has worked with his postsurgical patients before and we have to trust his instincts. His very experienced instincts. So, understanding this might yet come down a bit more, we can do this procedure for as little as five thousand dollars."

Patrick almost let out a sigh of relief. Five thousand? The limit on his Visa was six times that! He felt it was done, that Angie had won the day, Megan would have surgery soon.

But Lorraine put her hands over her face. . . .

"Don't panic," Angie said softly. "We're going to find a way. I have ideas. We'll talk about it later."

"That's half what the last doctor —"

"We'll get there somehow," Angie said. "There are lots of things I can do. Lots."

Catherine pulled the printed page from the printer. "Normally we schedule and ask for a deposit, but under the circumstances Dr. Hernandez has decided to forgo that technicality." She attached her card to the estimate and handed it to Angie. "Good luck with this. Let me know how it's going."

"Thank you," Angie said. "Let's go get Megan and head home. This was a very helpful beginning."

They were barely settled back in the Jeep when Patrick heard Megan's quiet voice ask her mother, "Am I going to get the operation?"

Angie turned immediately. "We have a few things to figure out first, Megan. I think I know some people who will help — but now that I know what the doctor can do, it'll be easier. I know it's so hard to be patient."

"It's hard," she admitted. "I wish I'd never of slipped."

"Well, accidents happen, honey," Angie reassured her. "I was in a car accident and broke my leg — and other stuff. It was hard for me to be patient while I was getting better, too."

And other stuff, Patrick thought. Like a

near-death experience, a swelling brain, a possibility of permanent disability and brain damage . . .

Patrick had spent the past few hours understanding and feeling Angie's vulnerability and it made him want to protect her in a way he'd never wanted to protect a woman before. Not even Marie. Yet despite her vulnerability, she fought to be strong and independent and his admiration for her only grew.

"Me and Frank, we talked about what we could sell. We have the land — his father was a homesteader, so we have land. But it's not great farming or ranching land and most of the maximum allowed lumber was sold off before it came to us — and no one's buying mountain land without a view these days. We talked to some real estate people — in a good economy, we could clear and sell parcels for houses, but not right now. . . ."

"You won't have to sell off your land," Angie said.

And Patrick wondered, *What has she got up her sleeve?*

"Ladies, I'd like to take you out for a nice lunch, my treat. I'm hungry and I know you are."

Looking in the rearview mirror, he noticed Megan get a startled look and then tug on her mother's sleeve before whispering in her ear.

"Oh, we can't let you do that, Patrick. You've already done so much, what with the driving and gas and all. I brought along enough money to buy us something we can just eat in the car. If you'll accept that, I'd like to treat. Please."

It was early afternoon and they hadn't eaten since breakfast, if they'd even had that. He understood the nerves prior to the doctor's visit, but now it was time to have a reward. And he thought he understood the problem. He pulled into the parking lot of a Red Lobster restaurant. The lunch crowd had already vanished and even the earliest dinner crowd had not arrived. He parked near the entrance and turned around to face Megan and Lorraine in the backseat.

"I'd like to do this for you," he said. "Megan, you've been very brave today and I think we should celebrate. If you'll stick with me, I promise no one is going to stare at you or ask you questions about your scar. I'll find you a place to sit, in a booth, so no one can even look at you. Not even the waitress. Trust me?"

It was a moment before she nodded.

"Good," Patrick said. "We're going to have

a nice lunch. We've earned it!"

He got out and opened the door to the backseat. Patrick pulled Megan out, positioned her at his side so that the scarred part of her face was next to him, put an arm around her to pull her close and led her into the restaurant. Angie and Lorraine were left to follow and once Paddy was inside with Megan he looked around a sparsely populated restaurant. The hostess approached and asked, "How many?"

"Four," Patrick answered. Then he pointed to a row of booths and asked, "Can we have one of those booths, please?"

"No problem," she said, gathering up four menus. "This way."

When they got to the booth, Patrick slid Megan in. The flawed side of her face was next to the wall, her back to the room.

He stood in wait for Angie and Lorraine, allowed Lorraine to slide in next to her daughter and Angie on the opposite side. When they were all seated, menus in hand, he looked at Megan and winked. She smiled at him and said, "Thank you."

"I'm completely exhausted," Angie told Patrick right after they dropped off Lorraine and Megan.

"I know," he said. "Hungry?"

"Not really — I had so much pasta for lunch. I wouldn't say no to a glass of wine by the fire, though."

"I have some of your favorite at the cabin. How are you fixed for adult beverages at yours?"

"Cleaned out."

"My place, it is," he said. "Need anything from home first?"

She shook her head. "I'm good. I'll run home in the morning to change clothes."

When they got to Patrick's cabin she pulled off her boots, sank into the leather chair by the hearth and leaned back while Patrick built the fire. "Aren't you exhausted, too?"

"Not really. It was a good day. I learned a lot."

"Then if you're not totally shot, I'm going to let you serve me. After you've built my fire, that is."

He laughed at her and continued his assigned chores. With the fire going strong, he handed her a glass of wine. With his boots off, as well, beer in hand, he slid behind her into the big leather chair, his long legs stretched out on the ottoman alongside hers. She sat in the vee his legs made.

"This isn't really a two-person chair," she pointed out to him.

"And yet . . ." he said.

"Why aren't you as whipped as I am?"

"Because I'm not an introvert. I watched you struggle. I hope you don't mind that I noticed — I think you did great. But I could tell that wasn't easy for you."

"Never is," she said with a shrug. "I'm much happier alone with a book. I'm trying to grow out of that."

"I'll help you search for funds when you have to get out there and thump for money."

"No! No, I'm going to do it. It's sometimes not easy for me, but I'm going to do it."

From behind her, he ran his knuckle along her cheek and chin. "Will you tell me when it would help to have me along? Because the priority here is Megan."

"Yes. Of course. But I'm going to do it. I'm not shy, it's just that it's easier for me in familiar surroundings, with people I know. With Lorraine's permission, I'm taking the before and after pictures Mel has on file to small and large businesses and ask for donations to the Megan Reconstructive Surgery Fund that my aunt Brie set up for me at Farmers Trust Bank. I'm also going to create a Facebook page that I can take down as soon as we have enough funding."

"Even though it's hard . . ."

"Even though," she said. "The thing is, I've always been okay with showing off my gray matter. I didn't mind if people thought it made me look dorky or dull — that only meant they'd leave me alone. But when I have to try to showcase my looks or personality, it's tough. I can't help but feel like I don't measure up. You know?"

"You don't give yourself enough credit, Ange. You measure up and then some."

"You're being very sweet. Is it because you think you're getting sex tonight?"

He laughed at her. "I assume I'm getting nothing more than the sound of your snoring unless you feel like sex. . . ."

"I don't snore."

"Oh, yes, you do. It's very cute."

"I doubt I'll be able to sleep while I'm with you now," she said. But a big yawn followed that statement, making them both laugh.

"I was very proud of you today," he said. "You knew what you wanted, what you needed, and although it wasn't easy for you, you got the job done. Very proud."

She turned her head to look back at him. "I don't know if you'll understand this, but since meeting you I feel like my best self is coming out. Maybe it's because of your confidence in me. It kind of trumps my own lack of confidence."

They talked for a little while, snuggled together in the chair in front of the fire. Angie hadn't realized she'd fallen asleep until she felt herself being lifted into his arms and carried to bed.

"Let me help you get comfortable," he said, pulling off her clothes. "Want a T-shirt?"

"Yes, please," she said, holding her arms out for him.

He stripped down to his boxers and crept under the covers where he curved himself around her back.

"Did you know I've never slept with a man before?"

"Sure you have. You had that ex-boyfriend."

"Mmm-hmm. But I didn't sleep with him. He couldn't get out of bed fast enough." She burrowed into his arms. "He didn't know what he was missing. Snoring or not, I've never rested better in my life."

It was quiet for a long moment before Patrick kissed the back of her neck and said, "Me, too."

After Angie had left in the morning, Patrick dialed Marie's cell phone.

"What great timing," she said. "I'm sitting

in the parking lot outside the day care at my mom's church. It's my old church, but from a long time ago. My mom convinced me to let Daniel go to day care a couple of mornings a week. She didn't want me to get too clingy right now and then get a job and suddenly shift him into full-time or almost full-time. She's right. He doesn't realize he lost a father. And he needs other children."

"Probably wise. How are you doing?"

"Up and down," she said. "You know — I have periods of thinking I'm doing better, then I have a couple of days I don't want to get out of bed. This is when having a two-year-old probably saves my life — my mom would let me lie in the bed, I think. But Daniel won't. How are you doing?"

"Okay," he said, feeling so guilty that his life had never felt better. "I got involved in a special project. There's a young woman here, a visiting relative of someone in town, actually. She's on break from med school and she helps out at the clinic and she became aware of a problem that needed fixing. A little girl with a bad facial scar and no money to repair it. So this woman took it upon herself to find funding through donations and I offered to help. It's kind of taking the focus off me and my self-pity."

241

"Really, Paddy? That sounds wonderful. Where did you meet her?"

"In the bar — the town bar. She's the niece of the owner. She's pretty young, but she makes up for it with a lot of courage."

"Aw, you sound so tender when you talk about her. . . ."

He wanted to tell her more — about Angie's accident, her struggle to recover, the issues with her family and her efforts to make her own way in the world. To pay back or pay forward. And he wished there was someone he could tell that his life had never felt this kind of peace, not even before his losses. But he said, "It's easy to admire her efforts. I would have seen that little girl's scar and just felt bad about it. Not Angie. She saw it and said, 'What can we do?' and got after it. She's trying to get financing for corrective surgery. I found out that rather than going back to medical school right away, she's going to give a couple of years to the peace corps."

"Do you think she'll get the funding?" Marie asked.

"She's making the rounds right now, going from business to business, from organization to club. She even put up a Facebook page that gives instructions for donating. Her aunt helped her set up an account for donations at a local bank. And what people don't realize about her is that it's actually pretty hard for her to put herself out there like that. She's studious, an introvert."

"What's the Facebook page called?"

"I don't know. I haven't even looked. I think it's probably Megan's Reconstructive Surgery or something. Now tell me what you're doing, besides sitting in your car outside day care?"

"People try to keep me busy," she said. "It verges on annoying, to tell the truth. From family and extended family to old friends from high school, I get invitations and visits and offers of things to do. I still need some time alone, though. I need time to grieve. According to my grief group, there's no bypassing it by staying active, even though some activity helps."

"You did go back to grief group," he said. "Did you confess about the Christmas presents for Jake?"

She gave a little laugh. "You'll never believe it — I confessed and three people in my group had done the same thing. Some people admit that years after losing a loved one like a sister or parent they still reach for the phone to call them, to tell them something, before they're reminded that, oh, yeah, they're gone. Right now I'm the baby, the newbie, but they talk about being changed and seeing their growth when someone with fresh pain comes to the group. There's only one thing wrong with this — I desperately want to graduate."

"I can imagine," he said. "And you will. We both will. There's a new, hopeful life out there for both of us."

ELEVEN

The rest of Angie's week verged on idyllic. After making sure her aunt Mel didn't need her help in the clinic, she drove into the coastal towns every morning. She went from business to business, large and small, showing a couple of pictures, explaining about Megan's situation. She was in restaurants, print shops and even tattoo parlors. Sometimes she collected cash — a few dollars here and there. Sometimes she gave account deposit information for Farmers Trust Bank. She found special support at the fire department — they offered to continue to collect for her. Then she went on to the police and sheriff's departments in Fortuna and Eureka.

The one thing she wouldn't do was post Megan's picture in a business window or on a bulletin board. Merchants could verify the legitimacy of the cause through the bank and Brie Valenzuela, attorney.

At the end of each day she went to the bank to make a deposit and get a balance. The first couple of days it was modest — a couple hundred here, couple hundred there. And the end of the day before meeting up with Paddy, she drove to the Thicksons' house to update them on her progress. Then on the fourth day, Friday, there was a huge surge in donations. Up to this point Angie had collected six hundred and change, when someone suddenly made a thousand-dollar deposit. It was an anonymous donation.

"How does something like this happen?" she asked the teller.

"Word of mouth, I'm sure," she said.

"Maybe firefighters or police — they said they'd continue collecting. But I'd planned to go back next week and see what kind of results they had."

"No matter who's responsible, the result is very nice," the teller said with a smile.

"I wasn't complaining," Angie said. "I'm stunned."

Angie was excited to tell Megan and her parents about the fund — which was nearing two thousand dollars — but she was even more eager to tell Patrick. They were spending the evening at his place tonight, and when she arrived, he was already cooking their dinner. She told him the news about the growing fund, and he was so proud of her, so happy for her, that he picked her up and spun her around.

As he served her dinner, she said, "A girl could really get used to this."

"So could a guy, but unfortunately there's that boat . . ."

"You ready to go back to the Navy, to the plane?" she asked him.

"Not sure yet. I've always wanted that life," he said.

"Even when it's dangerous?"

"Especially when it's dangerous," he answered. "The thing about a jet like that . . . you want the challenge it demands, and the rush is just unparalleled. The job it does can't be compared to anything else in my mind. But when there's a tragedy, like what happened with Jake, it shakes things up. I've had my doubts lately, wondered if I should move on to something with less rush and more stability." He looked into her eyes and said, "You know what I learned while sitting out some leave here?"

"I can't wait to hear."

"It's not something I'm real proud of, but it's a fact — I've always wanted Jake's life," he said.

Marie, she thought.

"You said you had a girlfriend. A serious

girlfriend," she reminded him.

"Sure, I was serious about her, but it wasn't mutual. And I wasn't like Jake — I wasn't insanely in love with her. Why'd I think that was okay?" he asked her. He just shook his head. "From the time I realized what Jake and Marie had going on, that was what I wanted. But I only admitted that to myself recently. Since he died, really. Most of my friends are married, most of them have ordinary relationships. They run hot and cold. A lot of them get bored or take their women for granted. But from the minute Jake and Marie got together, they were madly in love. Totally committed. I don't think that happens to too many people."

"It happens almost all the time in my family. There have been a couple of exceptions. My aunt Brie was divorced — her ex-husband was . . . *is* a real screwup. He left his second wife, too. But Brie's so solid with Mike, it's wonderful. Uncle Jack didn't get married till he was forty, never even had a close call. But as soon as he found Mel, there was no one else in the world for him."

"My brothers weren't exactly fast burners in that department. Well, Luke — he was married before. Briefly. And Aiden even more briefly. That would inspire caution in any man, I guess."

She put down her fork and tilted her head. "Every man and woman wants what your friend Jake had. Every single one. That's the dream, right? The kind of powerful love that lasts a lifetime? And no matter what you say about all the married guys you know who are bored or discontent or just too plain dumb to appreciate their good luck, I bet there are a lot of couples who appreciate their good fortune and treat their marriages very carefully." When he didn't say anything, she added, "I bet there are."

"My father was a blusterer," Patrick said.

"And mine is the studious and silent type, all too happy to let my mother dominate the conversation. But they hold hands. They love to travel together. They surprise me all the time. Once I saw him give her a pat on the ass in the kitchen and I thought, wow, they've still got it."

"I have to say, I never saw that at my house. My mother thought about being a nun. And my father was —"

"A blusterer," she said with a laugh.

Patrick held her hand across the table. "What do you want, Angie?"

"I never saw Jake and Marie together," she said with a shrug. "And I'm the last person to ask how to guarantee the future. I mean, didn't I get an up close and personal lesson in how unpredictable life can be? So, after falling in love, what I really want is a man who believes marriage can work. A man willing to try for that. A man who won't give up. Because I already know that if I make a commitment it would take a terrible string of crises to get me to give up."

"How will you know when you're in love?"

"I'll know," she said. "I'll absolutely know."

He smiled at her. "I want you to do something for me. I want you to take the weekend off. Come with me to Colin's tomorrow night — Luke, Shelby and their little boy will be there. Jillian's sister and her family are coming over. They've been baking and freezing rolls and breads for Jack to put in the town's Christmas baskets. The house is amazing, decorated for the holidays. You'll like them — they're nice people."

"I can swing through the coast towns for a few hours and then —"

Patrick shook his head. "There won't be time. I rented us a snowmobile. For Sunday."

"You did?" she asked, coming out of her chair. "You did!"

"We're wearing helmets," he informed her. "And we're going on an approved trail so

250

we don't run into any wire fences."

"Oh, Paddy, you are so cool. But I can still make a run through —"

He was shaking his head again. "Tomorrow we're going to sleep in, then lie around in front of the fire, have a big breakfast — not early. I know you don't like an early breakfast. Then we're going over to Colin and Jillian's. I'll give you a tour of the property on their little snowplow. You can see the greenhouses, the big Victorian they live in, the farm." He grinned at her.

"But, Patrick, I'm getting closer to the amount I need —"

He squeezed her hands. "We're going to play. Then on Monday you should call Catherine. Book the surgery for Megan because if you can drum up almost two thousand dollars in four days, you're going to get there, no sweat. And whatever else you need in the end to get it up to five thousand, I'm going to chuck in."

"Patrick . . ."

"The whole time I was dating Leigh, she dragged me to fundraiser after fundraiser, a slew of silent auctions, raffled prizes and fancy events that required big tickets for charitable contributions. I'm scared to even think what I shelled out and nothing I can remember felt as right as this does. Go with it, Ange. I won't get in your business and steal all your thunder in this campaign — you're doing great and I'm proud of you. But I want to have some fun this weekend and I also want to dump some money in the Megan fund."

"Wow," she said. "Do you realize how wonderful you sound?"

"Yes, I do," he said with a firm nod. "And I think I'm underappreciated."

"Well, we can't have that!" She stood up and lifted her plate and his. "I'll do the dishes."

Elbows braced on the table, fingers laced together, chin on his hands, he watched her clear away the dishes. But the minute she had them rinsed and in the sink, he stood up. He scraped the chair back loudly and when she turned to look at him, he was smiling that half smile and his eyes were smoldering. He approached her slowly, but then grabbed her up in his arms, lifting her off the floor. She laughed and looped her arms around his neck.

"Listen, mister. Don't think you can buy my love."

"I don't intend to. I'm going to seduce your love. Then I'm going to help buy you an operation."

■ ■ ■ ■

Patrick felt the soaring, heard the powerful engines, the g's pulling on him. The sky above him was the kind of clean blue you can only experience from a jet. The water below barely moved. Then he reached land that was brown and gray, mountainous and stark.

Nothing in the world felt so potent to him, yet even in his deep sleep he was afraid to feel it, to let it consume him. He felt he had complete control of a mighty machine, and yet . . .

Viper One, target in range. Descending to ten thousand feet.

He held his breath. Even in his sleep, he stiffened and couldn't breathe. And then it happened — just as the three Hornets passed over the mountain range with a large fortress in his sights, he felt his ship rock from an explosion, a blast of white light, flying debris, and he screamed. He banked away and brought the jet level, looking for a chute. *Jake! Goddammit, Jake! Where's the goddamn chute?*

He screamed his friend's name, sat up in bed, covered with sweat and freezing. Panting. Gasping.

And there was Angie, kneeling beside him, running her small hand over his back and whispering his name. "Shhh, Paddy, it's all right now. Shhh, just a bad dream . . ."

Just? he thought. Just seeing his best friend go down over and over again, his F-18 exploding, showering the other jets with debris, then dropping from the sky in a flat spin, another explosion on impact with the side of a big, brown mountain.

Patrick groaned and fell back against the pillows. He was shaking. He pinched his eyes closed and felt Angie pull the quilt over him, but she didn't lie down beside him. She gently ran her fingers through his hair, waiting for his breathing to even, to slow. When he finally opened his eyes she asked, "The crash? Jake?"

"Did I yell?"

"No. You said his name. You made a sound. You stiffened and clenched your fists and started panting. And you wouldn't wake up."

He gave a humorless laugh. "I was busy," he said.

"Does that happen a lot?"

He let his lids close gently. "Not since you," he said softly, opening his eyes again. "It's been a couple of weeks, I guess. That's why I won't stay with my brothers. I thought

I screamed. In the dream I scream. It's like the real thing."

She shook her head. "You didn't scream. I might not have known about the nightmare if I'd been in the next room."

"That's good to know."

"Can you talk about it? About what happened that day?"

He gave a shrug. "There's not too much to tell. We were locating a terrorist cell on the Libya border, flying in low, making our presence felt. There were reports of a terrorist training post. There had been heavy fire from that place — we'd had casualties and fatalities. There had been reports of a lot of grenades, IEDs, gunfire, ground missiles. A couple of sorties to the area reported surface to air Russian-made air heat seekers, which were evaded by jets. There were some close calls, near-misses, and then a NATO helicopter was taken down. We saw the flash, evaded, but the bastard got Jake's engine. And his plane just came apart — as if it were made of nothing more than plastic. I looked for a chute. I prayed for a chute. We thought we were clear but . . . We weren't clear."

"Then what did you do?"

"Went around, came back in and bombed the shit out of that place."

She was quiet for a second.

"It's what we're paid to do, Angela," he said.

"I know, it's just that I can't imagine seeing a friend crash and then getting right back to the mission. . . ."

"It was the only satisfying thing that happened that day," he said. But he turned his head away.

She put her fingers on his chin and turned him back. "Have I said how sorry I am for your loss?"

He gave her a small smile and pulled her down beside him. "You're a sweet girl."

"You don't treat me like a girl," she said. "If I were really a girl, you'd be arrested."

"But your uncle Jack was right, you know — I have issues."

"We all do, Paddy. Including Uncle Jack. My aunts, Mel and Brie, have had some issues of their own — really tough stuff to get over. You're not so different from the rest of us." She gave his neck a kiss. "Can you fall back to sleep?"

Sometimes he was afraid to sleep, which left him tired and angry. But when Angie was around, things didn't seem so cold and empty. "Snuggle up here, angel. Rock me to sleep."

"My pleasure."

But sleep was not what she thought would comfort him the most. She caressed him — his shoulders, his chest, his belly. She kissed his neck until he rolled toward her and took her mouth with a vengeance. His hands started to move and when she groaned her pleasure, he laughed deep in his throat. Any lingering trace of his nightmare was now gone.

They'd been together such a short time, yet it felt as if he'd known her a lifetime. They certainly got to know each other in a wonderfully intimate way. He grabbed her butt and turned her, fondled her, slipped his fingers into her and over her and got her wriggling toward a climax. She stroked him until he was moaning and reaching toward her.

"I'll be careful," he whispered, reaching to the nightstand for his condom.

"Please don't be too careful," she whispered back.

Again that sexy laugh. "Feel like a wild ride, do you?"

"Any ride with you is wild."

He knew every place to touch her, each erogenous spot that excited her, the movements that propelled her toward pleasure. When he hovered over her, spread her legs and entered her, she always gave him that satisfied sigh. When he rode her, she clung to him with a whimper of joy. He could always bring her to orgasm a couple of times before he took his own, and she couldn't possibly know how happy that made him. That she responded to him so totally, gave herself so trustingly into his hands, let herself go like that . . . He was so grateful. It made him so happy he had to remind himself not to utter *I love you.*

Instead, he said, "Angie, I've never been with a woman like you. You're everything. You're amazing. Thank you for loving me like this, for giving me all the sweetness you give me."

"It's easy, Paddy," she said against his lips. "You give it right back."

From her spot in bed, Angie could hear Patrick on the phone in the great room early in the morning. "Are you sure I didn't wake you?" he said to someone on the other line.

Marie.

"I just wanted to check in because I'm going to be busy most of the weekend — there's a lot going on at my brother's house. Big dinner with friends, the women are gathering up and baking stuff for Christmas charity baskets and the men will be doing some snowmobiling and hanging out. I wanted to make sure you have phone numbers for Colin and Luke. And you have this number if you need to talk — but I'll be at Colin's a lot. You know to call if you need me, right?"

He's hanging out with me, Angie thought. *But he doesn't want Marie to know.*

"Yeah, it should be fun. Do you have plans?" There was a pause. "Looking at houses? Wow, you're getting serious about putting down roots. Isn't it too soon for that? Shouldn't you wait awhile?" After another pause, "I know, the right house takes a long time to find. Are you getting frustrated, living with your parents?" And then he laughed. "I can appreciate that. I'm way beyond living with my family."

Angie burrowed down into the covers, listening. He wouldn't talk to Marie in front of her or within her hearing. He thought she was asleep. *Oh, Paddy, Paddy, what are you doing? Having your bad dreams and making love with me during the night, then calling Marie in the morning, almost like a guilty boyfriend?*

She knew she'd never be enough for him. He wanted her, yet he didn't think she could sustain him. He was looking for someone with experience at being a wife. She thought it might be a good idea to just walk away now, before things got even more intense, but she couldn't, she just couldn't. Not until the last possible moment.

"Are you feeling okay today?" Patrick said into the phone. "Well, I'll be there soon, sweetheart. We'll get through it." And then he chuckled. "Yeah, he was kind of an ass last Christmas, wasn't he? Would it help if I was an ass this Christmas?" More laughter. "I can probably do that without even trying. What? Here? Oh, this has been okay, all things considered. I'm glad I came. . . . good to see Luke and Colin. It's very cold, very white, sometimes very quiet."

All things considered, Angie repeated to herself. *Quiet? Except when you're crying out in your sleep or making me scream your name at your touch.* She turned over in the bed, pulled the cover over her head and blocked him out. He talked to Marie like a girlfriend he was tragically separated from.

Or . . . like a sister who had lost her husband.

She pulled the covers down, listening again. "Give the little guy a wop on the butt for me and tell him Uncle Paddy is on the way. I'll be there on the twenty-third. Try not to be in the middle of buying a house when I get there. I'll go looking with you."

And then he was back, slipping under the

covers and curling around her back. He nuzzled her neck, thinking he was nuzzling her awake. "I made the coffee," he whispered.

"Thank you, Jeeves," she said. "You're good to have around." She rolled over onto her back and met his lips, his arms around her.

"Didn't your mother make you coffee in the morning?"

"She did," Angie answered, breathless. "Somehow it wasn't the same."

He laughed deeply. "No?" He rolled with her until she was beneath him. He was ready again; he was ready a lot.

"I thought I heard you talking to someone," she ventured.

Not even slightly distracted, kissing her neck and cheek and temple, he answered. "I called Marie to check in because I'm going to be busy all weekend. I hope you're not too attached to this T-shirt. . . ."

"Did you get some sleep last night?" she asked.

"Plenty. Enough to take care of any morning needs you might have."

"Oh, Paddy . . ."

Angie also had phone calls to make. The best way to keep people who are inclined to get in your business from looking for you is to head them off at the pass. So she checked in with Mel and with Jack, gave them reports on her progress on Megan's behalf and explained she was spending some time with Riordans over the weekend, mostly at Jilly's farm.

And then there was her mother.

It was possible Donna had called her at the cabin several times already and had no answer. They talked almost every day and sometimes twice a day. This past week, while Angie had been busy thumping for donations, their conversations had been both brief and tolerable.

"How are you, Mom?" she said.

"Excellent, out shopping. But how about you?"

She explained the exciting success of her first week on the trail of money. "I can't tell you how the look on Megan's face made my heart beat. She looked so hopeful, so thrilled. I made so much progress, I'm going to schedule the surgery. There's no doubt I can make this happen."

"Oh, Angie, you must be so proud! What a wonderful way to spend a vacation!"

"Complete accident, but I agree. Nothing makes a person feel more worthwhile than being able to lend a hand."

"And so you are! This plays right into your future plans to make a full-time commitment to lending a hand."

Angie was silent. "Right," she said, thoroughly baffled by her mother's support. "Though I'm not quite sure how yet. That's going to take research and application."

"But there is no doubt in my mind you'll find the best possible route."

"All right," Angie said. "You're being completely supportive of an idea you hate. What's wrong?"

Donna laughed. "Listen, we had a tough go for a while, you and I. I attribute my less-than-ideal behavior to stress and fear — something you'll understand one day when you're a mother. And I know you won't believe this, but I realize I'm a strong personality. . . ."

"Oh, really?" she asked with a laugh.

"We'll have a frank discussion about that after you try managing a home, three daughters, three hundred students, a husband and a dean."

Angie laughed.

"Three brilliant daughters who are so easily bored they mix chemicals . . ."

"Right, I get it, Mom."

"And of the three, I have to get one who's gifted in science, one in music, one in athletics. I teach journalism — did I get a writer among you?"

"You're completely right — you've been screwed."

"Ange, I miss you. Not just because you're there in Virgin River, but because even when we were under the same roof, we were estranged. At odds. I want us to get beyond that. I take responsibility — I've been overbearing. You're an adult, so I'm officially backing off."

"Okay, you're really scaring me now. How's your health? Do you have a fever?"

Donna laughed. "Never better. My blood pressure is even down a little."

"No more talk about the psychiatrist?"

"Listen, if you ever sense you're having trouble with focus or memory or cognition, please let me know so we can get help with that before . . ." Donna took a breath. "No more. I'm leaving that to you. Unless there's an emergency, of course."

"Wow. Did my leaving town make this happen?"

"Perhaps," she said. "That and having you hang up on me. A lot."

"Mom," Angie dared. "I'm going to do things you don't always want me to do. I'm going to make decisions you sometimes don't agree with. You may even be right in your advice, but that doesn't matter to me. It's time I learned a few things on my own. Can you understand?"

"I can," she said. "But, Angie, please be patient with me. I'm doing my best. And I swear to God, you will have a child one day and you'll want that child to excel and have joy and never be hurt. It will sometimes put you on opposite sides. It's not easy. It's not."

Angie was silent for a long stretch before she said, "It matters an awful lot to me that you're trying. I appreciate that."

There was hardly a person alive who didn't find a visit to Jilly Farms purely magical. The big old Victorian on ten acres of farmland had roads leading around and through the various plots, sheds, greenhouses and fields, which were separated by snow-covered trees. The house was decorated for Christmas outside and in; Colin's artwork gracing the walls in every room except one — the lone painting in the dining room was a modern rendition of a Native American woman and child done by a friend of his, a famous artist.

Patrick drove Angie around the grounds in what Colin called the gardenmobile. They went inside greenhouses and marveled at indoor winter gardens. There were inactive steppe gardens on the hill, presently snow covered, but from March and April planting until September harvest they were covered with plants and vines. Fruit trees bordered the property; berry bushes separated gardens.

But even more fun than the house and land were the people. The kitchen was full of women — Jilly, Kelly, Kelly's step-daughter Courtney, Becca Cutler, whose young husband was Jilly's assistant and partner, and Shelby Riordan. Kelly, she learned, was a chef and she was the one directing the activity.

"I can help," Angie offered.

"Do you bake?" Kelly asked.

"Sure. Miserably."

They all laughed. "Then partner up with Courtney — she's getting scary good at this stuff at fifteen. She's working on sweet bread rolls — the biggest, softest, most delicious rolls in California — my great-grandmother's recipe."

"Right over here," Courtney invited, calling Angie down to the end of the work island. "Roll the dough balls about this size and we load them in the pan like so. Last fall Kelly, Jilly and I made tons and tons of zucchini bread, pumpkin bread and cranberry bread. Most of it we'll thaw for the

Christmas baskets."

"Who do they go to?"

"A lot of people! First of all, those who have fallen on hard times, especially the elderly who live off the grid in outlying areas. Then there are lots in town who barely squeak by. And this year we're putting together the baskets — er, I mean, boxes. Baskets are too pricey. We're putting them together here because there's so much more room than at the bar and because Jilly has ginormous freezers in the cellar. And pantry shelves for Kelly's canned goods and sauces and stuff that she sells all over the place. Jilly grows it, Kelly uses it."

"It's special stuff," Becca added. "Organic, heirloom fruits and vegetables. Very beautiful, healthy, delicious stuff."

Angie rolled dough and listened to them extol the virtues of the farm, of the retail food business. Patrick had disappeared — the men were staying clear of the kitchen. And then, quite suddenly, the landscape in the kitchen changed. A huge pot came out of the refrigerator and went to the stove, bags of greens and vegetables joined forces in an enormous wooden bowl, the last batch of bread was some fresh-baked French loaves that were sliced and slathered with a garlic paste. Angel-hair pasta was rinsed, plates and flatware went to the table.

"My God, you all work together like a machine!" Angie exclaimed.

"We've done this before, many times," Kelly said. "We're all kind of related, at least by work and marriage. And when you get down to it, we share a common purpose — keeping the farm going, the people fed well and the food at the dinner table five-star."

"Amazing," Angie said. "It's almost communal living at its best."

"Sometimes more than almost," Jilly said. "There have been many friends and family members under this roof."

"But Jilly would rather be in the garden or traveling with Colin," Kelly assured her. "Jilly is a master farmer and Colin is a brilliant painter, but neither of them is interested in running a hotel. For that, they need help."

The table was crowded for dinner. Angie had never before been terribly impressed with spaghetti and meatballs, but today she was awed. "This is the best I've ever had," she said. "The sauce is wonderful and the meatballs — God, they are perfect in every way."

Kelly took the opportunity to brag. "First of all, Jill grew these tomatoes and they're priceless. There's a farmer in the valley with free range turkeys for the meat — he's a love. I buy a lot of turkey meat from him. In fact, I like to pick out my turkey and —"

Several people at the table said, "Ewwww . . ."

"Well, I don't name them!" Kelly said.

"She picks her calves, too," her husband, Lief, said. "You probably don't want to know any more about this process. Chefs like to go to the wharves and smell the fish, grow their lobsters and select their shrimp and crab. She's very fussy about scallops but she'll take just about any duck I shoot."

"And deer?"

"She leaves the venison to Preacher."

"He's the best there is," Kelly confirmed. "But you're right about the turkey meatballs. And the sauce, my nana's — the best recipe I've ever used. Perfect. And there's tiramisu for dessert."

"You will die, it's so good," Becca said.

And it was during dessert that Patrick urged her to fill them in on Megan. Before they'd even picked up plates, everyone was eager to add to the fund.

Late that night, back at Patrick's cabin, Angie snuggled up against him in bed and said, "I envy them in a way. I mean, I don't want to teach or garden or cook, but still . . ."

"What do you envy, then?"

"They know exactly what they want. And who they want it with."

TWELVE

Luke and Shelby were the last ones to leave the Victorian after dinner. Luke held his hefty son; Brett's head rested against Luke's shoulder, sound asleep.

"He's going to fuck it up," Luke said as Colin walked him to their car.

"Luke!" Shelby admonished. "My God, I hate to even think what Brett's language is going to be like! Besides, what are you talking about?"

"Paddy," Luke said. "He's in love with her, with Angie. And he's going to move on without her."

"Did he tell you he's in love with her?" Shelby asked.

"He didn't have to," Luke said. "Right, Colin?"

"I'm pretty sure Luke's right. I've seen Patrick with other women. That last one, Leigh, he was with her for four years and we'd never have met her if we hadn't gone to Charleston. He didn't look at her like he looks at Angie. And when Angie looks at him, she lights up."

"I should have a talk with him," Luke said. Everyone laughed.

"How is that funny? That's not funny."

Colin put a hand on Luke's back. "Mind your own business. He'll figure it out."

"Maybe, maybe not. The Riordan men aren't known for figuring things out. And he's only got another couple of weeks here."

"He does look better than he did two weeks ago," Jilly said. "Better rested, I think."

"Of course he's rested. He probably hates to even get out of bed these days!"

"Oh, Luke," Shelby said. "Let's get you home before you say something stupid."

"I'm just making an honest observation," he grumbled. "I should really talk to him. . . ."

Since that first night together, Angie and Patrick hadn't spent a night apart. He loved falling into bed with her, loved waking up with her. He knew how much his heart would ache when they ended this, and he worried that it was going to scar hers. But she always reminded him that, even if they did have a future together, he would be deployed often. And she had plans of her own. So Patrick tried, somewhat successfully, to take this comforting routine at face value and not to think about it too much.

Right now, his relationship with Angie out in the open, life was good. They could spend time with his brothers and her family, have a beer or dinner at the bar without ruffling Jack's avuncular feathers. In fact, in the past week, Jack had become downright friendly.

Angie worked every day, though Mel encouraged her to take as much time to play as she wanted. But Angie was setting up a surgery and wanted to be one hundred percent involved. Megan was scheduled for the operation in one week — on the seventeenth. Angie planned to travel to Davis with her, to get her own hotel room so that after the doctor saw Megan, she could bring her home. Megan's mother would stay in Megan's room all night, along with Dr. Hernandez's nurse.

Paddy begged his way along.

"I'm not sure it's proper," she said.

"We'll get two rooms if you want," he said. "We won't use them, but we can get them. Let me do the driving."

They'd had such a wonderful weekend together, first with the group at the Victorian and then a day of adventurous snowmobiling. And always, no matter what went on during the day, they had that time together alone at night. And there hadn't been anymore nightmares.

But Patrick still called Marie daily, promising to be with her for Christmas when grief might hit her hardest.

On this particular day, he went to Fortuna to shop. He wanted to stock his refrigerator for that night. He was planning to meet Angie at the bar along with others from town. They'd have a beer or glass of wine, then she'd follow him home and he'd make her a special dinner — Italian beef that had been simmering in the Crock-Pot all afternoon, drowning in spices and gravy, potatoes whipped into silk, peas and carrots. He grabbed a chocolate cake, her favorite wine, his favorite beer, eggs, milk and a few other staples.

He had loved cooking for Leigh, too, but she never seemed to care much, always preferring dinner at a restaurant. Angie, on the other hand, seemed to enjoy everything he made for her and spending the time alone together.

Heading for his car in the grocery store parking lot, he heard a sound that stopped him in midstride. It was that telltale click of a dead battery. Click, click, click. And then a woman got out of her car and lifted the hood. She was a tall woman around fifty years old who looked good in jeans. She had short auburn hair and wore a leather jacket. She stared at the engine. Patrick had seen this before — she thought her problem might jump out at her.

He walked over, holding his two bags of groceries. "Battery," he said simply.

"I know," she returned, irritably. "Why now? I'm headed to my brother's and I'm almost there. I wanted to grab a few things — gifts for his family — and now the car won't start."

"Is he close by?"

She shook her head. "Another half hour or so up the mountain. But I can call him. . . ."

"Here's what we can do," Patrick said. "I can give you a jump and you can either carry on, let your brother help you. Or, I can follow you to the auto supply and put in a new battery for you. I have a toolbox in the Jeep." He gave a shrug. "If you need a new battery, which I'm pretty sure you will, you're going to have to come all the way back here to buy it, anyway."

"I have Triple-A . . ."

"It'll take them longer to get here than it will take us to buy and install a new battery.

Let's just do it."

She smiled very attractively. "I could pay you for your help," she said.

"I'm already paid pretty well. And I have a little time to kill. Let me bring around the Jeep, get your engine going and we'll get this done in no time."

She laughed and shook her head. "Just when you start to lose faith in human nature . . . You're very kind to help with this. Thank you."

"It's no trouble. I wouldn't leave you stranded. I'll be right back."

He stowed his groceries in the Jeep and swung around to park directly in front of her. He hooked up the jumper cables and, in no time flat, he had her car running.

"The auto supply is right up the street. Just follow me. This should be simple enough."

Less than a five-minute drive later, they were in the store together and he was helping her pick out a new battery. Although this didn't take long, they did have a chance to talk a little. She was visiting family for a few days; he was sitting out some leave near his brothers. He was a Navy pilot, she was a teacher. She said she hadn't been able to convince her husband to come along and was going to make sure he heard about this.

He said putting in a battery was simple, if she wanted to learn.

"I'd rather just make a phone call," she said.

"Well, if you're going back in the mountains, your cell won't work. I think you're probably lucky your battery went dead here in Fortuna rather than out on a mountain road somewhere, although as long as your engine was running, you were safe."

"But now I'm safer," she said. "I bet I can risk going to a florist before I get on my way."

"A florist, a deli, a dress shop, whatever you feel like." He tightened down the screw and said, "Start her up."

She got in the car, turned the ignition and the car roared to life. She left it running, but got out and faced him. "Are you sure I can't pay you for your trouble?"

He smiled and shook his head. "I'm overpaid already, seriously. I'm just glad I could help."

"You're a very impressive young man. I just wish I could wrap you up and give you to my daughter for Christmas."

He laughed and said, "I'm afraid I'm taken."

"Unsurprising." She put out her hand. "I'm Donna," she said.

"Patrick," he returned, shaking her hand. "Drive safely."

"I think I might look around Fortuna. I have plenty of time. It wouldn't hurt to grab a few things for my brother's children, since I'm surprising him."

"Enjoy," Paddy said, heading for his Jeep.

Patrick looked at his watch. That little adventure had only cost him forty minutes that he could certainly spare. Then it was home to set up his roast. Easily done. Then he peeled potatoes and got them underwater. He was cheating on the peas and carrots — frozen. But frozen was good. Angie, who loved everything, wasn't much of a cook. She was easy to impress. In fact, he couldn't think of a single thing he did that didn't wind her watch and he laughed to himself.

She was so good for his ego, an ego that had suffered the past year. He'd been feeling unsure of himself. A little lost, really. But Angie brought him back to life, made him smile. Laugh. Most important, with her he could revisit hopefulness. Optimism.

In record time, he was on his way to the bar. When he got there, he jumped up on a stool at the end, staying out of the way.

Jack slapped a napkin on the bar in front of him. "How's it going, pardner?"

"Good, thanks. Beer?"

"You meeting Ange?"

"Yep."

"Having dinner tonight?"

"I cooked," he said. "I'm a good cook."

"I'm sure," Jack said, placing the cold draft in front of Patrick. The bar hadn't filled up yet, giving Jack too much time to linger. "And after dinner?" he asked.

"Scrabble," Paddy said, lifting the icy mug.

"You two must be getting pretty good at Scrabble."

"She annihilates me. Every time. And I can spell."

"She's brilliant," Jack agreed. "So, when do you leave?"

"Ready for me to go?" Paddy asked.

"Not necessarily. If you're fool enough to leave her, I just want to be ready to scoop up my little girl and try to keep her from falling apart."

Patrick got serious for a moment, against his better judgment. "Jack, it has nothing to do with intelligence — it's just what I have to do. How this went was always up to her. I swear, I didn't manipulate her. I was honest from the start."

Jack sighed heavily. "I know. She was hellbent. Just try to be a little . . . I don't

279

know . . . sensitive."

"Absolutely. I think the world of Angie. She's the most amazing woman I've ever . . . But, see, that's not going to count for much because Angie has her own plans."

"So I hear. But just the same. Go easy, all right?"

Patrick wanted to say something like, *I wouldn't hurt her for the world,* except leaving her was going to hurt her to at least some degree. Despite her bravado, she was going to grieve him. He was definitely going to grieve her. He wanted to tell Jack he had regrets, which he did, and top of the list was his making a commitment to Marie, even though he knew it was the right thing to do.

"Hold her up, Jack," Patrick said. "She deserves better than some jet jockey."

"Probably right about that."

And right then, speak of the devil, Angie walked into the bar. When he saw her, he sat taller. "Look at her, Jack. She lights up the whole place. Have you ever seen anything more beautiful?"

"Not lately."

And in no time it was easy to see why Patrick was doing this — to be able to lift his arm to circle her shoulders, put a kiss on her cheek, bask in her smile for a little while. To feel that she was *his.* It brought such a rush of pride. He wondered if he'd ever felt this way about Leigh, but if he had, he couldn't remember it now.

Angie leaned toward her uncle and kissed his cheek, and even that brought Patrick pleasure. It made him feel a part of something.

Jack served her up a glass of wine and made small talk while he still could; soon the bar would begin to fill up with the dinner crowd and all those people from other towns and outlying regions who wanted to see the magnificent tree. And just before the sun began to set, there was a familiar face in the bar. That tall, auburn-haired woman from the grocery store parking lot walked into the bar.

"Donna!" Jack said, surprised.

"Oh, my God, *Mom!*" Angie said, horrified.

Instinctively, Patrick's arm went around Angie's shoulders and pulled her closer, claiming her. Protecting her. Because she was *his*.

He'll never let her go again, Jack found himself thinking. He'd seen it a hundred times in this town. The chemistry was just too damn strong; it rolled off them in waves. He wasn't sure how they could make it work if Patrick had a military commitment and Angie was hell-bent to join the peace corps or a reasonable facsimile. But he couldn't miss Patrick's proprietary action. *Publicly* claiming her in front of her mother.

The shock and awe on Angie's and Donna's faces told the tale — Donna did not know Angie was seeing someone. Well, Jack certainly hadn't wanted to tell her. Obviously Brie felt the same way.

He held his breath. He hoped his big sister would handle this wisely. Donna was a wonder woman, no doubt about that, but she seriously liked having her way.

She walked right up to Angie and said, "Darling. How I've missed you."

Angie let herself be embraced, returned the embrace, but then she said, "This isn't what I'd call giving me space."

"I won't be in your way. I might try to steal a few minutes here and there, but I didn't come here to hound you. I didn't have to teach so, on a wild lark, I just decided to drive up and take some time off."

"And you're staying where?"

"Jack's guesthouse, of course." She nodded at Patrick. "Hello again."

Now everyone but Donna and Patrick were startled. In fact, typical of this bar, the din quieted so that every word could be overheard. People actually moved or at least leaned closer.

"Again?" Angie asked.

"My car battery went out in the grocery store lot in Fortuna. This lovely young man not only got me going again, he helped me buy and install a new battery."

"Having no idea this could be your mother," he said. Then he grinned and added, "I would have helped her, anyway. In fact, I think she liked me."

Donna lifted her chin in agreement. "I had no idea that when you said you were 'taken,' the person who has taken you could possibly be my daughter. She never mentioned a young man in her life."

"For very good reason," Angie said.

Jack began wiping water spots out of glasses, an action that always occupied him when he didn't know what else to do. Donna might wisely let Angie off the hook for not telling about Patrick, but Jack didn't expect to get off so easily. "Did you call Mel or Brie? Let them know you were coming?" he asked.

Donna shook her head. "I didn't mean to sneak into town, really. I woke up this morning feeling kind of down, missing Angie and everyone so much. If I promise not to be any trouble, can I get a pass?"

"If you're no trouble, it might be the first time," Jack said.

"Patrick, excuse me a minute," Angie said. "Mom, we need to have a word. Let's just step outside for a minute." And without waiting for her to follow, Angie headed for the door. Donna followed, leaving Jack and Patrick at the bar.

Jack leveled Patrick with a narrowed gaze. "You know, I actually feel kind of sorry for you."

Patrick took a drink of his beer. "Yeah, right."

Angie stepped onto the porch, the collar of her jacket turned up and her hands buried deep in her pockets. She stared up at the beautiful tree, the bright star crowning its top. She heard the door open and close behind her and she turned around, shaking her head at her mother. "You have some explaining to do," she said sternly.

"It's exactly as I said — I wanted to see you, Ange."

"You vowed to let me have a little space, Mom."

"And I will, I promise. I had no idea what I was walking into, but I'll tell you this — I just couldn't stand the idea of us being at each other, estranged, angry. Especially with you bound and determined to move on to some new, strange life far, far away." Angie opened her mouth to speak and Donna lifted her hand. "I don't blame you, I don't. In fact, this sounds like exactly something I would have done at your age if I could have. I guess my worry comes from the fact that it's so soon after nearly losing you. Angie, I just want us to try to put our relationship back together before you head off to a new life. I realize I made a mistake in being so controlling. I made many mistakes. I'm sorry, I really am."

Angie put her hands on her hips. "Okay, who *are* you and what have you done with my mother?"

Donna's hands went to her hips also. "You know, I'm getting real tired of everyone acting like I'm impossible to deal with all the time! I'm trying. Don't I get credit for really trying?"

"Where's Dad?"

"He wanted no part of this. He's convinced we're going to fight."

"I'm not convinced we won't. Yet."

Donna relaxed her stance. "Well, we'll just have to see about that. Now, Ange, tell me about him. About Patrick."

"He's just a Navy guy on leave. He has to head back to Charleston before Christmas.

I've been . . . dating him. As much as one dates in Virgin River. The fact that he happens to be the most wonderful man who ever drew breath is just a bonus. I've been working on arranging Megan's surgery, but we spend evenings together."

"Evenings?" Donna asked. And at Angie's angry look and renewed stiff posture, she said, "All right, all right — not my business. You're an adult. It was a slip. Lighten up. My God, you'd think I was the worst mother imaginable!"

Angie thought back to all her mom had done for her, especially since her accident. "You're a wonderful mother and I love you. But it would probably be best if you turned around and went right back home before we clash. Big-time."

"Give me a chance, Ange. I won't crowd you and, if I do, call me on it. But play fair, sweetheart. You haven't been all that easy on me, either."

"Agreed. But this is different. I only have a little time left with Patrick and I like him. I like him so much — and he's special. It's understood we have to go our separate ways — he has a military commitment and I have goals of my own. But who knows? If you don't totally screw this up, maybe we'll stay in touch or something. Now, what do you mean by not crowding me?"

"Are you busy tomorrow?"

"Yes, I'll be at the clinic during the day and I hope that I'll spend the evening with Patrick as usual. But I can spare a little time. Just a little."

"Lunch at your favorite bar and grill?"

"I can do that," Angie said. "Now let's go inside. I'll finish my wine, you can have something to drink with us. Then we'll be leaving and you'll be headed to Jack's. I'll be at the clinic at nine in the morning. Seriously, Mother, if you mess this up for me, it'll be a long time before we're speaking again."

"You certainly found your mettle," Donna mumbled. "All right, all right. Consider the message received."

"Good," Angie said. She opened the door to the bar and held it for her mother to enter. They sat back at the bar.

"Something to drink, Donna?" Jack asked her.

"Merlot?"

"Coming up. How was the drive up?"

"Uneventful, until the grocery store parking lot."

"That new battery working out for you?" Patrick asked.

"Perfect. You really were sweet to go out

of your way like that."

"It was no trouble."

"And what are you two doing this evening?" she asked.

"Well, I have something in the Crock-Pot — since Angie was busy all day, I cooked. You're welcome to join us. . . ."

"I'm afraid my mother has plans, Patrick." Angie took a sip of her wine, then left it on the bar and stood. "And we should probably get going." She gave her mother a kiss on the cheek. "I'll see you tomorrow. Don't pick on Jack."

Angie and Patrick stood on the porch for a second to regroup.

"That was awkward," he said.

"My mother. There's a reason all her siblings call her a force of nature."

He laughed. "You haven't met my mother. *Nature* calls her a force of nature."

"At least your mother isn't here!"

"Ride home with me," he said, putting an arm around her. "I'll bring you back for your car early in the morning. Before the town wakes up."

"I'd like that."

When they were under way, he asked, "Are things between us going to change a lot with your mother here?"

"Not as far as I'm concerned. I'm a little

angry with her for coming without notice. If she'd called and told me she was missing me, that she was looking for a reunion to get back on good terms, I would have been honest with her. I'd have told her about you and asked her to hold off. I'll see her at Christmas. Even before I met you, I needed space. My mother's been driving me nuts!"

"Really? Like how?"

She told him about some of the arguments they'd had over the past few months. "She's convinced I've gone through a personality change since my injuries."

"I like your personality," he said, reaching for her hand.

"I realize I'm a little different. It's deliberate. I don't want to spend my life so one-dimensionally — I want more balance. I don't need another shrink to give me permission to do that."

"Another shrink?" he asked, looking at her.

"A little counseling after a fatal accident is reasonable, but my mother has trucked me off to more than one psychiatrist to check my brain. I think she wants the old Angie back. She'd gotten used to that person — the new me is someone she was unprepared for."

He gave her hand a squeeze. "I like the

handful I've got now. Did I tell you I spent some time with a shrink? After the crash?"

"No. How was it?"

"Boring. But that's how I managed to get assigned six weeks of leave. It was my PTSD. The nightmares."

"Are you different now?" she asked.

"Probably."

"I like you now, too," she said with a smile.

"Listen, don't make things harder with your mother than they have to be. I'm a flash in the pan — your family is forever." He turned onto the drive to his house.

"If she screws up this flash, I'm going to be furious."

"Nah, don't get mad. Everything will turn out. We'll manage just —" He stopped shy of the house and just stared. A very fancy RV was parked next to the house. "Oh, God, this isn't happening to me."

"What?" she asked.

"*My* mother."

"No way!"

"Way," he said tiredly.

She took a breath. "Talk about awkward."

THIRTEEN

"How long has this been going on?" Donna asked Jack.

"Since the day she walked into town," he answered. "The second she saw him. I couldn't have shot her out of a gun faster."

"And you didn't tell me because . . . ?"

Jack put down the towel and the glass he was polishing. "Listen, it's hard for me to see Angie as an adult — I keep flashing back to that little blonde in pigtails and glasses, taking apart anything that wasn't under guard, acing spelling bees, sitting on my lap and asking me questions I couldn't answer. I want her to be a child again, but she's not. She lacks experience, I know that. She's still a little like a fawn — kind of clumsy and immature in certain parts of her life. But, Jesus, Donna — do you remember being twenty-three?"

"Vaguely . . ."

"You were engaged! And we both know

you weren't exactly a virgin on your wedding night."

"Yeah, yeah, yeah — enough!"

"Mom kept saying, 'Not my Donna — she's too busy studying to have sex!' What a crock."

"I did study!"

"You were so damn smart you had time to make the honor roll *and* Tommy Maxwell! You somehow flew under the radar and Mom and Dad never monitored you the way you've strapped yourself to Angie."

"They had five kids! They were a little busy. And Angie — special circumstances. We used to be so close. . . ."

Jack leaned close. "I don't want her to grow up and have her own life, either, Donna. We always want our kids to stay young and innocent forever. But she isn't brain damaged — she's a twenty-three-year-old woman who's doing what comes naturally."

"And if I'm not ready?" Donna asked.

Jack took a moment. "You'll lose her," he said softly. "And I'm counting on you to come back when Emma's a young lady to remind me of this conversation." Then the door to the bar opened and Mel came in. "Thank God," Jack said. "The cavalry."

■ ■ ■ ■

Maureen Riordan was apparently not feeling as polite as Patrick had hoped — she checked the cabin door and, finding it unlocked, entered. With her was her partner, George Davenport. The two of them shared the big RV and drove between extended family and vacation spots. Retired senior citizens living in sin — and loving every minute of it.

When Patrick and Angie entered the cabin, they found George sitting in front of a fire and Maureen enjoying the kitchen, more spacious than that in the RV. "Mom?" Patrick said.

"Paddy!" she said excitedly. She rushed to him, though he held Angie's hand. "How are you, my love?"

"I'm . . . fine . . . Mom, what are you doing here?"

"I haven't seen you since Jake's memorial and have hardly talked to you at all. When I did talk to you, you just didn't sound yourself. I wanted to see for myself." Then she shifted her eyes to Angie and gave a smile. "Hello."

"Mom, this is Angie LaCroix, here on vacation, visiting her uncle, Jack Sheridan."

Maureen put out a hand and her smile widened. "Ah, Jack! A fine man. So nice to meet you, Angie. I'm Maureen. And this is George. Paddy, I'm so glad the door was unlocked — I think that's my beef recipe in the Crock-Pot. I started the potatoes and lucky for you I had homemade rolls in the freezer in the RV. I found the cake — if I'd known, I'd have baked one for you."

Patrick was thinking that if he'd known, he wouldn't have left a forwarding address. "I take it you're free for dinner."

"We wouldn't want to impose," George said. "Kind of looks like date night . . ."

"You're not imposing," Angie said. "We were going to have dinner and play Scrabble."

Patrick glared at her.

"By all means, join us," Angie said.

"But you're hooking up the RV at Luke's, right?"

"Of course we will. We're not going to be able to get to Luke's tonight, as it is. That snow over the dirt on that narrow drive of yours — I think it's best to wait until morning."

"Morning?" Patrick said weakly.

Maureen just laughed. "We'll stay in the RV, of course. I can't tell you how wonderful it is, driving your home around the country."

"Mother, do Luke and Colin know you're here?"

"No, not yet," she said, looking surprised. "I intend to see them, of course, but you're the one leaving to go back to Charleston soon. I just couldn't help myself. Paddy, I've been worried about you."

"I'm fine," he said.

"I just want to spoil you a little bit, honey."

His mother was the last person Patrick was in the mood to be spoiled by. But Angie was shrugging out of her jacket, letting Patrick take it. "I'll help set the table," she offered.

Patrick just stood there and watched as his mother swept Angie into the kitchen, chattering away about getting the recipe for the rolls from Kelly and explaining Kelly's connection to the family — Colin's girlfriend's sister. Angie got right into it, explaining she had just helped bake the same rolls for the Christmas baskets. At that, Maureen became very excited — she and George might even be able to help with the baskets this year.

"Just shoot me," Patrick muttered.

George put a hand on his shoulder. "I'll get her out of here early," George said. "Right after she does the dishes, because she's going to insist on doing the dishes."

"Why didn't you make her at least call?"

"Make? Is that Latin? Son, you don't make Maureen do anything."

"Then how do you propose to get her out of here early?"

George gave a shrug. "I'll do my best, son. Anything short of faking a stroke."

Patrick loved his mother. Of all the Riordan boys, he might be the most agreeable to spending time with her. Aiden would be next — he was patient and took very good care of their mother when Paddy was unable to be in contact with her. That's what Patrick would do. He would call Aiden. Everyone called Aiden when there was a problem in the family. Sean, stationed not far from Virgin River, was pretty good with her because he was manipulative and pretty. But Luke and Colin? Useless.

Patrick sulked a bit during dinner, though even he had to admit the company was good, the food excellent and the stories of Maureen and George's recent travels seemed to amuse Angie and her laughter never failed to charm him. When Maureen and George got around to asking Angie about her family and about her visit, to say they were impressed with her project to help Megan would be an understatement.

"We can contribute," George said.

"It's funded," Patrick said stubbornly. "The job is done and all that's left is the surgery. Right, Angie?"

She smiled at him. "If you say so, Paddy."

George suggested to Maureen several times that they turn in and leave these young people alone, but Maureen always had one more question, one more comment. By the look on George's face, he was getting precariously close to faking that stroke.

"Well, Angie starts her day early — I'd better get her home." Patrick didn't wait for an argument. He went for their jackets and was shuffling her out the door.

"I hope I'll see you again soon," Maureen said.

"I'm sure of it," Angie replied warmly.

And before they could bond any further, Patrick got Angie in the Jeep.

"Holy cow, Batman — were you afraid I'd invite them to move in?" she asked.

"Yes! I've never been less happy to see my mother! We'll stay at your cabin tonight."

"Oh, Paddy, we can't do that," Angie said. "Your mom is right on the property. You and your Jeep have to get back. You have to spend the night at home tonight."

"Are you *kidding* me?"

"I wouldn't kid about a thing like that. And I can't spend the night with you while your mother is in the next room."

"She's in the RV next door and she sleeps like a dead person! I would know — I was the fifth Riordan to sneak out at night!"

"Not tonight," Angie said.

"But you said your mother being here wouldn't change things. . . ."

"Entirely different — my mother is pushy."

"And my mother *isn't* pushy?"

"Well, I'm going through a rebellious stage. My mother expects me to act out."

"Think about what you're saying," he begged. "We don't have that many nights left together."

"I know. But family is family — forever, as you pointed out. Be nice to your mother. I want her to think highly of me. To respect me. I just think that as long as she's here, it's probably best that we don't spend the nights together."

"But Maureen and George aren't even married! They're living together in that RV, sleeping in the same bed. They wouldn't judge us. Come on. . . ."

"I'm sorry, I just can't."

"I'm getting that damn RV hooked up at Luke's before breakfast," he muttered. "And I'm getting her out of town right away."

"Don't you dare be mean to your mother. She's wonderful."

"Yeah, yeah . . ."

He begged and grumbled the rest of the way into town. Then he kissed her silly up against her car in the glow of the monstrous Christmas tree and it still didn't work. Finally he let up. "Call me when you're home and your fire is lit."

"I will. And if it's any consolation, I'll miss you tonight."

"I'm not letting her ruin this. I need to be with you."

When Patrick got back to his cabin, there were low lights shining from the RV, thank God. He went directly to his phone and called Aiden.

"Hello?"

"It's me. Mom and George came to Virgin River. You have to get her out of here. Right away."

"Why? What's the big deal?"

"I'm seeing someone. A serious but unfortunately not long-term thing. I'm going back to the ship, she's headed for the peace corps. So we have a finite number of days together. *Nights* together. And she won't stay with me or let me stay with her while my mother is here!"

"Oh, I heard about this. Jack's niece . . ."

"The men in this family are worse than a bunch of old women. Listen, call Mom and tell her you need her. Cough or something. Tell her you're waiting for test results to see if you're dying. I'm begging you."

"Sorry, Paddy — I've got a full plate. I'm pulling a lot of OB call so I can take Christmas off."

"Do something! I'm sure you owe me!"

"What exactly is the problem? Don't want your girlfriend to get to know your mother? Because women tend to like Maureen."

"It's worse than that. I told you — she won't spend the night with me while Maureen is here! She's afraid Maureen might somehow know what we're doing! It's absurd — I'm sending Maureen and George to Luke's first thing in the morning but meanwhile, according to Angie, the lid is not coming off the cookie jar. Aiden, I have less than two weeks with this girl and I really like her. She's taken a lot of the ache out of me, she's so special. Get our mother out of here!"

But all Paddy got for an answer was laughter.

Donna sat at a table in the corner near the fireplace. She nursed a cup of coffee while she waited for Angie for their lunch date.

When she walked in looking so fresh and happy, Donna just marveled that she'd had anything to do with the creation of this amazing human being. She said a silent prayer — *Please, God, let me be wise and kind for once in my life, please.*

"Something has made you very happy," Donna observed.

"Sometimes things just come together. We're all set — surgery is Friday morning and it's all paid for."

Donna shook her head in wonder. "How did you do it, Ange?"

"Dr. Temple helped me find a willing surgeon and many things were discounted. Then I just rounded up the donations. The big boost was an anonymous donor who gave us a thousand dollars — boy, would I love to meet that guy."

"Could it have been Patrick?"

She shook her head. "No, but Patrick gave at least as much. He's the one who said to book it, and he'd pick up the tab for whatever was left on the bill. Every day that I went to the coast towns and hit up the public servants and business owners for donations, Patrick went to the grocery store — he cooked dinner or we met here and I gave him a rundown of my day. And you know the miraculous part? I don't even dread it anymore — putting myself out there to strangers. I'm growing out of that, at last." She laughed and said, "How did a daughter of Donna Sheridan LaCroix come out so timid?"

"Anything can be overcome, I guess. So, what's next?"

"Well, this place is not without work to do. We're going to start getting together the Christmas boxes for people who need a hand. Jack usually does it here in the bar, but the project has grown. Patrick's brother lives in a great big Victorian with tons of room. His girlfriend's sister is a chef and a bunch of women have been baking and freezing things. People have been leaving nonperishables here and at the church for weeks already. Preacher and Jack like to get those food boxes out before Christmas — there are needy people here and there."

"You didn't come up here to relax, I guess," Donna said.

"I get plenty of rest, so don't —"

"That wasn't a criticism, Ange. Far from it. I couldn't be more proud of you."

Angie sat back in her chair as if surprised. "Thanks."

"Even though I protested, your uncle Jack and aunt Brie were right — we needed a little distance, some perspective. Plus, you look wonderful. Healthy and strong and effervescent. I suspect a certain young man might be responsible for the effervescence."

"Well, that may have stalled just temporarily — Patrick's mother surprised him with a visit last evening. She and her partner, George, have an RV and they travel around, visiting and vacationing. They're retired."

"Please don't tell your father! He has aspirations toward an RV and I can't even think of actually living in a cramped space like that."

"But you love traveling with Dad!"

"I do, but I'm not one for roughing it."

"You should meet Maureen. You have things in common. She's here because she was worried about Patrick. Couple of nosy, in-your-business mothers."

Donna frowned. "Worried?"

Angie explained about Paddy's best friend's death, which precipitated this leave from the Navy. "It took its toll, but he's going to be all right. We have a lot in common that way."

It was not lost on Donna that Angie's eyes took on a proud shine when she talked about him. No argument from Donna — this was the young man who helped a stranger in a parking lot. "Fate is wonderful sometimes," she said. "When you decided to come up here, I thought you might be bored."

Angie shook her head. "Of course, his leave will be up soon."

"Then you should enjoy the time you have," Donna said.

"Mom, have you been *hypnotized?*"

"Why do you say that?"

"You haven't been yourself. You're different."

How to phrase it? Donna asked herself. "You're the guinea pig, Ange — getting me in shape for your younger sisters. It's time for you and I to meet on a new playing field and no one prepared me for this. While you're growing up, you need someone to raise you, to keep you from falling off the cliff now and then, to herd you, help you make good choices. And now? Now it's time for you to see me in a different way. I want to be entitled to an opinion now and then without offending you. I want to be there for you when you need me but you don't have to answer to me. I want to be in your path but not in your way. You're officially on your own. So how do we do that?"

"Feels like you're doing it. . . ."

"But there's a fine line. Let's try looking at it in a role reversal — when you think

I'm slipping or sick or hurt and can't take proper care of myself, will you step in? Will you have a board meeting with your sisters and say, 'Mom is short of breath and sometimes confused and in denial and Dad is useless with health issues — we have to stage a takeover and do something or we might lose her.' Will you, Ange? Because I used to talk to my friends about child-raising issues and now we're talking about looking out for our elderly parents. Things change and yet stay the same. I want to be there for you when you need me, but I also want to be able to rely on you because there's no question I'm going to need you. We have to make the transition somehow. We have to do it as friends. We have to rebuild our trust."

"Mom . . ."

"I know — I'm bossy. It's been pointed out to me for over fifty years now. It wasn't easy to be the oldest of five kids or be a working mother with three little girls. I might've taken on a few controlling issues. But Jenna and Beth will graduate from college before very long and I desperately want this monkey off my back. I want to learn how to be a good partner to my adult daughters."

Donna watched Angie as tears came to

her eyes.

"Please don't cry, Ange. I'll be banished if you cry."

"Oh, Mom, that's just so sweet! You're not exactly known for being sweet. . . ."

Donna rolled her eyes. It was going to be decades before she grew out of that reputation. "Who held you while you cried when that asshole stood you up on prom night? Who fired MCAT questions at you to help you get ready for the test? I've worked on countless science projects and checked over more homework than a sane woman can bear. Please, can you cut me some slack?"

Angie laughed. "Damn Beth and Jenna. I'll get you all fixed up and they'll get the benefits." She wiped at her eyes and that fast Jack was beside their table.

"Donna, did you make her cry?"

"No!"

"No, Jack — we were making up, actually," Angie said. She took a breath. "I'm going back to the kitchen to get a bowl of soup. Want one, Mom?"

"Thanks, honey."

As soon as Angie was in the kitchen, Jack bore down on Donna. "What was that?"

"New rules of engagement, Jack. I need my daughter in my life and I'm just arrogant enough to think she still needs me. I threw myself on her mercy. I think she was touched, actually."

"Is that right? Will you be leaving now?"

She shook her head. "I need to stay awhile. And I'm going to do what I can to be supportive without interfering."

"Why don't you get back to the family and leave that to us — me and Mel, Brie and Mike."

"Because, Jack. My little girl is in love with a fine young man. It's going to really sting when he goes. And he has to go, we all know that. I want to be here for her if she needs me."

FOURTEEN

Angie introduced her mother to the Riordans, including Maureen and George. They all had dinner together in one of those fantastic gang meals hosted by Jilly, cooked by Kelly. And the next night, Jack's was full of family and friends. On both nights she went home alone, convincing Patrick that if his mother called or dropped by, she wanted him to be there. One more night and she'd be going to Davis, so on this night she was back at the cabin early so she'd be able to get up early. When she pulled into the clearing, she burst into laughter.

There sat the Jeep. Smoke curled from the chimney and the Christmas lights were turned on. Now one of the smaller pines wore lights and balls — Patrick had been at it again.

She walked in and found him sitting on the sofa in front of the fire, stocking feet up on the chest, a small glass with some dark amber liquor in it. His travel duffel sat just inside the door.

"You trimmed my tree," she said.

"That's right. And I'm going to trim you next." And then he smiled that lopsided smile and his green eyes glowed in the fire-light. "Everyone knows we're going to bed early so we can get up at 4:00 a.m. to drive to Davis. No one is going to call or come over. It's just you and me. You're not getting rid of me this time."

She shrugged out of her jacket and kicked off her boots. "What have you got there?" she asked, indicating the glass.

"I little brandy to warm your mood and help you snuggle up next to me, which by the way I want to do every night until that black day comes when we have to go back to reality."

She saw the brandy and a glass sitting on the counter, waiting for her. She poured herself a small amount and went to sit with him. "What did you do with yourself today? Besides trimming my tree?"

"I spent plenty of time with Maureen, George and my brothers so we'd be left alone tonight. And I copped a container of Kelly's duck soup for when we're hungry later. I borrowed a thermos from Jilly for coffee for the drive."

She touched his beautiful face. "You're doing a very good job of making yourself unforgettable, Paddy."

"You'll forget me in no time, babe."

Angie knew better, but she wasn't going to show her weak side. She opted in this relationship knowing the facts.

Soup followed brandy and bed followed soup. Patrick undressed her and touched her slowly. Carefully. When he slipped his hand below her waist he smiled. "I wish you could really know what it means to me, that you're ready for me the second I touch you."

She laughed softly. "Patrick, I get ready at the sound of your voice. And it's not something I do on purpose, either. That line from the movie — 'You had me at hello' — they weren't talking about what people thought." And then she laid a deep kiss on him, sliding her hand over the bulge in his pants. "Hello," she whispered against his lips.

He moved over her, gently building the tension in her with fingers and lips until she was asking, *Please please please,* and he laughed low in his throat. Then he satisfied her, leaving both of them panting.

"God," she whispered. "How do you do it?"

"I listen to you," he whispered. "You tell me what you want. Need."

"I never say a word!"

"You sigh. You moan. Your body lifts to me. You wrap yourself around me when you're ready. You're responsive and have a powerful language just for me." He kissed her deeply. "For right now, for this little space in time, you belong to me and I belong to you."

"Does a small part of you wish, for just a second, that Christmas wouldn't come this year?"

He brushed back her hair. "It's not a small part of me, honey. And it lasts all day long."

Deep in the night, Patrick found himself transported to the carrier. It was predawn and the mist was rolling over the deck. He was crouched, preflighting the Hornet, kicking some tires. He'd been here in the middle of the night before but this felt strange — he was alone with the jet. No fuelers, mechanics, techs. Just Paddy and his plane — and it was eerie and quiet.

Patrick looked up and there he was again, leaning against the jet. Jake. Grinning. He was wearing his flight suit and holding his helmet. "Hey," he said.

Paddy stood up to look him in the eye. "What do you have to smile about?"

"Good to see you, too."

"You're not real," Paddy pointed out.

Jake laughed and shook his head. "I'm as real as you want me to be, man. Listen, it's time for you to cut me loose."

"Am I keeping you from something?"

"No, I'm keeping *you* from something. Paddy, wake up. Do what you know you have to do."

"I can't wake up."

"Paddy, it's all right. Wake up."

"I can't wake up. I'll do it — just don't worry. I'll do it. I'll take care of her. Don't go yet. Tell me what it's like."

"You're kidding me, right? It's like heaven, man, which is a miracle in itself. I was not slotted for heaven. Not as exciting as the Hornet, but I get by. Paddy, wake up and do what you have to do. Paddy, wake up. Wake up. Wake up."

His eyes popped open and he was looking into Angie's large, brown eyes. She was up on her knees, looking down at him. He took a breath. "Whoa."

"Nightmare?" she asked him.

He shook his head. He ran a hand through his hair. "You're going to think I'm crazy. It was Jake."

She dropped down so she was sitting on her heels. "You were talking to him. What did he say to you?"

Aw, he didn't want to tell her that! Jake wanted him to go to Marie and Daniel, to take care of his family since he couldn't. "He kept telling me to wake up."

"Um, that might've been me. You were doing some thrashing around and mumbling. Did it look like him? Sound like him?"

He nodded. "If it's not weird enough to see your dead best friend in a dream, we were on the deck of a completely deserted aircraft carrier. A ghost ship. Dreams are weird."

"You didn't seem scared, but you were struggling. Was it a good visit?"

"Angie, it's not like it really happened."

She gave a shrug and snuggled up next to him. "Never know," she said. "It's almost time to get up."

He pulled her closer. "I'm sorry I woke you. Sometimes I can be a real load to sleep with."

She giggled. "Right. Sometimes you're nothing but trouble."

They were all at the surgical center by 8:00 a.m. It took only a few minutes for Lorraine to sign all the releases and give her daughter a kiss before sending her off with a nurse to be prepared for surgery. She had barely cleared the waiting room when Dr.

Hernandez came through the door. He was wearing scrubs and drying his hands on a towel.

"I'm sure it's been explained to you, Mrs. Thickson, that we're going to give Megan a mild sedative now and within a half hour anesthesia will be administered. The procedure will take an hour, possibly two. It's not complicated at all, but we don't hurry where facial nerves are involved. You can wait here or you can go out and come back in a couple of hours. She'll either be just coming out of surgery or waking up. There will be bandages, but they're coming off tomorrow."

Lorraine nodded.

Then he looked at Angie and said, "Will you come back with me?"

She was a little confused. "Sure." And she followed.

Dr. Hernandez sat on a stool at a stainless-steel counter in front of a computer. He was typing something in. He turned toward her and gave her a smile. "So, the intel on you is that you're very smart. So Dr. Temple tells us."

Her eyes grew round. "I get by," she said.

He chuckled. "Have you ever observed a surgery?"

"I saw a knee scoped," she said.

"Ah, mechanical engineering," he said with a grin. "Would you like to scrub in with me?"

"Me? But I don't know anything about this!"

He stood up from his stool. "You won't be asked to do anything. We're going to keep you out of the way — on the outside of our sterile field with the circulating nurse. But perhaps you'll be able to catch a glimpse of what's going on and it may interest you. Unless you don't think you're up to it . . ."

"I'm up to it!" she said.

"Even though this is your young friend?"

"But she's going to be fine."

He gave a nod. "Completely fine. There will be more blood than a knee scope, however. . . ."

"I'm good," she said. "Let me run and tell Paddy and Lorraine where I'll be." She dashed to the waiting room before he could change his mind.

She tried to be calm but could feel excitement bubbling over. Sure, she had decided to forgo medical school for at least a couple of years, but for a girl who grew up taking things apart and putting them back together again, this sounded like *fun*. "And I'll be right there when Megan wakes up. Why don't you two go get some breakfast or at least some coffee? We have Paddy's cell phone number if you're needed."

"I'm not sure I could eat," Lorraine said.

"Even more reason — get something in your stomach to keep you calm and alert."

"I've got this," Paddy said, taking Lorraine's elbow. "There's a Denny's on the corner. We'll be back in an hour."

"Thank you. Let me get going — I don't want to hold them up."

She no sooner walked through the door when she found herself in the custody of the circulating nurse named Denise. "We're going to scrub together, Angie. And you're going to stay close to me during the procedure." Denise handed her a couple of hair bands. "Can you put up your hair so that none is trailing out of the cap?"

"Sure," she said, working it up to the top of her head. "This is so nice of him! How could he have known I'd give anything to watch?"

She laughed and said, "Great instincts, that one. This way."

While they scrubbed hands and forearms, Denise went over a few guidelines and asked some questions. "Does the O.R. make you nervous, Angie? Because I understand you've been through some dramatic surgeries of your own."

"And so grateful," she said, running the brush around and over her nails. "Those surgeries saved my life."

"Do you get light-headed at the sight of blood?"

"I haven't," she said.

"No PTSD from your accident?"

"Not the usual kind," she said with a laugh. "I'm doing pretty well."

Denise smiled. "Good for you. I wouldn't have thought otherwise. I'll put a piece of tape on the floor in the O.R. — that's your marker. Stay behind the tape. I think you'll be able to see what's going on. Maybe not everything. A lot of the doctor's work is so detailed it seems like magic. And he'll be wearing loupes — glasses with two and a half times magnification lenses, so he'll have a much better view."

"Do you work with Dr. Hernandez often?"

"Pretty regularly. It's not easy because everyone likes working with him. You'll see, he's a prince in the operating room. Very professional. And he's a gifted surgeon. If I ever needed that kind of work done, he would be my first choice."

"Flirt," Dr. Hernandez accused as he walked up to the sink beside them and began his scrub. "When we're in the O.R., it's all right to ask questions, Angie. I may not answer immediately or give instruction or long complicated answers, but it's all right. Denise might also have an answer to a question."

"Thank you," she said

When they were gowned and masked, they went into the O.R. Megan was asleep, the nurse anesthetist monitoring her vitals. The O.R. tech who would assist the doctor had his gown and instruments ready. Once he was suited up, he drew a couple of lines on Megan's face. It began so quickly, Angie was shocked.

"I've completely excised the scar down to its base. I'll raise the flaps on either side. May I have a double hook?" he asked his tech. "In a young healthy patient, we don't have to worry about ischemia."

"Ischemia?" Angie quietly asked the nurse.

Dr. Hernandez answered her. "Compromised circulation to the tissue.

"Now the flaps are raised and you can see this allows closure without tension. The key to a good scar is minimizing tension. If it's tight, the scar will widen."

He talked a little about what he was doing, but to no one in particular, not in a tone that lectured. She leaned close, wanting to absorb it, wanting to get her hands in there. "5-0 Monocryl, please. Next I'll close the deep dermis, which will provide strength to the repair. I'll close the skin with interrupted 6-0 Prolene. I like to take sutures on the face out early. With a good, deep closure we can take the sutures out in five days and Steri-Strip." Angie was leaning so far over the tape on the floor that a couple of times Denise grabbed the back of her gown and pulled her.

The stitching fascinated her — fast, small loops that he slid under and over the excised scar.

"My aunt Mel suggested you might have to do something to the other side of her face to keep her features proportional. . . ."

"Not on a patient this young with such healthy skin. Perhaps on an older patient with redundant skin, but Megan will be fine with this repair."

By the time the doctor was finishing, an hour and twenty minutes had passed. Before a bandage could cover it, she dared a closer look at the wound. "Wonderful!" she said under her breath. Megan already looked a world better than she had.

"Flirt," the doctor said. "Let's get her to recovery. And, Angie, follow me."

She wasn't sure why he wanted her, but

she already knew she'd follow him anywhere.

He stripped off the gown, cap and mask
and she mimicked. Then he went back to
that computer. He indicated a stool beside
him and she sat.

"We'll let her wake up, get a little oriented,
then you can go get her mother. Now, what
did you think?"

"Denise was right — like magic. Just
watching those stitches — how long did it
take you to be so fast, so perfect?"

"Years and years of stitching pigskin and
other practice fields. All that during residency — med students just float around,
studying different medical services — three
months here, three months there. But while
magic is flattering, did you see what was
happening? The separation of the skin from
the deep dermis? The lifting of the lid?"

She nodded. It was fabulous.

"I do face lifts, scar repair, reconstruction,
a number of things. The most satisfying to
me is when I can take a patient from the
fear and loneliness of disfigurement to a
more normal appearance. Have you ever
seen the face of a child who's had a run-in
with a vicious dog?" He shook his head
sadly. "To be able to use my skills to help
an impoverished child is gratifying. I was

320

glad of the outcome today and hope she is, as well."

She nodded, mesmerized.

"Dr. Temple tells me you have plans to take a break from med school to do some time in the peace corps," he said. "Do you mind if I ask why?"

It took her a moment to find her voice. "I want to make a difference. Like Dr. Temple does," she said, her voice hardly above a whisper.

"Dr. Temple is able to give time to movable hospital organizations that travel places where locals would otherwise not be able to have the life-saving surgery they require. Near and far — from rural U.S. towns without neurosurgeons or facilities to international sites. There's a community of doctors who like to balance their practices with some pro bono work."

"How does someone like me volunteer?" she asked.

"One goes through a rather lengthy application process. Many doctors give a year or two to humanitarian efforts ranging from Doctors Without Borders to UNICEF. Some of us have a week here and there to give and are more inclined to privatized efforts. There is a senator's wife, an R.N., who puts together three or four projects a year and she recruits a number of specialists. We've gone as far as India and Africa with her nonprofit traveling hospital. I like to go to my home country — a poor village south of Mexico City."

"Do these groups need someone like me?" she asked earnestly.

He looked at her levelly, his black eyes intense but his smile gentle. "These groups need doctors, Angelica," he said very softly, using the Mexican derivative of her name. "If you want to make a difference . . ."

"You've been talking to my mother," she said, but she smiled.

"Has your mother been harping on you to go back to school?"

"Oh, yes."

"Think about that option. Dr. Temple brags about you, about your future and your determination. About your potential. It's just a suggestion. As a med school dropout you'll never be allowed to run those sutures. And you'll never be able to afford to give as much as you want to give."

She bit her lower lip against saying what she wanted to say — that she wished desperately she could be the one to help, to do the most difficult, taxing job, to fix the scarred face of a child who couldn't otherwise have the help, that she envied his ability to do such intricate work.

"My great-grandmother used to tat. Make lace," she said.

His grin broadened. "I know what it is to tat. It's a very delicate pastime. Did you learn it?"

She shook her head. "Not yet," she said. "But I think maybe I will."

"You're very young. You have so much time, thank the saints. I didn't get to medical school until I was twenty-eight — it was an uphill battle."

"And why did you choose plastic surgery?"

"Because it's difficult and beautiful. I love the challenge and the outcome. It called to me." He turned to the computer and logged on. "If I can help with your decision in any way, please call me. For now, go see if Megan is alert. When she is, you can find her mother. One night with the nurse in the hotel, a checkup in the morning to make sure she's stable, then you can take her home with some postsurgical instructions."

Even though he seemed distracted by his typing, she said, "Thank you, Dr. Hernandez. You've done so much today, for Megan and for me."

He turned and gave her his attention again. "Keep in touch."

■ ■ ■ ■

After making sure Lorraine had some solid breakfast in her belly, Patrick took her back to the surgical center with a to-go coffee. He excused himself to make a phone call. As he paced up and down the sidewalk between the building and the parking lot, he phoned Marie.

"Well, hey," she answered. "You're calling from your cell phone."

"I've got good reception. How are you doing?"

"I'm having a good day today. I did a very brave thing — I made a deposit on a house."

"A . . . *house?*"

"That's right. Small but very nice, near my parents and brother and in a very good school district on the likely chance I'm still here in a few years. I can't wait to show it to you, Paddy. I think you're going to love it."

"You couldn't wait for me to get there?"

"I had to jump on it! It's a foreclosure and came at an excellent price and the repairs are not too extensive. In fact, this is going to sound a little crazy, but getting this house in shape, it gives me something to look forward to."

As he paced, he ran a hand through his hair. "Damn, I wish you could be just a little more flexible. . . ."

"In what way, Paddy? I have to have a home. I don't want to live with my parents forever."

"I had this idea that maybe I could convince you . . ." Unsure of how to word it, he let his voice trail off.

"Convince me of what?"

"I have to ask you something. Do you ever dream about Jake?"

"Oh, no! You, too?"

"You do?"

"Oh, Paddy, I conjure him, that's what it is. I miss him. I'm going to miss him for a long time — probably long after I'm over him! So you see him, too?"

"I'm not convinced I conjure him. What does he say to you?"

"It's all memory stuff. It's private moments. And sometimes he tells me I'm pretty. The thing that disappoints me and makes me cry and know that it's my conjuring — he never talks about Daniel and he was gaga for his son. What does he tell you?"

He took a breath. Better to be honest. "To take care of you and Daniel."

"Aw, how sweet is that! And I know you'll always be there for me, Paddy."

"I'll be there in less than a week. When do you close on that house?"

"Within thirty days. We're putting a rush on the closing to see if I can get the keys right away. I was hoping that just after Christmas I could get moving on the interior. Listen, I can't wait to show you, but I completely understand if you want to reconsider spending Christmas here in a little motel down the street from my parents."

He was quiet for a moment before he said, "I'm looking forward to seeing you, Marie. I miss you."

"And, Paddy, I miss you, too! I just don't want to take you away from your family."

"You don't know the half of it," he muttered, thinking of Maureen and George.

"Say, how's it going with that little girl? Did you work out the surgery thing?" Marie asked.

"I told you about that?"

She laughed. "In detail. I donated to the cause."

"You did?"

"Absolutely! I don't know if you even realize it, but the way you talked about that young woman, Angie, it was with such tenderness, such respect and admiration. I really hope you don't lose track of her. She might be just the kind of woman you should

326

stay in touch with. Did the little girl get enough funding for the surgery?"

"I'm standing outside the surgical hospital now, waiting for the operation to be over."

"Oh, that's wonderful! You've made my day!"

"Marie, how much money did you give the cause?" he asked.

"It's not important, Patrick. Just a little something from Jake."

"Jake?"

"There was a widow's benefit and life insurance. I put some of it in a college fund, some down on the house and I thought — this is important to Paddy, Jake would approve. I admire you, Patrick. What a great way to spend some leave. Spreading some goodwill, paying it forward."

"I have to get back to Charleston soon."

"Of course — but you'll find out your new assignment soon, right? I know there's no big gray boat in Oklahoma City, but maybe you'll get something awesome, like Hawaii. I wouldn't mind visiting Hawaii."

"Marie . . ."

"What?"

He took a deep breath. "Listen, we should be together. Me and you. If you can't do any more Navy, I get that — it's not your fault. Let's mull this over a little. We'll talk about it at Christmas and decide. I can get out of the Navy."

"Paddy, are you thinking this way because of Jake?"

"No, I — I mean, maybe part of it has to do with Jake. But I really want to be close to you and Daniel. I want to be able to look after you properly."

"And I don't know what I'd do without you, but . . ."

"Is there any possibility you could live in Charleston again?" he asked. "Because I admit, I want the best of both worlds. I want you and Daniel and I want the Navy and that damned plane. Marie, I really care about you."

"And I really care about you," she said. "Listen, Patrick, it's too soon for me to think about the next man. Probably years too soon. Right now I feel like there can never be another man for me. As much as I love you, you're my best friend, Paddy. I don't want to go back to Charleston with you. The memories there . . ."

"It's too soon, I know. You need time. But think, Marie — this is sensible. Practical. Logical. We're in sync, you and I. I want to do the right thing for us. That's all."

"Sometimes I forget," she said quietly.

"You suffered a grave loss, as well. But that doesn't make us destined to be together, Paddy. Listen, will you do something for me? Will you text me when the little girl is out of post-op, when the doctor says the surgery was successful?"

"I'll call you," he said.

"Sure, just let me know."

"I'll call you," he repeated.

"Then we'll talk soon. You're wonderful to help with the surgery. You're almost the most wonderful man in the world."

"Almost?" he asked with a laugh.

"It's good if you keep trying for perfection! Goodbye, Paddy."

FIFTEEN

By just after lunch Megan was settled in a queen-size bed in a Marriott in Davis. Her nurse was with her, as was her mother, but it was Angie she wanted to speak to. "You saw it?" she asked. "All of it?"

"I did," Angie said. "It was amazing. Once the swelling and bruising is gone it's going to look wonderful. I think you're going to be very happy."

Later that day, Angie sat cross-legged on her hotel bed with Patrick's cell phone in her hand. He had gone out for sandwiches while she used his phone to give Mel an update. She told her all about the surgery and her front-row view.

"How did you like that?" Mel asked.

"I loved it," she said, her voice quiet. "It got me thinking . . ."

"About?"

"What it must feel like to have the power of healing in your hand."

"I imagine it's incredibly humbling," Mel said. "Knowing where to use it, spend it, exercise it."

Patrick returned shortly after her phone call. They both sat on the bed, eating their sandwiches and sipping their sodas quietly. When they were finished and the wrappers tossed, Patrick laid down on the bed, hands laced together behind his head, staring at the ceiling. Angie was looking off at nothing in particular.

"Tired, babe?" he asked her.

She focused on him for a moment. "Did I ever tell you that I love jigsaw puzzles?" He just shook his head. "Do you?" she asked.

He gave a shrug. "I think I could find something a little more exciting to do."

She flopped down on her stomach, her chin braced on her hands. "We don't have all that much in common, do we?"

"Scrabble," he said with a small smile.

"And maybe one or two other things. But I love jigsaw puzzles. I put one together once that was the size of the dining room table. My mother stopped me before I tried one as big as the family room floor. My family would try a few pieces now and then but it was mainly all mine."

He ran a hand over her hair. "Got a little OCD going on there, honey?"

"Oh, yeah, piles of it, I'm sure. But I don't do the kind of fun things you do — I don't want to speed or jump out of planes or take tight turns. Patrick, have you ever felt your life changed by a few words?"

He was still stroking her hair. And he was thinking, *Do what you have to do.* Jake's instructions. "Like what?" he asked her.

"Dr. Hernandez put me in that O.R., let me watch him take apart a face and put it back together. Then he talked to me. He belongs to a small group of medical professionals who donate time and energy to people all over the place. I asked if they could use someone like me and he said, 'They need doctors.' " She frowned. "I guess I was wrong. I'm going to have to finish school, after all. If I could ever do what he does . . ."

They were both silent for a while, looking into each other's eyes. "USC?" he finally asked.

"I guess so. If they haven't given up on me."

"You'll find the best place," he said. "I have to admit, I like this idea better. You have a lot to offer, Ange."

"So do you, Paddy. What do you suppose becomes of us now?"

"It sounds like we have a good few days,

then begin new lives." He gave her shoulder a squeeze. "Going to be a doctor! A surgeon! How am I not surprised?"

"Patrick, do you think we'll . . . Will we stay in touch?"

He couldn't stop stroking her hair. "Would that be a good idea?"

"I hate the thought of not ever knowing where you are," she said. "What are we going to do?"

"Ange, I made a commitment to a man who's dead. I gave my word. I don't think there's anything to do but carry on. I should have fought this thing harder, this thing we have. I never wanted to hurt you, to disappoint you."

"Just tell me this — are *you* going to be hurt or disappointed?" she asked.

"I'm going to be grateful," he whispered. Then he pulled her down beside him. "Come here. Let me hold you. It's all I've got."

Angie refused to give up or give in. If there was one way she wanted Patrick to remember her, it was without pity or regrets. She slapped a smile on her face. She teased him and laughed with him; she slept curled up beside him and asked herself how to best memorize the smell of his skin, the texture of his thick hair. She wanted to never forget how bright and sharp his green eyes were or the way his hands felt when he caressed her. She wondered if, when he let go of her and went away, she would ever find a love like this again.

The ride back to Virgin River was quiet — Lorraine held Megan while she slept, and Patrick and Angie didn't want to disturb her. When they arrived at the Thicksons', Angie helped get Megan settled on the couch before leaving them. Her little brothers edged close with caution, peering at the new incision on her cheek.

"How about a beer?" she said once they were back in the Jeep. "It's been a very long day."

"My place or yours?" he asked.

"Jack's?" she suggested. "We can have a beer, catch him up on the condition of our little ward and flip a coin to see where we go next. Maybe we can grab some dinner from Preacher. Neither of us should have to cook tonight."

"Sounds like a plan."

They got to Jack's just ahead of the dinner crowd and jumped up on stools that sat side by side.

"Well, my missionaries have returned," he said, giving the bar a wipe and putting down a couple of napkins. "What's your pleasure?"

"Cold draft," Angie said.

"I heard from Mel that things went very well," he said while drawing up a couple of beers.

"I don't think it could have gone better. But, Jack, it was an emotional landslide."

He leaned both hands on the bar and looked at them. "Well, I'm afraid there's more where that came from. Ange, your dad and sisters arrived in town this afternoon."

"What for?"

"Your mom didn't want to leave you before you were ready to go. And she didn't want to pressure you into driving back to Sacramento. So Sam came, too."

"Grandpa?"

He gave a nod. "With the back of his truck full of presents. Looks like Christmas is at the Sheridan house this year. Your other aunts are missing out, but then you were with them at Thanksgiving and it seems to be their year for their in-laws, anyway. . . ."

She dropped her head onto the bar and moaned. Patrick gently rubbed her back. "Aw, babe. It'll be okay," he whispered to her.

"We'll see," Jack said. Then, uncharacteristically, he poured himself a draft. By way of explanation he said to Patrick, "Your brothers arrived about the same time."

"What?"

"Aiden and Sean. And wives."

"Get out!"

Jack nodded. "And of course Red — little Rosie." Jack looked at Angie. "Wait till you see the green eyes in that family — it'll blow your mind."

"But they have reservations of some kind — San Diego. The whole family is spending the holiday there."

Jack shook his head. "Not anymore, cowboy. They're so interested in knowing you're doing all right, they're canceling. Losing the deposit and everything."

"That's insane! Why would they do that? They've been talking about it for a year!"

"Loyalty," Jack said. "Sounds like they care about you. And since they can't get you to San Diego, San Diego is coming to you." He grinned, a bit evilly. "Happy holidays, son."

Paddy dropped his head into his hand. "Holy Mother of God," he muttered.

"Yeah," Jack said. He lifted his brew. "Here's to family."

He drank alone.

Exhaustion fled as Angie and Paddy

grabbed their takeout and headed for her cabin. Too many Riordans knew where his was. "I'm serious," she said. "I say we make a run for it!"

"You think they're going away?" Patrick asked. "They're not going away!"

"I was talking about *my* family. We can make a break for it. While there's still time!"

"We have Riordans on our tail now! They'd follow fucking bread crumbs! I'll never shake 'em now."

"At least my family is afraid that if they get too close, I'll have a meltdown. I have a feeling your family is willing to risk it."

"Here's the deal, Angie — we can be nice to them but we are *not* giving up our nights together! Do you hear me on that? Because the way I see it, we have four nights left and if I have to rent a fifth wheel and take you out in the woods —"

She burst into laughter. "Who knew you were so sex-crazed?"

"Hah. Like you aren't?"

"I don't think I'm quite as desperate as you are."

"Sure could've fooled me," he said. He pulled into the clearing of her cabin, threw the Jeep into Park and jumped out. Before she could even get out, he was at her side of the Jeep, pulling her out and lifting her into

337

his arms. "Hang on to the takeout," he said gruffly, carrying her up the porch steps.

She ran a knuckle along his rough cheek. "Are you angry?" she asked.

"I'm a little irritated, yeah."

"Well, put me down. I want to tell you something." When she'd landed on her feet on the porch and stood looking up at him, she said, "I want to meet them. I know it doesn't really mean anything, but still, I want to. Even though we're going off in different directions. I want to see the green-eyed family. I want to spend some more time with your mother — Jilly says everyone adores her. Your mother must really be something. . . ."

"She can be a real pain in the ass."

"Then there's my mother," she said with a laugh. "You've met her, but I'd love you to meet my dad. He's a very nice guy. And my sisters — they're growing into interesting young women, if a little high maintenance. Wait till you see how little we're alike. And, oh, Paddy — my grandfather is the most wonderful man. You shouldn't miss out on meeting him."

His anger began to flee as he looked into her eyes with tenderness. "Ange," he said softly. "I don't want this to be harder than it has to be. We should be alone. We shouldn't get too involved with each other's families."

She tilted her head and smiled. "How do you think you'll make it any easier? Patrick, you know I love you. Yes, you do," she said to the shaking of his head. "But on the morning of the twenty-third you're going to drive out of here as you promised you would do and I have no idea what will come after that. I don't know if you'll write or call. I don't know if you'll think about me sometimes or if I'll just be out of sight, out of mind. But it's almost Christmas and, before you go, I just want to enjoy the holiday spirit. I want us to help deliver the Christmas boxes, go to a couple of parties, sing around the tree, eat some great food and —" she smiled into his eyes "— and make love all night long. I don't know if you'll store up the memories, but dammit, I will."

They spent Saturday night at the cabin, such a brief space of time. On Sunday, they went to church where they spotted a couple of the Riordans — Sean, Franci and Rosie, George and Maureen. There were plenty of Sheridans present and a great reunion took place between the sisters. Angie was right — they were incredibly different. Jenna was as tall as her mother, slim and auburn haired, Beth just average height and slightly rounder with dark hair.

Sam, over six feet with thick silver hair, grinned and took Patrick's hand in a hearty shake. "Well, son, so good to meet you — I've heard a lot about you!"

Patrick cast a glance at Angie.

"Not from her." Sam laughed. "Jack was telling me all about you. My daughter, Donna, was impressed with your goodwill and I thank you for helping her with her car."

"It was nothing."

"There aren't many people who would bother," Sam said.

And just like that, Patrick's mother and George joined them, Sean's family were added, introductions were made along with plans for those present to go over to the bar for breakfast. Tables were pushed together, omelets were ordered, laughter filled the bar. Once everyone was served, Jack joined them and it seemed he had a story about every person at the table.

"Sean here — he ran into his old girlfriend in Arcata and, to his surprise, found out she had a little girl with his green eyes."

Franci gasped. "Do we really have to tell *that* story?"

"That's one of the good ones. Wait till you

340

meet Aiden, Dad," he said to Sam. "He had the distinction of knocking out his future wife before he could properly meet her."

"Quite the caveman, is he?" Sam asked.

"Jack shouldn't have opened this door," Donna said. "The Sheridans have no shortage of stories on him."

"Not in my house," Jack said fiercely.

"I think it would be fun to get the Riordans and what we have of the Sheridans gathered in the same room," Maureen suggested.

"It would have to be a damn big room," Patrick muttered, not really into this idea.

"The bar won't work after dark," Jack said. "Too many out-of-towners head up this way because of the tree."

"We have the Victorian," Sean said.

"We're not limited to after-hours — we can come up with daylight diversion," George suggested. "Anyone up for a good, old-fashioned hayride? Or would that be sleigh ride? Jack?"

"Buck Anderson hauls kids around on the back of his hay wagon every year. He pulls it with a tractor. It's nice and big."

"Will you call him, Jack?"

"Hey!" Patrick protested. "Does anyone care if Angie and I have *plans*?"

Everyone looked between one another,

then expressed a unified "No."

Angie grabbed Patrick's hand under the table and said, "I think it sounds wonderful. I'm in."

By the end of breakfast, and after a lot of suggestions and plans, a couple of ideas began to take shape. An afternoon hayride if Buck Anderson could be convinced and an evening at the Victorian, gathering the whole crowd. When the group was breaking up — some to help deliver Christmas boxes and others on their way to visit with friends and family, Donna separated Angie from the crowd. Off in a far corner in the back of the bar Donna asked, "How are you doing, sweetheart?"

"I'm okay," she said.

"Are you annoyed with everyone for making plans when you only have a few days with Patrick before he goes?"

She shook her head. "Not really. I told him — I want to spend time with his family. Even though he has to leave, it's the only time I'll ever know them. And knowing them is knowing him. Don't you think?"

"I do, honey."

Jenna and Beth were there, as if drawn by a magnet.

"He's beautiful, Ange," Beth said.

"Hot," Jenna agreed.

"I know. But Mom told you, didn't she? I don't get to keep him."

"Bummer," Jenna said. "That's going to suck."

"Probably." Then she looked at her mother. "I'm going back to school, Mom. After the holidays I'll check in with USC."

Donna put a gentle palm against her face. "I support whatever decision you make, Angie."

"Thanks, Mom."

"At the end of the week, we'll be around. We can be close by or we can disappear if you feel like being alone. We'll do Christmas with Jack. You can join us or not — it's up to you."

"I don't want you guys to have an unhappy Christmas because of me."

"No matter what kind of holiday we have, we stick together."

Patrick realized he hadn't called Marie since the day of Megan's surgery. So much had happened; so much family had invaded. When he did call her, she didn't pick up. He didn't have cell reception in the mountains and only a very limited amount of time alone when he could place the call from a landline. So he did as she requested and texted that all was well.

He had come to his cabin for a shower and change of clothes while Angie visited with her mother and sisters for a little while. This afternoon would be the hayride with as many Riordans and Sheridans as could be rounded up. Just to clear his head so he could enjoy his time left with Angie, he called Marie's mother to leave her a message.

After a brief cordial chat, he asked if Marie was there.

"No, Patrick, I'm afraid not. I'm watching Daniel while she shops. She's with a friend who's a decorator, picking out and pricing all kinds of things for the house. It turns out she's going to have to completely re-carpet and tile, not to mention paint."

So she was really into this new house. Should she have done something like that so soon after Jake's death? "She's not picking up when I call," he said.

"Is that so?" Marie's mother said. "That's odd — I called her not ten minutes ago to ask her what Daniel should have for lunch, since he turned his nose up at leftover spaghetti."

"Can I ask a favor? Will you please call her again and ask her to call me right away? I'm only at this number a little while and I really need to speak to her. Tell her it's important."

"I can try, Patrick. But chances are if she's not picking up your call, she's out of range. She never has her phone turned off — she has a two-year-old. I'll give her another try now."

It was barely five minutes before the phone rang and he grabbed it.

"Well, stranger — what's so important?" she asked.

"I thought you'd take this as encouraging news — my entire family showed up in Virgin River. Since I wouldn't go to San Diego with them, they came here."

"Oh, I'm so glad to hear that!"

"You're much happier about it than I am," he said. "But I knew you would be. Now you can relax — I've spent time with the family. I'll see you in a couple of days. I get the impression from your mother that you're all excited about the house."

"It's going to be a lot of work, but I welcome it. Something positive to look forward to. I can't wait to see you. I know it's only been a few weeks, but I miss you like crazy!"

"Just a couple of days more."

The hay wagon was loaded with people — even Jack took the afternoon off so he could help Mel watch the little ones. In addition to Sheridans and Riordans, Noah Kincaid and his wife and kids came along, since their family had such a close relationship with Maureen's partner, George.

The entire town was alive with Christmas — as the wagon rode down the main street, everyone came outside to wave and join in carol singing. They laughed at one another's off-key voices and a few friendly snowball fights broke out along the way. The Riordan men regressed a bit, running alongside the wagon and firing snowballs as though they were missiles, and eventually ended up rolling in the snow, stuffing snow down one another's jackets and pants. It didn't stop until Luke's wife, Shelby, got hit square in the back of the head by a really wet one.

"That's it!" Luke shouted. "The next one to throw a snowball has to deal with *me*!"

Through hysterical laughter, Angie was able to count the sixteen snowballs that hit Luke in every part of his body.

After the ride, everyone separated to rest and change for the evening gathering at Jilly and Colin's Victorian. Patrick and Angie went first to her cabin where her shower and dressing was delayed when she was tossed on the bed and her body covered by his.

It didn't take much more than a couple of kisses and a little touching to coax her into seeing things his way. She soon found herself naked and locked in the arms of her lover. For a good half hour, he concentrated on studying her body in a way that brought both of them to shuddering satisfaction followed by soft kissing.

A little breathless, Patrick suggested, "We can call in a no-show. Just say the word."

She shook her head. "It's fun to be together with our families. And it distracts me from the inevitable."

The visit to Patrick's cabin for his change of clothes was much more efficient, and soon they were joining the others at the Victorian. They were too many for a sit-down dinner — Shelby's family had joined them, as well as Walt Booth and his lady friend, Muriel, Walt's daughter and her husband and children and, of course, Jilly's sister, Kelly, and her family. Kelly did the basic cooking — a large prime rib roast and a turkey — but everyone brought something to eat so it was a very full house and heavy table. It shaped up like an old-fashioned town party, and the only person missing was Preacher — someone had to run the bar for

347

all the out-of-towners. In fact, Jack recruited a couple of guys in town to serve so he could sneak away for a few hours.

Desserts were laid out and everything was starting to quiet down when Aiden put a hand on Patrick's shoulder. "Let's check out a cigar."

"It's cold out there!" Patrick said.

Aiden laughed. "I'll keep you warm." With his hand on Paddy's shoulder, Aiden directed him to the back door and they grabbed their jackets off the hook on the way out. Aiden pulled a couple of cigars and a lighter out of his pocket, clipped the ends and handed one off to Patrick. When a few puffs had them going, Aiden asked, "How are the nightmares?"

Patrick's eyes shot to Aiden's. "What nightmares?"

"Don't kid a kidder, Paddy. You went through a traumatic event. The life of your closest friend was lost. I was a Navy physician for years — I know how it goes."

"An OB! You're an OB!"

"Yes, I was a women's doctor. *And* also the doctor on a ship. Oh, wait, that's right — women don't have combat issues." He shook his head.

"I didn't mean that. Of course they do. But . . ."

"But I made referrals and had to know what I was dealing with. Even if I hadn't had medical training in this, between Luke and Colin and their disasters, I'd be up to speed. So? Nightmares? Depression? Anger? Denial? Anything?"

Patrick studied his cigar. "I had some bad dreams. It's better."

"Yeah, good. Colin says you're headed for Oklahoma. Jake's widow lives there."

Patrick gave a humorless laugh. "Bunch of old women . . ."

They were quiet for a moment. Finally Aiden said, "I like your girl. Sweet."

"Not my girl . . ."

"You doing her for fun? Does she know that?"

He looked at Aiden with barely concealed rage. "She's a good woman. It's just a thing, all right? Totally consensual."

"Look, I know you came here for a break, a chance to take stock of your life. Have you had a chance to do that?"

"Until all of you showed up, that's exactly what I was doing!"

"Really, Paddy?" Aiden asked, his voice quiet. "Make any progress on that? Because last I heard, you still weren't sure what you wanted. You used to be sure."

I used to have a best friend, Patrick thought

miserably.

"I only met Jake once," Aiden said. "He was a lot like you, though. And if you'd gone down, you wouldn't have wanted him to rethink his whole life trying to compensate for losing him. Know what I mean? There's nothing you can do to bring him back, Paddy. You have to grieve the loss, but you'll never change the course of events. He's gone now. I've said this before but I'll say it again — I'm really sorry, man."

"Yeah, thanks," Paddy said.

The back door opened and Sean came outside.

"Oh, brother," Paddy said.

Sean just smiled. "Franci hates cigars. Got one more?"

Aiden supplied him, handing him the clip and lighter. Once he got the cigar going, Sean said, "Paddy, you're not really going to give up that sweet little beauty, are you? She's crazy about you."

"It's really none of your business," Patrick returned.

"When has that stopped anyone?"

The door opened again and Luke came out. Before the door could close on him, Colin held it and joined him. Without a word, Aiden supplied two more cigars. "That's it. I brought five. If anyone else shows up out here, they're on their own."

"If anyone else shows up out here, just shoot me," Patrick said.

No sooner had he said that than Walt Booth and Sam Sheridan came outside.

"Sorry, man — my brothers ran through all the cigars," Aiden said.

Walt pulled a couple out of his pocket. "Not to worry, son. I'm always packing."

A minute later, Jack and Paul came outside. "General," Paul said. "What are the chances . . . ?"

Walt supplied a couple more.

A minute later brought Bob, Angie's dad. Walt pulled a cigar out of his pocket and Bob put up his hands. "No, thanks. I don't feel like putting up with Donna tonight."

Mike V came outside. "You left me alone with all those women!" He accepted the cigar that Bob had declined.

"Yeah, this is my idea of a Christmas party," Jack said, puffing. "Forest ranger might get a little excited, but that's okay. So," he continued, turning to Patrick, "rumor is, you're still leaving day after tomorrow." He shook his head. "I'll believe it when I see it."

"I made a commitment. Not something I take lightly. And before anyone asks — Angie has been completely aware of this since the very first day we met. She understands. She approves. And she has plans of her own — she's headed back to med school. She's very motivated. More now than when she got here. So you see? We both have our plans. I'm not saying it's all that easy, but it's decided and accepted."

It was quiet for a long stretched-out moment.

"I have ten bucks that says he never gets out of town," Walt Booth said.

"I go with Walt," Sean said. "For twenty."

"Twenty says he gets as far as the airport," said Jack. "Trust me, I've watched this place over the years — men hardly ever get away. They try, though."

"Put me down for a hundred that takes him all the way to Charleston before he figures it out," Luke said. "My little brother is book smart, but that's where his smarts end."

"Gentlemen, as much as I enjoy your humor, I'm out of here," Patrick said, then he stalked back into the house.

SIXTEEN

Patrick didn't have the heart to tell Angie they were wagering on whether he'd actually leave town, leave her, as planned. If it weren't for the fact that his brothers didn't actually start it, he'd be feeling pretty unforgiving toward them. In fact, if not for his mother, he might not even offer them a goodbye. But there was his mother. And though she was a tough old broad, when her boys were unhappy with one another, it tore a little at her heart.

Patrick wanted to make his departure as easy on Angie as possible. Though she put on the strong, resilient act, he knew it was going to be hard for her to say goodbye. He knew because it was killing him. So he went through the details of how his last day would be spent. He was just about packed up — a bachelor never completely unpacks and tends to travel light — and he was going to make a run over to Luke's to tell his mother goodbye and not to worry. It was an important ritual — mothers liked to worry. He'd favor Luke with a handshake if they crossed paths.

After bidding his family farewell, Angie could have anything she wanted from him until he had to leave. As it turned out, all she asked for was his chili, a beer and a quiet night in, which suited him just fine. They opted for her cabin. He would leave first thing in the morning, run by his own cabin to get his things and then head for Oklahoma.

The first order of business was visiting his mother. She'd sent all her sons to war at one time or another; she'd tried to pull each one of them through a laundry list of crises. "Just remember that I love you, Paddy," she said. "Take care of yourself."

He had to give his brothers credit — the joking was over. "If there's ever anything you need, you know how to reach me," Luke said. "Don't hesitate."

"Thanks."

"Keep the greasy side down, man."

"Aw, that's not the fun flying," Paddy said.

At the Victorian, as predicted, he found the rest of them. "No partying or playing tonight, gentlemen. I'm making Angie a pot of chili and we're going to play a little

Scrabble. Then I'm out of here. Aiden, thanks for the cabin. It almost feels like home."

"My pleasure. And listen, if you need more time, let the Navy know. They'd really rather have you washing battleships than messing up one of their pretty F-18s if you're not ready for that duty."

Patrick laughed.

"If you need something, call me first," Colin said, putting out his hand. "I think I owe you big. I owe all of you big, but if I remember . . ."

"I remember," Patrick said, taking his hand in a firm shake. "I came to your rescue when you were strung out on Oxy and you threw me out. Threw my clothes on the lawn."

"Did I apologize for that?" Colin asked with a grin.

"Not that I can recall."

"Good. It's better to just return the favor."

And then there was Sean. "Listen, Paddy — I know we butt heads sometimes. Okay, Riordans butt heads regularly. But you know we've got your back. Right?"

"Right," he said, shaking Sean's hand.

"You lost a good friend — I can't say anything that will make that better. But your

355

brothers are always there for you. Sometimes even when you'd rather we'd just go away."

"Considering the number of times you losers have had me on the other side of this equation, I'm just going to say thank you. And move on."

Then it was time for the really hard part. His last night with Angie.

Patrick was ready to call on every ounce of courage and compassion he could muster to get her through the night and his early-morning departure. But he'd been woefully unprepared for the fact that Angie would prove to be the really strong one.

"You know how there are people in your life that change everything?" she asked. "The kind of friend without whom you can't make a paradigm leap into a new realm, into unchartered territory and new possibilities? The kind of friend who you're always your very best self with? Was Jake that kind of friend?"

"He was."

"Before you go, I want you to know you've been that kind of friend to me," she said. "I came up here to get away, struggling to know myself better, working on where I'd go next, trying so damn hard to change.

And you encouraged me every step of the way."

"Ange, you had all that, you were all that without me around — it was just time. . . ."

She shook her head. "With you on my team I felt so much was possible. You backed me in everything. You're a wonderful partner. Paddy, you showed me a whole new world. I'll never settle again."

"Never, ever settle, babe," he said. "You're too good."

"If Jake meant as much to you, I can sure understand why you have to head to Oklahoma. If you owe him as much as I feel I owe you, you're doing the right thing."

He shook his head. "And here I thought I'd have to prop you up."

"Nah, I'm not sorry. This has been the most wonderful month of my life."

And now Patrick owed her. You hardly ever run into the kind of person who can really hold you in an open hand, never threatened or competitive, always loving you enough to want you to have everything you've imagined possible. Angie, only twenty-three, had that down. She was all selfless love. She was going to leave her mark and the world would be a better place for it.

"I want you to know . . . letting you go to

do what I have to do — I haven't faced anything harder," he told her.

"You're strong, Paddy," she said. "Just believe in yourself the way I believe in you."

He held her through the night. When he found he couldn't sleep, he just inhaled her scent and told himself he'd rest later when he couldn't savor the moment anymore. He'd sleep when she was out of his reach. But this time they had left, he wasn't about to waste it.

In the wee hours before dawn, he slipped out of bed, dressed quietly and went back to her. He kissed her sleeping eyes. Without opening them, without looking at him, she said, "Just kiss me, tell me you love me and go."

He sat on the edge of the bed, slid his arms under her, lifted her against him and covered her mouth in a powerful, deep, emotional kiss. She didn't open her eyes; she didn't choke on a sob. "I love you," he said against her lips.

Her small tongue licked in his taste. "And I love you."

Patrick had plenty of time before he needed to be at the Redding airport. He could even swing through his cabin for a shower and change of clothes, grab his duffel and, if he felt like it, stop somewhere for breakfast. Even with time on his side, he moved as if through quicksand.

It felt as if there was now a second person he'd had to permanently give up. First Jake, then the person who was best able to get him beyond Jake: Angie. Sometimes life really threw a lot of rotten apples.

He brewed his last pot of coffee in Aiden's cabin while he showered. After dressing, he stuffed yesterday's clothes in his duffel and tossed it by the door. Then he sat by the now-cold hearth and drank a cup.

He couldn't stop thinking about her. She'd shown him more support, understanding and encouragement in a few weeks than Leigh had delivered in as many years. How was that possible? He kept asking himself if Angie simply turned him on, making him think all these things when really it was just about lust. But what came to mind was the way she held him after a nightmare, while Leigh had never even called after Jake's death. He thought about reaching into Angie's hair and finding a bald spot and hearing her say, "Shunt." He remembered seeing her in those scrubs and booties after Megan's surgery. *It went very well — she's waking up now.* And when the Riordans and Sheridans gathered at the bar and the stories began she laughed until tears were running down her cheeks. She had leaned over and whispered to him, *I think I might've wet my pants.*

He'd never had anyone in his life like her. Never would again. He felt inside the way Jake would act when they were getting back from a deployment — like an animal, insane for his woman.

His coffee was cold. He looked at his watch — he'd been sitting there just thinking about her for a long time.

He looked at the ceiling. "Crap. Buddy, I'm sorry," he said aloud.

Then he went for the phone.

"Marie, sweetheart, I'm going to miss my plane. I'm really sorry."

"Not a problem, Paddy," she said. "There will be other times, other planes."

"That's the thing, Marie — I'm actually not going to make it for Christmas. I got caught up in something. I know I'd promised to be there, but —"

She laughed. "Paddy, I got so tired of trying to convince you this wasn't the place for you to spend Christmas, I stopped trying. You just don't take a hint!"

He was stunned. "Don't you love me anymore?"

"I will always love you, Paddy. You're one

of my dearest friends. And if you ever need me — call me."

"I wanted to be there for you," he said. "I promised Jake."

"And you have been there. You stood by my side while we eulogized him. You held Daniel while I received the flag. You came to Oklahoma to be sure I was okay. You call almost every day to see how I'm doing. What more could you have done?"

He sat down weakly and ran a hand through his hair, which had grown thick and long in the six weeks the Navy hadn't been looking. "Well, my plan was to try to convince you we could make it together, you and I. All you had to do was keep an open mind."

"I don't want to go back to Charleston," she said.

"Even if I said I wanted to marry you?" he asked.

"Oh, for God's sake! I'm not going to *marry* you! I love you but I'm not *in love* with you. More importantly, you're not in love with me!"

"Are you absolutely sure?"

"Yes!"

"Jesus, Marie — I gave Jake my word! If anything ever happened, I'd look out for you!"

"Right. So, if anything ever happened to you, was Jake on the hook to look after anyone?"

"Well, there's my mother . . . but I have brothers. . . ."

"Looking out for someone doesn't mean committing a life to them, Paddy! Damn, you men never listen. You've been looking out for me every day that Jake's been gone. But you still need counseling. Grief counseling. You're hanging on to Jake through me and guess what? I'm just not strong enough to carry you. I have my own grief to work through."

"No," he said, shaking his head. "I was trying to keep you upright for him!"

"And what's the difference?"

"Aw, Marie . . . Am I completely screwed up?"

"No more than expected. Paddy, let him go. Miss him with me, that's all. Call me sometimes, all right? Visit now and then, but not for too long — I intend to eventually have a life. It might not be as great as the one I had with Jake, but I have a son to raise, a little boy who looks just like his dad and is smart as the devil. I'm not going to raise him in a gray cloud of longing. I want to tell him about Uncle Paddy and the things you and his dad used to do. I'd like you to be there at his high school graduation. But not as a replacement for his father. We need you for who you really are. Daniel's godfather. Jake's best friend. My best friend."

He was quiet for a moment. "You sound fierce. I've never heard you sound like that before."

She laughed, but there was a hitch in her laugh. "I guess Jake grew very perfect in your memory. But then, you weren't usually around for the fights. . . ."

"Fights?"

"Paddy, you were with him at the bar while I was in labor! He kept telling me to hang in there."

Patrick ran a hand around the back of his neck; he hung his head. "Yeah, poor form . . ."

"If you hadn't gotten him out of there, you might've been the one having to say 'breathe' and 'push.' "

"God," he muttered, remembering. "I haven't been thinking clearly."

"I know. All this talk of taking me back to Charleston to live there in your house with you . . . Please. No. Maintaining a good relationship is hard enough when you actually marry someone you're crazy in love with — why would I risk my future to a friend who means well? That's not the recipe for a happily-ever-after. Paddy, please, let go and find your own girl. Jake's girl is moving on as best she can."

Again, he was very quiet.

"Well, to be honest, I did meet a girl. . . ."

"Thank God."

"She's amazing. I said goodbye to her this morning so I could catch my flight to Oklahoma. But I've never met anyone like her — she doesn't let anything stop her. She's so young, but still unbelievably brave and determined. Kind of like Jake and I used to be back in those Academy days — even though we were scared to death, we tried not to let it show. She's powerful like that. Full of love and goodwill and a desire to make a difference, to live a positive and authentic life. And she's also beautiful and funny. She's small and looks like she could be fragile, but don't be fooled — she's strong. Stronger than I am."

"The girl who made the operation happen."

"Yeah, that's her. She took it on without being asked and she did it. She's good to the marrow of her bones. Kind and loving."

"Exactly what you need," she said, but her voice had grown thick.

"Marie? Are you crying?"

In a voice so soft he could barely hear, she said, "He used to say things like that about me. . . . Go get her, Paddy. It'll be worth it. I promise you."

Angie allowed herself to cry once Paddy had left, but she knew that wallowing wasn't going to make this any easier. So she showered and dressed and just before noon, she called her uncle Jack's house and her aunt Brie answered.

"What are you doing there?" Angie asked.

"Your mom and I are whipping together an early dinner while Mel cleans up after us. Jack's going to be here this afternoon, but he and Mike are going to work the bar at around six — that tree keeps it hopping until late. Are you okay?"

"Yes, I'm fine."

"Did Patrick leave?"

"This morning."

"Will you come over? Join us?" Brie asked.

"Sure. But I'm coming back here to sleep, so let's not even argue about it."

"I thought it was pretty clear, you're on your own," Brie said. "Come on, baby. Come to your auntie Brie. I'll let you try on my clothes and wear my makeup," she said, bringing to memory the days when Angie was a little girl and Brie a young woman.

Angie laughed, but there was a lump in her throat. "See you, then," she said. But she wasn't sure she could hold it together with her family. If they felt sorry for her, she might crumble.

When she got to Jack and Mel's, she let herself in. There was lots of activity in the kitchen and dining room; Emma and Ness were running through the house. Grandpa was tucked away in the recliner in the corner, dozing, the newspaper spread over him like a blanket. Angie's sisters were sitting on the floor in front of the fireplace and they instantly shot to their feet and stared. Tall, lean, nineteen-year-old Jenna had her hands in the back pockets of her jeans; twenty-one-year-old Beth crossed her arms protectively over her chest and hugged herself. Both of them looked as though they'd just witnessed an accident.

"Don't baby me," Angie said. She hung her jacket on the coat hanger by the door and pulled off her cowboy boots. "Don't feel sorry for me."

Her sisters just looked at each other. Then her again.

Donna came from the kitchen, wiping her hands on a dish towel. "We doing okay?" she asked Angie.

"Okay." Then she went to sit on the floor

in front of the fire where her sisters had been. They immediately joined her with very expectant looks on their faces. "If you two make me cry, you're history," she warned her sisters.

She saw her uncle Jack come out of the kitchen holding a stack of plates for the dining room table. He stopped short when he saw her, lifting his heavy eyebrows. She gave him a smile and a wave.

"Was it horrible?" Jenna asked. "Letting that hunk of burning love go?"

"Jenna, have you ever actually had a boyfriend?" Angie asked.

"Are you kidding me?" Beth asked. "She's had seventy-two or so. And none as fine as that Irish dude you caught."

Angie circled her raised knees with her arms and put her head down. "Temporarily caught. He's on his way back to the East Coast, I'm on my way back to school and that's that."

"But what was he like? Really?" Jenna asked.

"He *is* the best man alive," Angie said with a small smile. "You guys got to know him a little — what did you think?"

"I think I would have followed him all the way to Charleston," Jenna said.

"That's the thing — I wasn't invited. He

has other plans. . . ."

Uncle Mike came from the kitchen with three glasses of white wine and some snacks on a tray — torn hunks of bread and a plate of artichoke spinach dip. Jenna took it out of his hands and brought it to the floor in front of the fire. "The help around here is outstanding."

Mike gave a snort, but he put his big hand on top of Angie's head. A comforting hand. And she reached up and gave the hand a pat.

When he was gone Jenna asked, "Were you in love with him?"

"Stop it," Angie said.

"Can't you talk about it?"

"Maybe next week. Talk to me about something else. What are the family plans?"

"Well, in support of our emotional cripple of a sister, we're having Christmas here. Are you going to come home with us right after? Or are you still on romantic hiatus?"

"You're being kind of bitchy," Beth told Jenna.

"Sorry. I was looking for some details. Didn't I tell you every detail the night I lost my virginity?"

"And every time after," Beth put in.

Jenna made a face at that sister, but to Angie she said, "And you had that gorgeous man all to yourself for a month and haven't said a word."

"Give her a week," Beth said. "Where did you come from, really? Are you adopted, Jenna? You shouldn't be so pushy."

"I'm not talking," Angie said. Then in a quiet voice she added, "My heart hurts. And I don't want to cry in front of everyone. So please, Jenna — stop being such a brat. Just tell me what's in the news or something."

"What's in the news is that we are stuck in Virgin River where the one single guy has officially fled and the big event to look forward to is the Christmas Eve children's pageant at the church." She took a gulp of her wine. "That's the news. Drink up."

Beth and Angie both laughed in spite of themselves. And once they got off the topic of Angie's romance, they yammered like girls would. They sipped their wine; Beth and Jenna ate the dip and bread. Angie just wasn't ready to eat. Someone yelled, "Dinner in thirty minutes," but the girls had formed a tight, protective little circle in front of the fireplace and were somewhat oblivious to the rest of the house.

Angie noticed it was getting dusky outside and she was surprised she'd made it through the day without him. There was a small table between the great room and dining room set for David, Emma and Ness and it brought to mind all those years of setting up the adult table and the kids' table for the holidays. She remembered being the first of ten grandchildren to graduate to the adult table, an event that filled her sisters with jealousy and loathing.

She abstractly noticed Mel rounding up the kids for their dinner, getting them settled at the table. Mike and Brie were carrying dishes and plates of food to the table. And some fool was honking a horn outside.

Jack went and opened the front door to see who was making the noise. "Holy shit," he said. He turned and looked into the great room. "Ange. It's for you."

She got slowly to her feet, Jenna and Beth scrambling to get up and follow.

When Angie got to the front door, she couldn't quite take it in. Five cars, all lined up in front of the house, people standing beside them. Not just people. Riordans — the whole family — brothers, wives, their mother, George. A couple of kids — Rosie and Brett. And in the front, Patrick.

"You have to give me another chance, Angie," he said loudly. Then he spread his arms and said, "I come with a lot of baggage."

Her hands crossed over her chest. She was afraid to move, to think. Then suddenly she

370

was nudged from behind and she stumbled forward. She looked over her shoulder and Jenna shrugged.

Patrick was walking toward her. She took a couple of steps toward him, standing at the edge of the porch. "Why are you here?" she asked.

He put a foot up on the porch step. "A better question is why did I leave?" He shook his head. "I was just confused. Ange, I was a fool to think I could leave you. And now I'm running out of time — I should have started begging you to take a chance on me at least a week ago. Angie, baby, I love you. I don't even want to try to make it without you."

"But, Patrick — there's Marie!"

"She's my friend, but I don't love her. Not that way. And she doesn't love me. I don't know what got into me. Listen," he said, crossing his forearms over his raised thigh and leaning toward her. "I'll help Marie and Daniel whenever they need help. I'll be the kind of friend Jake would have expected me to be. But you've made me believe that I have much more to offer than just friendship — to the right woman. And if you think I'm worthy, you're the woman I want a life with."

"We've only known each other a month,"

she said. "And I'm supposed to go back to school. . . ."

"I knew how I felt in only a week. I tried to talk myself out of it — it makes no sense, except I can't stop it. I want you, if you want me, too. I'll make sure you still get to school — and I'm up for an assignment. Maybe I'll get to the West Coast. If not, there are awesome med schools on the East Coast and I have to believe any one of them would kill to have you. It's not like we have to wait until all that's behind us, we can face this together. There could be challenges, but couples do it all the time — get married, fulfill their ambitions, work as a team. By the time you're finished with med school and residency, I'll be retiring from the Navy. We'll be ready for the next stage — there might even be something we can do together to make a difference. Maybe there are humanitarian organizations that need both doctors and pilots."

"Married?" she asked weakly. "But there could be separations . . ."

"Oh, guaranteed! But millions of military couples have weathered that storm successfully. I don't want to rush you, babe. I'll wait for you if you need time. Time to be sure of me, of us. It's not an easy life in the Navy, I know that. But what the hell —

there is no easy life." He smiled at her. "You'll see — I can be almost as brave and strong as you. The only thing I'm not sure I'm strong enough for is a life without you in it."

Angie heard a little squeak behind her and turned to see the entire Sheridan clan stuffed into the doorway. Jenna had her hands covering her mouth, tears running down her cheeks. "Wow," Angie said. "Looks like I come with baggage, too."

"Yeah," he laughed. "I feel your pain."

"Are you sure about all this, Patrick?" she asked.

"I didn't even begin the drive to the airport, Ange. My legs wouldn't go. I started wondering how I was going to leave you over a week ago — and it just isn't in me. Trust me, I'm sure." He looked over his shoulder. "If you just say yes, maybe we can ditch the entourage and go find some place alone. We have things to talk about. We could pack you up, make some plans, say some more goodbyes and see if we can get a flight out of California. Before you're due back at school, we'll have a good idea where I'm going to end up. Please, Angie — come with me."

She took another step. "Of course I'll come with you."

He took her hand and pulled it, kissing her palm. "I'll do everything I can to deserve you." Then he pulled her into his arms, lifting her off the ground and kissing her deep and long. In front of God and everyone.

Jack dropped an arm around his sister's shoulders and said, "You know, it's hell being right all the time. The strain is terrible."

"Right," she said, wiping her eyes.

"Brie," he yelled. "Throw another potato in the soup — we've got company!"

The Riordans began walking up to Jack's house. Paddy and Angie never broke their lip-lock, not even when Aiden gave Patrick a pat on the back as he passed.

Luke was the last of the brothers to pass them. Jack was holding the door for him. "Check that one off," he said, glancing over his shoulder at Patrick and Angie. "Kid's got good taste."

"I'd have to agree on that," Jack said.

ACKNOWLEDGMENTS

Three very special people helped me with necessary research for this story. Ellen Hedden, MSPA CCC/SLP, walked me through the recovery process for traumatic brain injury, including the struggles the families of survivors encounter. Ellen has compassion so rich and deep, her patients are so lucky. And I am lucky to call her friend.

Candace Irvin, a former Naval Officer and currently a romantic suspense writer, helped me become familiar with Navy terminology.

And Goesel Anson, MD, a gifted plastic and reconstructive surgeon, walked me through one possible procedure for reconstructive surgery.

Of course, any mistakes or artistic license for the sake of story and drama would be all mine, not these experts who were so generous with their time and knowledge.

I would like to also acknowledge the support of a few friends. We share writing victories and stumbling blocks, laugh together, prop one another up and lend a hand when a hand is needed. Thank you to Susan Andersen, Kristan Higgins, Colleen Gleason, Deanna Raybourn and Jill Shalvis.

To my editor, Valerie Gray, and my agent, Liza Dawson, I thank you from the bottom of my heart. Believe me, I never take for granted one second how lucky I am to have you on my team.

ABOUT THE AUTHOR

Robyn Carr is the *New York Times* and *USA Today* bestselling author of over forty novels, including historical romance, series romance, and a thriller. Originally from Minnesota, she and her husband, Jim, live in Nevada. They have two grown children. Visit her website at www.RobynCarr.com.